EYEBALL TO EYEBALL

"Are you going to kiss me, or look at me?"
Diana said.

David Loring took a breath and crossed the
inch-wide chasm to put his mouth on
hers. He found himself staring at her staring
at him, eyeball to eyeball.

"One of us is going to have to close his
eyes," she said, her mouth moving against
his.

He closed his eyes.

A mistake. Because on a trail of vicious violence
and infinite evil that led from a Texas backwater to a Colorado mountain resort . . . from
real estate scams to the fine art underworld
. . . from hot kisses to cold killing . . . the first
rule of survival was to keep your eyes open
at every blind turn. . . .

CRIMINAL
INTENT

CRIMINAL INTENT

Michael L. Monhollon

To Teague & Janet,

Some light reading for when the kids are in bed. Enjoy!

Michael L. Monhollon

12-9-92

Ⓢ
A SIGNET BOOK

SIGNET
Published by the Penguin Group
Penguin Books USA Inc., 375 Hudson Street,
New York, New York 10014, U.S.A.
Penguin Books Ltd, 27 Wrights Lane,
London W8 5TZ, England
Penguin Books Australia Ltd, Ringwood,
Victoria, Australia
Penguin Books Canada Ltd, 10 Alcorn Avenue,
Toronto, Ontario, Canada M4V 3B2
Penguin Books (N.Z.) Ltd, 182–190 Wairau Road,
Auckland 10, New Zealand

Penguin Books Ltd, Registered Offices:
Harmondsworth, Middlesex, England

First published by Signet, an imprint of New American Library,
a division of Penguin Books USA Inc.

First Printing, October, 1992
10 9 8 7 6 5 4 3 2 1

Ⓢ REGISTERED TRADEMARK—MARCA REGISTRADA

PRINTED IN THE UNITED STATES OF AMERICA

PUBLISHER'S NOTE
This is a work of fiction. Names, characters, places, and incidents either
are the product of the author's imagination or are used fictitiously, and
any resemblance to actual persons, living or dead, events, or locales is
entirely coincidental.

For Rachael

1

1

A silver-framed photograph of the two of them together was on a dresser in the boy's bedroom: Leo in red-striped swimming trunks, his torso tan and lean, a few strokes of curly hair between his pecs; the boy in a Speedo swimsuit. Leo's arm was thrown casually across the boy's shoulders in what could have been mistaken for manly camaraderie.

Leo, a.k.a. Leonard Nash, now held in the county jail on ninety-seven charges of fraud, embezzlement, racketeering, and assorted other felonies, had put the boy up in the studio apartment. Clark Holland was seventeen; he couldn't have afforded it. The whole place was decorated in black and white and shades of gray. There was very little litter around. No dishes were in the kitchen sink. The wastebaskets were empty, except for a single crumpled tissue at the bottom of the black and white wastebasket in the bathroom. There were no books stacked around the chairs (no books at all, only magazines like *GQ* and *Esquire*), no clutter of papers on the coffee table, nothing to give any feel for Clark as a real person who sweated and blew his nose and needed something to occupy his mind.

Mick got a look at all of it one Friday morning between eight and nine o'clock. Clark was out. Mick had watched him go, then used one of Leo's keys to let himself into the apartment. He had to try a couple to find the right one.

Several days after Leonard's arrest, when Mick was sure the police were paying no particular attention to Leo's house, Mick had gone through it carefully. Getting into Leo's house was no problem. Mick had a key, had had it for years because they were friends and had been since they were kids. Now Mick was in a position to exploit his old friendship.

In one of the drawers of Leo's massive roll-top desk, Mick found a ring of more keys, and he took it, sure that it was Leo's duplicate set, that one of the keys was a key to Clark's apartment. He was not disappointed.

Mick ended his search where he had started it, in the boy's bedroom, looking at the photograph on the dresser. It was impossible for him to have neutral feelings about that picture; just looking at it caused him to clench and unclench his fists, caused air to course audibly through flared nostrils. He knew the man in the photograph was "Leo" to the boy, not only because of gossip he had picked up recently, but also because that was the name on the letters he had found tied with a ribbon in the box underneath the bed.

For twenty-five years he had called the man Leonard. They had gone to high school together. Though Leonard hadn't played football—really, he wasn't big enough for that in those days—he had run track, and there was no one faster at the hundred-yard dash. Mick had gone to all the track meets to watch him run. Leonard had been at all the football games.

Standing braced before the picture, Mick felt a stab of acute grief at the loss of what had been a great friendship, of what had at least seemed a great friendship, even if it had been founded on deceit and treachery. They were drinking buddies through their twenties; they picked up women together. When one of Leonard's business deals got too rough for Leonard to handle alone, Mick was his muscle. When one of Leonard's partners or suppliers or customers needed encouragement of a certain brutal nature, Mick provided that encouragement. The payoffs supplemented his income as a roughneck and eventually permitted his retirement from the oil derricks.

Several years ago, though, it had begun to seem to Mick unlikely that the good times could last. Leonard got too greedy; he plunged too deeply into flimflam ever again to surface. And then, and then . . .

He could hardly bring himself to think about it, his discovery of Leonard's other life—Leonard's life with Clark and, he now knew, with others before Clark. This other life contradicted everything Leonard had ever said, everything the two of them had believed in together. How it had taken Mick so long to tumble to it in a town of eighty thousand people, he didn't know. Everyone said the town was a goldfish bowl, with every affair, every indiscretion, every rivalry a matter of common knowledge. One exception to that, apparently, was the homosexual community, which was far more insulated than he ever would have guessed.

Mick came to hate Leonard too much even to confront him with what he knew, so the warmth between them became politeness, and the politeness became a chill. Mick had avoided confrontation; he could not have faced it. Besides, revenge was sweeter. Oh yes, revenge was sweet. Leonard was now held on the top floor of the Pepper County Courthouse, an oven in August, and for eight days he had received not a ray of sunlight. Sweet revenge. A smile played around Mick's lips as he thought about it, and at last he could turn away from the picture of Clark and Leo in their seminude embrace.

His stomach gurgled, and he realized he had not eaten breakfast. His wristwatch told him it was nearly nine-thirty. His search had not turned up what he was looking for, which meant he was going to have to talk to Clark. The boy had visited Leonard at the courthouse every day this week. The two were talking about something.

Clark was dawdling, though, making Mick wait for his breakfast. "It is an indignity up with which I shall not put," he said, quoting his favorite line from Winston Churchill. He could come back. There was nothing to prevent him from doing that.

Clark had gotten to the landing outside his apartment at five minutes before nine o'clock that morning, but he had not gone inside. Ever since they had arrested Leonard at Dallas-Fort

Worth Airport, four hours' drive up I-35, he had been paranoid. They had detained him, too. For hours they had questioned him, and he lived with the feeling that they were watching him, that everywhere he went, someone followed. Whenever he returned to his apartment he experienced a feeling of violation. He would know that someone had been in his apartment while he was gone, that someone else's hands had poked through his clothing, that someone else's face had peered from his mirrors. It was infuriating. He fumed over imagined violations of his right to privacy until finally he remembered a trick he'd seen once in a spy flick. That night at three A.M., he used a cheese knife to smear a half-inch line of tree resin on his door and door frame. When he left his apartment, whenever he left his apartment, he would pull a long, curling hair from the top of his head and, as casually as he could (he might be watched), slap it against the resin on the molding and the door. The August heat kept the resin tacky enough to hold the hair. That one unbroken hair, stuck in the yellow, glinting streak of resin, gave him some feeling of security again, some feeling of control.

Until now. Returning from the International House of Pancakes, he saw that the hair was broken. It was there, but a full quarter-inch was missing from the middle. Someone had been there; perhaps someone was still inside. Breathing rapidly, so rapidly that dark spots appeared in his field of vision, he retreated from the door. For more than half an hour he watched it through a giant holly bush at the corner of the next building.

He saw Mick leave the building and lock it, saw Mick hesitate and pull a piece of hair from the resin. He heard the harsh sound of Mick's laughter. Mick knew his trick now.

It gave him the shakes. He knew Mick, knew who he was to Leo, but that only made it worse. For the first time, he had an idea of how the cops had known to look for him and Leo at Gate 11 of Dallas-Fort Worth Airport. His sense of violation deepened.

He watched Mick cut across the grass to a BMW parked by the curb at the edge of the apartment complex. Then, despite his fear, Clark went back inside his apartment. He knew what Mick was after. It was the money.

The first thing Clark did was to get his largest butcher knife from the kitchen and tuck it into the waistband at the small of his back. He had to be careful with the knife there, the blade pressed against him, but he wanted the knife within easy reach.

He called Trevor, to see if he could go over there for a while, but Trevor didn't answer his telephone.

Which was good, he decided. He wasn't going to be driven out of his home. Mick was big, sure, lots bigger than he was, but no one was so big that a butcher knife between the ribs wouldn't stop them. And Clark was fast. He'd handled himself in lots of dicey situations before, as had any gay growing up in Redneck, U.S.A. If Mick came back, Clark would be ready.

Midafternoon found him drowsing on the couch, lying on his side to keep the hilt of the knife from digging into his back. It was supposed to be over one hundred degrees out there today, and though his air conditioner ran constantly, it was a little too warm inside the apartment.

It had been warm inside the airport that day, too. For the past month, the whole state had sweltered in the worst heat wave in Texas history. In memory, Clark is sitting by Gate 11, a pretty seventeen-year-old with dark blond hair lying in curls on his forehead. He is conscious of the way he looks, for it is the way Leo will see him, the white flight bag between his feet, the bag's straps held in both hands between his knees. He is pretty.

Glass walls allow a view of the runways, though the view is constricted by the huge 747 parked at the gate. The plane has the markings of Trans-World Airlines. The boy, watching it from a seat in the no-smoking section, expects to be on it soon. When Leo comes.

"Is everything set?" a man said.

"Leo!"

And Leonard Nash sat beside him. He was wearing black alligator boots, olive drab slacks, a blue-and-white-striped shirt that had no collar. On his wrist he wore a gold Rolex.

"Bags checked?" Leo asked.

"Uh-huh."

"Good boy." He laid a hand on Clark's wrist. The hand lingered a moment, almost tenderly— Clark would always remember those tender moments—then tightened perceptibly. Clark was instantly alert. A man in a brown suit had stopped just inside his field of vision on the right side; now another man turned toward them, his back to the glass wall overlooking the runway.

Clark's heart lurched with an instant's apprehension, but the man in front of them merely stood with arms folded, apparently looking past them.

Clark glanced at Leonard, who exhaled softly and rubbed his hands together as if to dispel the perspiration on them. It was impossible that anyone had tracked them here; Leonard had told him that. It was just their nerves.

"They're supposed to start boarding in ten or fifteen minutes," Clark said to comfort Leonard. Once boarding started, Leonard would be making one last trip to an airport locker for his all-important carry-on, just as they had discussed.

"Good. Good," Leonard said.

The man in the brown suit who had appeared on their right was leaning against the gate counter, waiting to speak to the ticket agent, so he was all right, too.

But Clark's heart had taken on a faster cadence, and his happy thoughts were failing to slow it. " 'Ay attention," Leonard said quietly, without looking at him and without moving his lips. He leaned forward to adjust his thousand-dollar boots.

"Oh, my feet have been killing me," Leonard said in conversational tones. Out of the corner of his eye, Clark saw him lean over until an airport locker key fell from his shirt pocket and into his hand. Leonard placed his hand again on Clark's forearm and squeezed hard enough for Clark to feel the imprint of the key.

Clark put his hand over Leonard's and smiled into his eyes. Leonard withdrew his hand from beneath Clark's, leaving the key in place and the whole of his fortune in Clark's right hand. "Sunshine and surf," Leonard said. "I'm looking forward to it." Clark's heart was pounding like a trip-hammer.

"Do we have company, Clark?" Leonard asked. "What do you think?" The man at the counter was looking at them now. Leonard smiled genially and gave the man the finger.

The man by the plate glass started forward.

A hand closed on Leonard's shoulder, and a voice behind them said, "Mr. Nash, I presume?"

Clark stood up without his flight bag and, looking about him vaguely, tried to wander off.

"We'd like you to come with us, too, if you would, please."

Leonard, they handcuffed on the spot, and two men walked beside him. Clark walked beside the third, his hands free, but the other man's hand resting lightly on his arm.

He kept his hands open to allay suspicion, the fingers of his right hand curled naturally. Against his right palm his thumb held the locker key. Whether they knew he had it, he did not know. That they would know soon enough unless he did something, he did know.

They passed the restrooms and the gift shop. Another waiting area opened on their right. The men holding onto Leonard's elbows were on Clark's left. The man holding his arm was on his right, boxing him in.

His eyes focused on a potted tree against the wall they were approaching. The man on his right was bigger than he was, but there wasn't any choice. When they got there, Clark shoved him into a pregnant woman holding a baby against her chest. Out of the corner of his eye, Clark saw the baby going up, the woman going down, Clark's guard reaching out to both in an effort to save them. Clark took two steps forward and cut right, tripping over a big blue suitcase pulled along behind a flight attendant and going down. With both hands he reached out ahead of him to catch himself, and both hands hit his target, the pot the tree was sitting in, his left hand clutching at the porcelain side, his right hand plunging deep into the soft, artificial loam.

His head hit the carpeted floor as he felt his hands dragged behind him. Cold handcuffs bit hard into his wrists, and he was hauled savagely to his feet.

Leonard was lying facedown on the tile floor of the walkway, one foot of the man in the brown suit on his lower back, a .38-caliber revolver pointed at the back of his head. When Leonard raised his head, his nose trailed bright blood.

The pregnant lady sat with her legs straight out before her, and she cooed comforting things to the baby she clutched to her breast. The baby stared bright-eyed about himself.

They jerked Clark forward so hard that his head snapped back. He didn't mind. In fact, he was smiling. The locker key was safe. They did strip-search him, but uselessly. Through all the hours he spent locked in the small, stuffy airport office, through all the hours of questioning, the key was safe.

For nearly twenty-four hours after they released him, he stayed in Dallas. He moved his car from the airport parking lot to a residential street and then crisscrossed the city, switching cabs, looking always though the back window for some sign of a tail. He entered Neiman-Marcus nonchalantly through the front door and scurried for the exit in the back. On foot he circled city blocks and cut through alleys. Always he stared at those around him, picking out individual faces from the crowd, alert for any flicker of special awareness.

In time he knew he was not followed. He returned to the airport, walked back and forth past the potted tree near Gate 11. He had been so long—suppose the key was no longer there? And did he dare to fish for it before dozens of staring eyes? And suppose the police were still here, searching, or even awaiting his return? He had no choice. Sitting with studied weariness beside the potted tree, he worked his hand into the loam. He found the key, the number of the airport locker engraved upon it.

He got Leonard's heavy carry-on from the locker, and he got out.

It was the sound of another key in the door of his own apartment that interrupted his reverie and sent him scurrying toward the door, checking the knife in the waistband of his pants, pulling out his shirt to hide the knife handle.

Mick had waited until dusk. In the distance, people moved like shadows across the grounds of the apartment complex, but Mick knew that he was no more than a shadow to them himself. He heard Clark's feet on the tile floor on the foyer, just as he realized he had the wrong key in the lock. One hand on the knob, he stepped back to watch the peephole darken as Clark checked him out. With his other hand, he sorted out what he hoped was the right key. Clark didn't open the door; instead, the peephole brightened again as Clark's head moved away from it.

If Mick had rung the doorbell, he would have expected Clark to recognize him and throw open the door to find out what tidings Mick brought of the beloved Leo. Too late for that now. If he had rung the doorbell in the first place, he would have given up even the possibility of surprising Clark inside the apartment.

He rang the doorbell now to keep Clark's mind occupied as he put the new key in the lock and turned it. The door opened a crack, but Mick found he was pushing against Clark, braced against the other side. Mick smiled at the thought of Clark trying to hold the door against him. He applied his shoulder, and, sure enough, there was Clark straining mightily to hold the door, his face red beneath his blond bangs.

"Hey there, precious," Mick said to him. "Aren't you going to invite me in?"

The boy stepped away from the door. "I know you. You're Mick."

"Uh-huh, friend of Leo's. Shouldn't that make you glad to see me?"

"Don't call him that."

"Leo?"

"Nobody calls him that but me."

Mick smiled at him, his eyes hard. "You weren't the first I heard it from," he said.

"What do you want?"

"To talk."

"What about?"

"Money." He put his hand on Clark's shoulder in a friendly gesture, but he gripped the muscle at the top of Clark's shoulder between his thumb and forefinger when he did so, which took a lot of the friendliness out of it. If Mick got too friendly he wasn't going to get any information.

Holding Clark by the shoulder, Mick led him out of the foyer into the living room. All the floors on this level of the studio apartment were tiled in black and white, and great fluffy throw rugs were scattered about like muppet turds.

Clark's head was twisted toward his shoulder in ineffective defense of the trapezius muscle; the effort distorted his gait enough to make him a cripple. He was wearing loose cotton pants and a black, long-sleeved jersey. His yellow hair was combed forward in soft waves.

Mick sat him in one of the leather easy chairs, white in keeping with the apartment's monochromatic design. He released the boy's shoulder and walked around the glass-and-chrome coffee table to sit on the arm of the white leather sofa. The boy's eyes darted here and there as if he were trying to come up with a plan. His breathing was clearly audible in the high-ceilinged room.

Mick wasn't too worried about any plan Clark might come up with. Clark was about five-nine and slight of build. Mick, by contrast, was several inches over six feet in height, and he weighed two hundred forty pounds, none of which was fat.

"I thought you were a friend of Leo . . . Leonard's. How come you're hassling me?"

"I'm not hassling you, I just want to make

some conversation. You know, the thing that really surprised me about Leonard's arrest was that nobody seems to have recovered any money. What do you think, was Leonard leaving the country with nothing or what? It doesn't seem like him. I mean, how was he going to live?"

Clark's gaze seemed fixed on Mick's nose, which had been broken repeatedly in childhood and never set properly. It was the one feature Mick was sensitive about. "This is about money?" Clark said. "I can't believe you're here about the money. I mean, man, Leo thinks of you as his friend."

"Yes. And I have always thought of my friend Leonard as a heterosexual. Life is full of these little disappointments."

"Slimeball."

"Slimeball? Ooh, that's pretty harsh. I hope I can stand up to it." Mick took a pair of pliers from his hip pocket.

He studied Clark meditatively. Clark's eyes had focused hard on the pliers, which Mick held in his right hand, opening and closing them casually.

"I understand you were at the airport with friend Leo when they picked him up," Mick said.

"What do you know about it?" His voice was a whisper, nearly inaudible. Mick smiled.

In a slightly stronger voice, Clark said, "You ratted on him, didn't you? He trusted you like you were his own brother, and you ratted on him." The anger that sparked in his eyes seemed to give him strength. Mick pressed on.

"Did Leonard send his money on ahead of him,

or was he taking it with him? I'd swear he had to be taking it with him."

"If Leo had money, do you think he'd be cooling his heels in a jail cell? He'd make bail and be out of here," the boy said with a sneer.

"Huh. Bail, you know, is set at a million dollars. It may be that he doesn't have quite a million dollars. It may be that he doesn't even have the ten percent for a bailbondsman. But let's say he does have the money. Leonard has one hell of a lot of creditors out there, and if he posted a million-dollar bond, all that money would be out there in the open where his creditors could get at it. Might be worth a short stay in a jail cell to avoid that."

Clark didn't say anything.

"If Leonard did have a large sum of money with him at the airport, and you were with him, and the money didn't turn up on his person or in his luggage, it stands to reason that you must know something about it. Why did the cops let you go, boy?"

"They didn't have nothing on me."

"I believe you."

"And I don't know nothing about any money. I told them that, and they searched me, and they searched my car, and when they didn't find nothing, they let me go. Just stay in Texas, they said."

"Makes a good story, but I don't believe it. I believe there's a substantial sum of money out there, and I believe you know where that sum of money is."

"Well, there ain't no money, and I wouldn't tell you anyway." Clark started to stand, but only got halfway up before Mick had reached across the coffee table to grab hold of his cheek with the pliers.

"Do you see how the second part of that sentence negates the first?" Mick said, squeezing just hard enough with the pliers to hold onto its plug of cheek. "Do you see? 'I wouldn't tell you anyway' doesn't mean anything at all unless there is in fact money, unless there is money and you know something about it."

Clark had frozen in place, halfway out of his chair. "It hurts," he said woodenly. Mick squeezed a little tighter and twisted the pliers a quarter-turn. Genuine alarm showed for the first time in Clark's eyes.

"I don't want to hurt your face, boy. If you tell me about the money, then I'll leave. You'll still be healthy, and this whole unpleasant incident will be no more than a fading blemish on your day."

"I don't have the money."

"By which you mean it isn't here. I know it isn't here." If the money were here, it meant that he, Mick, was a nincompoop for not finding it when he searched the place this morning. "What I want to know is where it is."

"Suppose I don't know."

Still holding onto his ounce of flesh, Mick walked around the coffee table so that he was standing above Clark. "Oh, that's the really unfortunate possibility. Because, how can I know that you're telling the truth? I'd have to pull a plug out of your cheek here." He released his hold and grabbed a piece of the other cheek. "I'd have to pull a plug out of this cheek, too. I'd have to yank a plug off the inside of your biceps here, maybe a plug out of your thigh . . ." He had Clark thrashing about in an effort to escape the grip of the pliers. Mick held onto that last plug of thigh and squeezed it. "You don't know anything about any money, and by the time I leave here there'll be pieces of you lying all over this floor."

"There's a key inside my right front pocket," Clark squeaked. "It's the key to a safety deposit box I rented Monday."

"Ah, yes."

"The number's on it."

"Yes, so it is."

"The bank's First National."

Mick let go of the boy's thigh. "See, that wasn't so bad, was it? You've got a little red spot on your face there. You may have a bruise on your leg. But we both came out of this pretty good, don't you think?"

He pocketed the key and turned toward the door, thinking: *Why does it have to be a safety deposit box? Why do I have to get the key so late on a Friday?*

"Oh, Mick." The boy's voice was high-pitched, and, as Mick turned, the boy launched himself, shrieking. His right fist was in the air, coming down.

Mick didn't see the knife until it was all over. He blocked the descending arm at the elbow as a matter of course and drove a short jab into Clark's ribs. The kid doubled straight over. As he came up, Mick hooked his right hand into the side of Clark's face, swinging hard enough to spin Clark around: When he pitched forward onto his face, it was away from Mick. Clark's head bounced on a fluffy throw rug, which was probably all that saved his head from splitting open. That was good. Already Mick had begun to realize he could need Clark to get into the safety deposit box.

When Clark did not move, Mick turned him over, and that was when he saw the knife. The steel-and-hardwood handle protruded from Clark's throat. The blade was buried.

Blood erupted suddenly from around it, spurting up into Mick's face with its first pulse. Mick stumbled back, throwing Clark back onto his face, swiping with his free hand at the blood that obscured his vision.

He had to stay back to keep his feet out of the spreading pool, but he stood over the body, blinking, trying to think, trying to see. Maybe they would think Clark fell on the knife by accident, and maybe they would think he caved the side of his face in when he hit the floor. Maybe pigs could fly. Hoo boy, hoo boy. Nothing he could do about the body. It looked as natural as it was going to look where it had fallen, best to leave it. His prints, where had he left his prints? At least the blood wasn't on his shoes. His car was out there, though, so he couldn't spend very much time here, had to get out, had to go. First things first. *Have to do some quick housecleaning, then I can go. Ah, the stench, enough to make you sick. Ah. Oh. What did he . . . Oh, crap!*

He left thirty minutes later. It was fully dark by then, and nobody saw him go.

2

The August sun, filtered by the rose-colored blinds, scored bright bars of light on the taupe carpet. It was Saturday morning. David Loring threw aside the pin-striped sheet that covered him and swung his legs off the modular sofa to sit up.

He sat for a moment with his elbows on his knees, his fingers buried in his thick, sandy hair, which pointed stiffly in all directions. Then he left the living room and went to the partially open door of his bedroom, where he peered through the crack to see if slipping into the room to get some clothes would be expedient.

On the left edge of his double bed, Rhonda Hazelhoff lay on her stomach, the tangled sheet exposing part of one leg and rising only halfway up her back. There were sun freckles on her shoulders. Her face, turned toward the door, was pressed hard against the mattress, giving her face a puckered look, and her closed fist was beneath her chin.

Quietly he pulled open the top drawer of his chest of drawers to get a pair of white socks, the second drawer to get a T-shirt. His Nike Air Stab running shoes he got from the closet.

Holding everything in a bundle under one arm, he closed the bedroom door softly behind him and slowly released the doorknob.

The doorbell rang. His head swung toward the front door.

The peephole stared brightly at him, sparkling in the morning sun.

He wanted no visitors, not now, with Rhonda in his bed. Rhonda had been out of his life so long that few of his current friends even knew her.

Against the front door he hesitated. If he looked, his visitor would see the peephole darken and know he was there. If his visitor were a motorcycle gang armed with knives and clubs, it would understand his not opening the door. There were others who might not be so understanding.

The doorbell rang again.

After a quick glance back at the bedroom door, still closed, he looked through the peephole. What he saw within the round field of vision was not encouraging: a slender girl with tawny, shoulder-length hair, her face and figure subtly distorted by the fisheye lens. Ordinarily he was encouraged by slender girls with tawny, shoulder-length hair, but this was Marie, wearing faded Levi's and a white sleeveless blouse that buttoned up the front, and he was dating Marie. She was looking to her left, so that he saw her in profile, and he pulled back before she could notice the telltale darkening of the peephole.

Before he could slip outside and forestall her,

she rang the doorbell again, and Rhonda called to him from the bedroom. "David?" she said.

"David?" Marie said from outside the door.

The bed gave a loud creak, and in his mind's eye he could see Rhonda padding barefoot across the carpeted floor. In his mind's eye she was naked. He was letting this get complicated.

Marie knocked on the front door, the sound taking on in his mind the inexorable thudding of imminent doom. Oh, for that motorcycle gang armed with clubs and knives!

The front doorknob rattled. The bedroom door gave a creak as it began to open. David bolted.

Across the living room, reaching through curtains to fumble one-handed with the lock on the sliding-glass door, still clutching T-shirt, shoes, and socks against his chest, pushing finally through the curtains and dropping his clothes in a jumble to the floor of the balcony. Free! He was free. The white incandescence of the morning sun was blinding.

He was pushing the door closed when he saw his shadow on the carpet inside the apartment, visible even through the gauzy curtains. They could see him from inside the apartment. Not free.

He shoveled socks and shoes and shirt off the edge of the balcony and, as he hooked one foot over the rail, heard his shoes slapping onto the cement patio of the ground-floor apartment below him. His toes on the edge of the balcony, his heels hanging in space, he looked down. Diminutive wicker furniture was visible between his feet, no one sitting in it, thank God. How far was it down there? He was going to kill himself.

He heard the front door of his apartment open. Women's voices. *Oh, David, thy name is mud, thy name is dung, thy name is sewer*, he thought.

He crouched, grasping a bar in the railing with his right hand and placing the other hand flat on the cement floor of the balcony. As he dropped, the metal edge of the balcony struck hard against his left wrist, and with his right hand he let go of the rail, clutching frantically at the edge of the balcony with his fingertips, the edge of the balcony already beginning to slide away from him as he looked down through his legs, twisting slowly in space. It wasn't so far, just a few feet, really. He would just miss the wicker table.

He dropped.

Because he was six feet tall and his extended arms gave him another foot-and-a-half extension, he only fell three feet. *A good high curb is enough to panic me*, he thought with disgust, dancing to escape the pins and needles exploding up from the concrete patio into his feet and ankles. Maybe not such a high curb.

He bent to collect his shirt and socks and shoes, and as he got the last shoe saw a pair of delicate brown feet, brown calves, brown thighs, followed by the rest of the woman. She was fortyish and sun-darkened; dry, deep lines radiated from the corners of her eyes and bracketed her mouth. Her brown hair was shoulder length and curly, and strands of gray were sprinkled through it. Her eyes were reddened and the lids puffy, suggesting to David that she had been crying.

Despite the aging that had taken place in the woman's face, her legs were those of a twenty-year-old, slender and hard. Her tan looked all the darker in contrast to the white terry-cloth robe that just reached the top of her thighs and hung open to show a vertical slit of a navel suspended midway between the top and the trunks of a scanty, diagonally striped bikini.

"I'm David Loring," he said, dropping his shoes and his shirt again to pull on his right sock. "Your upstairs neighbor. I, uh, just thought I'd drop by."

"So to speak." She sniffed loudly, not looking at him.

He glanced up at the balcony, which was empty. "So to speak," he agreed. "I appreciate you not screaming or shooting me or anything." He got his other sock on, and both of his shoes.

"You're welcome," the woman said. "I'd offer you some lemonade, but you look like you're in a hurry."

David was standing with his T-shirt, pushing his arms into the sleeves before raising his arms overhead and lowering them to the side to pull the shirt over his head. With his hands, he pulled down the T-shirt to cover his abdomen. "I guess I am."

"Drop by again when you have more time."

He nodded vaguely, looking around him. "I guess I was planning to jump your fence."

"Feel free." She crossed to the wicker recliner, set just outside the shadow of the privacy fence, and shed the robe. She paid David no attention as she settled herself, sniffling a couple more times, and he decided he had been dismissed. He pulled himself up onto the two-by-four plate that ran along the top of the fence and jumped down.

Unsettling woman, he thought. Shaking his head, he started jogging down the sidewalk that ran between the apartment buildings. There was a sound behind him, but before he could glance behind, thin, bare arms had encircled his knees and squeezed, and he was going down. He skidded to a halt on the concrete sidewalk, his palms and one elbow taking most of the damage as he tried to catch himself and tried to shake off his tackler.

It was Marie. "You son of a bitch," she said.

"Me!" He was sitting up, she was sitting up, their legs were getting tangled. "What the hell do you think *you* . . ."

"Do you service the whole neighborhood," she said. "Or just the girls in that one building?"

"Ooh. I, uh . . ."

"Don't tell me about the girl upstairs, just tell me about the one downstairs."

He smiled reflexively, buying time. "There's not much to tell, I—"

"Let me guess. Her T.V. was on the fritz."

He had been about to say that her T.V. was on the fritz, but it seemed unwise to adopt that explanation now. "No, her toilet wouldn't stop running," he said. He needed just enough detail to be convincing, and he made a stab at supplying it. "The arm on the ball cock was a little bent, okay?" It sounded even lamer than he expected. Besides, he now realized, Marie had trapped him. Despite what she said, it was the girl upstairs that really needed explaining.

"She just called you, I guess, and you came down to fix it." Her ardor seemed to have cooled, and he thought in that instant she was buying it.

"Sure, why not?" he said.

"And naturally, the shortest distance between two points is a straight line."

She had seen him jump from the balcony. "Oh."

"Yes, oh. I see it pretty clearly, I think. Knowing your neighbor was trapped beneath you with a bent ball cock, you leaped to the balcony, vaulted the rail, and dropped to the patio below so as to waste no time." She held up a hand to forestall anything he might say, but, really, he hadn't thought of anything he could say. "Let me finish. She was there on her patio to meet you, bent ball cock in hand, so you could take it from her immediately, wrestle it back into shape, then vault the fence and trot off on your next mission in your quest to save Earth. That's the story, isn't it?"

Though his reflexive grinning hadn't done him much good so far, he didn't seem able to stop it. "Marie, I—"

He made the mistake of touching her shoulder, and she flung him off, climbing to her feet. "Damn it," she said. "I liked you. Why did you have to turn out to be such a rat?"

She strode off down the sidewalk, and he sat, befuddled, and watched her go.

It was Rhonda's fault. For four years, nothing but sporadic phone calls, and then she turns up. Four years of "Hi, it's me. I'm calling from Oklahoma City. Do you remember Larry, my old friend Larry, whom I used to talk about incessantly? I'm staying with him." "Hi, David. Rhonda. I'm spending the next month or two with my old college roommate in Abilene. Jennifer?'' Tears sometimes, when things were going badly for her. She had been born with the curse of too much money, and no job could hold her in place for very long. He himself had been unable to hold her in this backwater, oil-rich, southern Texas town for very long.

He ran through a modest residential neighborhood laid out on deliberately curving streets, as far as he knew unique in the otherwise gridlike layout of the city. When he got to Forty-fifth Street, he turned south to run between huge square tracts of golden-grassed prairie. His apartment was only a half-mile from the southwest corner of town, and the transition from town to countryside was abrupt. To his left the sun gleamed on the great grain elevators that towered along the town's southern border.

He ran on the left side of the road, midway between the white line marking the road's edge and the double yellow line in the center. On both sides, tall grasses came to the very edge of the pavement.

Ball cock, he had to say *ball cock*. Marie had taken the word and by force of repetition had rendered it obscene. Clever, when you thought about it; Marie was a clever girl. So of course he had alienated her completely, he should have expected to do that. The great mystery was how he had managed to avoid doing it sooner.

Though Rhonda just turned up last night, and I'm blaming this on her, remember?

And what about Rhonda? Did she just need a place to stay this month, or was she thinking that after four years it was time the romance

was rekindled? Did he care? It was all too easy
to remember the first time they had flown a kite
together, the trip they made east to see New
York, the hike through the rare snowfall for gro-
ceries. What he needed to remember instead
were his own best interests, and involvement
with a girl crazed with wanderlust wasn't con-
sistent with those interests.

An approaching pickup swung out into the
other lane to pass him. In the cab sat two
middle-aged men wearing baseball caps and old
T-shirts. A rifle hung on the gun rack behind
their heads. The driver waved as they passed,
and David lifted a hand to them in return. It
was the easy friendliness of the Texas countryside that had attracted him to Texas in the first
place. In town people didn't wave as they
passed, there were too many people, but out here
it was different. Texas towns were isolated pockets of concentrated humanity on a vast, sparsely
populated plain.

He cut over to Washington Avenue for the run
back into town, breathing in the moist, warm air
through his nostrils, expelling it through his
mouth. When he reached Washington, he glanced
at his watch. Twenty-six minutes. It was time
to put the hammer down.

He stretched out his stride to eliminate the
bobbing. His breath was coming easy. With the
effortlessness of a god, he floated above the tar-
mac, and the wind was in his ears.

When he returned from his Olympian flight,
Rhonda was in his kitchen breaking eggs into a

clear glass bowl. On the stove bacon fried. The grease bubbled and popped.

He stood for a moment in the kitchen doorway. Her jeans were snug, and she was barefoot on his blue-and-white linoleum floor. Her brown hair was tucked behind her ear on the side nearest him and hung in a curtain beyond her face. She had clear skin, sun-reddened over the cheekbones. Her nose was upturned slightly.

She looked up, and he moved out of the doorway.

At breakfast they sat in high-backed chairs of oak at the round oak table in the dining area. David leaned over his plate, weight on his elbows, not looking at Rhonda as he ate. The bacon was crisp but not overcooked, and a light coat of grease glinted from it. She always had been a good cook.

"Is it all right?" she asked once.

He nodded, not looking at her, and wedged half a slice of Branola bread into his mouth to preclude further discussion.

"I stink," he said when he was finished with his food. He put his fork down on his plate, now clean but for a few spots of bacon grease, a few crumbs of Branola, and a faintly yellow egg residue over one-third of the plate. He picked up his grapefruit juice, drained the glass, and plunked it down on the table.

"I'd better shower."

And he locked the bathroom door behind him to stave off any thoughts she might have of joining him.

*   *   *

So laconic, he was, and so unlike himself! The problem was that it had all been said, said long ago and repeatedly. "Let's *not* get married right away," he had said. "We can have a long engagement."

"Okay by me. Let's have a long engagement. I consider us engaged."

"Not with me in Texas, and you in O.K. City."

"I intend to marry you, David."

"When?"

"As soon as I feel ready."

Another time, she had said, "Don't think you're the only one who's sad. I feel sorry for what has happened to us, too."

"You talk about it as if it were an act of God, not something you did."

"It was an act of God. These feelings were spinning around inside me, this uneasiness about the thing we were about to do forever."

"Meaning marriage."

"I felt like I was suffocating. I had to cut and run, that was no decision."

"Maybe the most important decisions in life are made with the guts rather than the head. That doesn't make them any less our decisions."

"This was more infection than decision."

"So you're coming back?"

"Soon. Soon."

And so she had, almost four years to the day after her departure. What were her intentions? He didn't know.

He cut off the water and toweled himself savagely with the big beige towel. What were *his* intentions? That was what he had to get clear on.

*   *   *

When he came out, she was in the living room, on the couch, her left arm resting on the overnight case beside her. She looked up at him, he in his shorts and rugby shirt, long sleeves pushed up to the elbows. Her gaze was fierce and her dry eyes shot through with fine crimson threads.

"I'm not going to force myself on you," she said, and when she spoke he could see her pain. "I'm back, if you want to try again. If you don't, tell me, and I'll go, and I won't trouble you anymore."

He looked at her, opened his mouth, and found himself unable to speak. Balanced on an emotional fence as narrow as the blade of a knife, he tottered toward rejection, toward acceptance, toward rejection again. He could say nothing.

She stood up, finally, the overnight case held high against the side of her chest. "Good-bye, David."

And she walked past him into the entrance hall and through the door of his apartment into the growing August heat.

The door she closed carefully behind her.

And he could not speak, not to call her back, not even to say good-bye.

3

ick saw Rhonda leave David's apartment,
though he took little note of it. He was sitting in the living room of a second-floor

Mick saw Rhonda leave David's apartment,
though he took little note of it. He was sitting in the living room of a second-floor
apartment in the next building, watching Diana
through a gap in the gauzy curtains that covered
the sliding-glass doors. A three-hundred-dollar
pair of field glasses brought her to him, revealed
the light, downy hair on her stomach, made ma-
jestic peaks of her breasts.

He had been obsessed with Diana ever since
she had come to see him after Leonard's arrest.
Mick had always thought her sexy, had always
admired her class—the way she wore her clothes
and the way she held her body. Leonard was a
pig. He had been so undeserving of her, so unap-
preciative; of course, Leonard liked boys.

Now that Mick had taken Leonard's freedom,
now that he was going to take his money, it only
made sense that he walk away with Leonard's
woman as well. Diana didn't seem to like him
much at the moment, but she could learn. That
was the great thing about women: They could
always learn.

*   *   *

As Mick's binoculars roamed over every contour of her body and lingered at the edges of her bathing suit, Diana lay with her eyes closed against the sunlight and against her own tears, unconscious of the attention she was getting. Before her mind's eye was Leonard's picture as she had seen it upon unfolding her newspaper that day, inexplicably a copy of the very photograph she kept on her dresser. Transposed into newsprint, the flashing smile seemed muddied; the intent but guileless eyes were shadowed. "Leonard Nash Arrested," the caption proclaimed, and the picture was transformed magically from a publicity still to a mug shot.

A tear slipped out from beneath one eyelid and ran down along the edge of her nose. She had not been all that surprised at the newspaper's recounting of swindles and frauds. For months Leonard had become progressively more hated and more reviled. The fact of the arrest was a shock. At first she had not even known where Leonard was being held.

Tentatively, she sought out Mick. He had always made her uncomfortable, but whatever there was to know, he would know it. Because he didn't answer his phone, she had to drive out to the isolated circle of condominiums to the northwest of town. Driving all the way out there emphasized to her Mick's aloofness. Everyone else she knew lived in the southwest quadrant of the town. Mexicans lived in the north, along with a large Vietnamese community. Blue-collar workers lived in matchbox houses and trailer parks in the southeast. Almost everyone else, all the professionals and the white-collar people, lived within a patch of about two square miles in the southwest. Not Mick.

Mick's car, a big, dark blue BMW, was parked at an angle in front of his condominium. Diana pulled in beside the big car and went up the flagstone walk to Mick's door. Even from the stoop, she could hear the doorbell sounding within, chimes but not the usual chimes: dit-dit-dit-dah. And she thought immediately of Beethoven. No one came to the door.

Dit-dit-dit-dah.

It was his car, she was sure. She went around Mick's building, along the sidewalk that ran between it and the building next to it. A man and a woman were playing tennis on one of the tennis courts. The man was coming in behind every serve, and his opponent was lobbing her returns over his head with telling effect. The man continued stubbornly to come in behind his serves. The game was soon over.

"What are you looking at?" the man called irritably to Diana, who stood with the fingers of one hand laced loosely through the chain-link fence.

She was taken aback that he had noticed her at all. "Nothing," she said, shaking her head, moving away.

As she approached the rectangular swimming pool, long enough for swimming laps, a big man pulled himself dripping from one end of the pool and came toward her. In his wake he left huge wet footprints on the white cement, along with a splattering of dark drops of water. He laughed when he was close enough to her to recognize her, and his laughter, like his voice, was harsh, disconcerting. "I thought I recognized your voice," he said. "Did you come to watch me swim? I'm afraid you're late, you just missed me."

She took Mick's hard, wet hand as she came closer. Mick and Leonard had been friends from childhood, but that didn't make Mick her friend. Though it was early afternoon and the sun was high above them, his big shoulders blocked the heat of the sun from her legs, and his shadow was chilling, even in the midsummer heat. "I think that's the most obnoxious man I ever met," she said, sotto voce, nodding at the tennis courts.

Mick, who had stooped above her to catch her words, straightened and looked past her at the couple on the tennis courts. The man and the woman were both watching them, racket heads resting on the green-painted asphalt of the tennis court.

Mick raised a hand above Diana. "How you doing?" he called in his grating voice.

The man coughed. "Fine, Mick. Doing fine." He motioned to his opponent, and the two of them approached the net.

"Do you know him?" Diana whispered. She glanced upward at his face, handsome but for a incongruously red and twisted nose, but most of her attention remained fixed unnaturally on his broad, gleaming pectorals. It was the first time she had seen him so nearly naked, and still he was holding her hand. Making no real attempt to keep his voice down, Mick said to her, "I played golf with him once, a pick-up game at the club. He's one of those guys who shot a round at par once, years back, in a wonderful streak of luck, and he takes that as his usual game. From then on he's scowling all the time because his game's off."

"He sounded scared of you." Diana glanced again at his face; then her gaze became fixed on the great plates of muscle that covered Mick's abdomen. His body was so much easier to look at than his face.

"Maybe I'm a scary guy." He released her hand then, chuckling, but with a hand on her shoulder he guided her to one of the lounge chairs that sat in a row along the side of the pool.

When Diana looked at the tennis courts again, the two players had gathered up their rackets and their racket covers and their gym bags, and they were heading off the courts—put to rout, midmatch.

"You should have brought your bathing suit. You could sun a little," Mick said.

"I came over because . . . didn't you see today's paper, Mick?"

"Ah, yes. You're here about Leonard. I was hoping you had come to see me."

She looked at him sharply, trying to penetrate his pale, gray eyes. There was no warmth of color in those eyes. She had never run into Mick without Leonard, she realized suddenly. "He's in jail," she said. "Don't you care?"

"Maybe he deserves to be in jail."

Diana's legs were extended on the lounge chair, and though she sat upright, her posture now seemed too casual for comfort. Mick sat sideways on the lounge chair beside her, his elbows resting on his thighs. The chairs were close enough that if she adopted the same posture, they would be sitting with their heads as close together as a pair of lovers.

"Diana," Mick began. He rested the tips of his fingers on her bare leg, just above the knee, and she seemed unnaturally aware of his hand, of the veins that stood out like welts on the backs of his hands and along his marbled forearms. "Did you notice where he was arrested?" Mick said.

"At Dallas-Fort Worth." Matter-of-fact.

"Attempting to board a plane for South America. Did you think he was going alone?"

She opened her mouth, hesitated. Said, "What are you saying? That he was running off with another woman?"

Mick smiled down at her thigh, where almost absently he was making tiny backhanded strokes with the tips of his fingernails. There was an uncomfortable electricity between them; angrily she shifted her leg to break contact. Mick looked at her mildly.

"No, I'm not saying that," he said.

"Good. I wouldn't have believed you."

"He was running off with a boy named Clark Holland."

"Clark . . ."

"The high school kid who runs errands for him."

"I don't believe you."

"The boy has a pet name for him. He calls him Leo."

"Why are you saying these things? I've met Clark Holland. The boy calls him Mr. Nash."

"Only in public, Diana. Think back. In all the years you've known him, did you never have any thought, any passing fancy, that maybe he had an unhealthy interest in men? Not all men, no, but little men. Delicate men. Pretty men."

"No." But she had hesitated.

"He was leaving you, Diana, running out on you, and taking his catamite and his ill-gotten fortune with him."

Diana swung her legs off the lounge chair and stood up, but before she could move away, Mick had stood up, too, and they were standing against each other, her blouse and the cuffs of her shorts brushing his bare skin. He held her in place for a moment, his big hands on her shoulders. "I'm sorry to be the one to tell you," he said, but she could tell it wasn't true.

She jerked away from him, hitting the lounge chair behind her so that its legs scraped along the cement patio. She ducked her head, turning it so she wouldn't have to look at Mick, wouldn't have to look at any part of him, as she hurried away.

When she reached her car she couldn't drive. She could only sit and blubber, her head resting against the top of the steering wheel.

Diana got up from her chaise lounge and went inside, crying again. Mick lowered his glasses. What he had told her that day had had its desired effect: It had driven a permanent wedge between Diana and Leonard. Diana was going through the mourning process; getting over Leonard, though obviously she had some more getting over to do.

"Hey, Otto, come here a minute. I'm leaving these binoculars here on this table, because I'm probably going to be back to use them from time to time. Maybe you'd like to glance out your window occasionally to see what's going on down there, and if you see anything interesting, call me."

"Okay." Otto crumpled his beer can and lobbed it at the trash can near the TV. He grinned. "It's not like I haven't spent plenty of time looking at her before this."

Mick scowled. Otto had been his weight-lifting partner about ten years ago, but he never had had any class.

"You're lucky my apartment is so well placed," Otto said.

"Yeah, yeah. Thanks for the key. I'll be back."

"Thanks for the beer," Otto said, and he patted the case on the floor beside him.

The sun had left Diana feeling dazed. Entering her air-conditioned apartment, she blinked in an effort to adjust her eyes, but her furniture sat in shadow. Inside her bathroom, she stepped out of her bathing suit and toed it into the corner of the room. The tile floor was cool on her bare feet.

She had to get over that guy. The relationship had only been a waste of, what, six years? Uh. The fine spray of water was cool on her face and shoulders. Concentrate on that, on the clean feel of water on her sun-heated body: an animal pleasure, but a real pleasure just the same.

The heavy towel was coarse against her skin. That, too, was good. The problem was that images of Leonard prompted images of Clark and, worse, images of the two of them together. When by an effort of will she pushed away those thoughts, she found herself remembering Mick and their last upsetting encounter.

She did have one pleasantly interesting thing to think about: There was that guy who came sweeping down from his balcony onto her patio this morning. What was the story behind that?

She made a real effort to call up his features as she pulled on her panties and fastened her bra. He was a good-looking guy. He lived right above her, apparently, and that raised possibilities.

Except, how old was he? Thirty? If he were only thirty, he was kind of young.

4

There were two men at the scarred wood table. "You want me to do what?" Cecil Armstrong said in a flat voice. He was the other man's lawyer, and, in keeping both with his profession and with the August heat, he wore a khaki suit, white shirt, and striped tie. Though it was hot here on the top floor of the Pepper County Courthouse and Cecil was sweating, his body betrayed him with an involuntary tremor.

"Represent Clark Holland," Leonard said.

"Who is dead, according to this morning's paper."

"Right. Here is his power of attorney, which he executed just this week."

"It gives you power of attorney."

"Well, no, actually. It's made out in blank. You'll have to type your name in. This was typed on an IBM Selectric, so if you can match that . . . What am I telling you for? You're the lawyer."

Cecil sighed and let his gaze slide away from Leonard's eyes. Leonard had the all-too-common misconception of what it was that lawyers did: They were the masters of the game called Lie, Cheat, and Steal, old hands at corner cutting and misdirection, and they fed on that complicated but lawful beast, the technicality.

He looked back into Leonard's pale brown, almost yellow eyes. There was no point in telling him that a dead man's power of attorney was without value; to Leonard, it would be a triviality. "What is it you want, Leonard? What's this about, really?" he asked.

Leonard's eyes had not left his face. "I want the contents of Clark's lock box at the First National Bank," he said.

"And what gives you the right to those contents—this power of attorney?"

"Clark's will."

"Which is where?"

"In your possession."

After a tired moment of silence that Leonard no doubt intended for dramatic effect, Cecil raised his eyebrows to let Leonard know he was waiting for Leonard to explain himself. Leonard's files were voluminous, and over the last several months most of them had filtered into Cecil's possession. Back at the office there was a storeroom devoted to them. To find there was a will buried among the other papers was no great shock.

Leonard smiled, enjoying his imagined suspense. "It's in the box of files marked Lazy Y Ranch, in a folder bearing Clark Holland's name," he said.

"Huh."

"It names me executor, too. I'll be wanting you to probate the will for me."

"But first you want the stuff in this lock box."

"Yes."

"Why?"

"It's valuable. There may be people out there who know about it and are angling to get it. I want you to get there first."

"What people?"

"Any people. Clark Holland's murderer, his roommate, his old girlfriend—anyone."

"What's in the lock box?"

"Get it and see."

Cecil looked at him. Today Leonard was wearing olive green chinos with a razor-sharp crease, and a linen shirt that remained crisp somehow despite the heat. In jail only a week, his heavy tan had not yet begun to pale.

"Who killed Clark Holland?" Cecil said. The murder had become news only that morning, and the body could not be more than hours cold.

"I don't know," Leonard said.

"Who do you think killed Clark Holland?"

"I don't know."

"Speculate."

"I can't."

"Is it possible that someone killed him who was after the stuff in this lock box, this valuable stuff you've told me about?"

"I don't know."

"It is possible then."

"I didn't say that."

"You didn't say it wasn't possible."

"Look, why are you cross-examining me? I'm your client."

Cecil sighed again. Leonard was his client. His fee was secured by a first deed of trust on a big block of slum housing on the east side of town. Leonard was in bankruptcy, and the law firm of

McKinnon, Armstrong and Cuneo was soon to be a slum lord.

Cecil took the power of attorney from the table, refolded it, and slipped it into an inside pocket of his suit jacket. "I'll take this," he said, looking not at Leonard and his pale, earnest eyes, but at the wall behind Leonard. The walls here were metal, painted an institutional green. "And if the will says what you say it does, I'll probate it for you. I'll make sure the bank knows the lock box is part of Clark Holland's estate—if it is—and that will effectively seal it for us. For now, though, the stuff in the lock box stays where it is."

"You can't do that, Cecil. You're supposed to be representing my interests."

"I am representing your interests, and I'll keep on representing your interests. I'll represent the hell out of every lawful interest you have."

"What does that mean? Every lawful interest I have? Are you saying I'm some kind of crook?"

"A grand jury has said it. That's why you're awaiting trial up here on the seventh floor of the courthouse."

"And you say it, too, that I'm a crook."

Cecil pushed himself away from the table, his wooden chair squeaking back on the grimy tile floor, and he stood up. "I'm not saying it, Leonard. You're the one who grabbed hold of the phrase 'lawful interest' like I'm not permitted to distinguish between lawful interests and unlawful interests. It may be that part of my representation of you is helping *you* to distinguish the two. All I'm saying is that you're not going to use me as a cat's-paw to carry out every little piece of business you have in mind without me exercising my own judgment. That's going to have to be good enough for you, because there's not a lawyer in this town who's going to tell you any differently."

"All right, all right," Leonard said, holding up his hands. "I just wanted to be clear on things." He didn't get mad. Leonard, in Cecil's experience, was a man who never got mad, who never showed any real emotion. Life for Leonard was one of uninterrupted gamesmanship. Sometimes Cecil speculated that Leonard was not really a human being, but an alien actor of monumental talent wearing a human costume cunningly detailed.

Leonard's calm in the face of Cecil's own heated outburst left him feeling overbalanced and awkward. He tried to speak calmly: "If it turns out that Clark did own the contents of the lock box and that it did pass to you on his death . . ."

"Doesn't the ownership of the lock box . . ."

"Determine the ownership of the contents? Not necessarily. If it did pass to you on his death yesterday, that was well after you filed your bankruptcy petition . . ."

"Two months after."

"Yes."

"Which means my creditors are out of it. It all belongs to me."

"Assuming that Clark did not acquire this stuff from you, assuming he was not merely holding it for you, assuming . . ."

Leonard was nodding vigorously, waving him to silence. Cecil left off with his qualifications. "Just how valuable a lock box are we talking about here?" he asked again. Several of Leonard's creditors were good friends of his. He had taken on Leonard as a client despite that apparent conflict of interest—after full disclosure—because that same conflict would have existed for just about any lawyer in town.

"Open the lock box . . ."

". . . and I'll see. I know. Are we talking on the order of five thousand dollars or fifty thousand dollars?"

Leonard's mouth was a thin pale line.

"Or five hundred thousand or five million?"

Leonard smiled. "Somewhere in there," he said.

"Somewhere in there," Cecil said. Somewhere between five thousand dollars and five million. He stood up to go. Leonard stood with him, smiled at him, patted his shoulder.

Cecil's gaze fixed on Leonard's temple, as if his gaze were a laser and he could, with sufficient concentration, bore into Leonard's cranium and see the pattern of Leonard's soul. He saw only skin and hair.

Cecil sighed and shifted his gaze, feeling helpless and hapless. Leonard's head made a better door than a window, as his father would have said.

At his car, Cecil Armstrong stopped and looked back across the lush, green lawn at the courthouse, which shone white against a sky of flawless blue, reflecting sunlight so strongly as to be painful to the eyes. In Pepper County, this courthouse was the tangible manifestation of Justice, which Cecil believed existed as the courthouse did, high and shining white. Yet the walls of the courthouse corridors were dingy and the floor tiles bore the permanent stain of grime, symbolic of . . . what? The difficult, shoddy compromises necessary to obtain even the rough shadow of Justice? Was Justice's edifice a whited sepulcher?

Ah, he was sick and weary of spirit. Most mornings he woke feeling keenly the pang of disappointment at finding himself still in the world of the living rather than in that final place of rest and surcease. It was one-forty-five on Saturday afternoon, less than twenty-four hours since Clark's murder, and already Leonard was maneuvering for the contents of a lock box that had been in Clark's possession.

From the newspaper article, Cecil knew that Clark Holland had been seventeen years old, old enough to have testamentary capacity, not old enough to have accumulated much of an estate unless it was by inheritance. The source of these lock box valuables was likely to have been Leonard himself. If it had been, those valuables now belonged—probably, almost certainly—not to Leonard but to his many creditors.

It required looking into. Cecil had filed an asset schedule with the bankruptcy court that had not listed the contents of any lock box, and he was not going to participate in a fraud on the court. There would be time enough to get tough with Leonard when he knew the truth—something he couldn't learn from Leonard, who couldn't distinguish truth from a bag of warm donkey droppings.

On the drive back to the office—the town was

small enough that it only took five minutes, hardly time enough for the a/c to start blowing cold air—Cecil sweated and mopped his face with a white cotton handkerchief. A traffic light ahead of him turned yellow and then red against him, and he stopped the car, a little too suddenly. The fact was, he had had a sudden fear of the car failing to stop and rolling gently into the intersection, where a semi thundered ponderously by. His heart rate double-timed briefly.

My God, my God, he thought, feeling breathless. *I am coming apart.*

He had been having these weak spells a couple of times a week recently, and he did not know why, did not *want* to know why.

Why him? Why had Leonard come to him? Leonard had limited use for men with scruples or even for men who might have scruples. And Leonard would not have moved so fast, would not have called him at home on a Saturday with mingled promises and threats, all tinged with desperation, unless he considered this lock box at risk. Cecil wiped his face again and shoved his rumpled handkerchief into his jacket's side pocket. Leonard had set him on yet another quest, and he was tired of quests.

Suppose. Suppose whoever killed Clark knew about these hidden valuables and had gotten the key to the safety deposit box from his corpse yesterday. Suppose Clark was not personally known to the bank officer who would be in charge of the lock boxes on Monday morning, that this bank officer would not remember Clark's death from Saturday morning's paper. Suppose the unknown killer would be able to fake some identification identifying him as Clark and would have the brass nuts necessary to use it.

He drove to the office even though it was Saturday. Though he rarely had the energy to go to the office on Saturdays—at forty-eight, he rarely had any energy, which made him wonder what loss of energy fifty-eight would bring—the other lawyers would be there. His law firm consisted almost exclusively of six-day-a-week lawyers. For them, as it had once been for Cecil, law was not a living but a life.

Not that Cecil had any other life; there was no one at home waiting for him, and there had not been since the divorce. His only daughter would be in her third year of college at the University of Alaska, of all places, and she spent her summers there. His wife had returned to Dallas, where she had grown up, though as far as he knew she no longer had any family there. Still, the old house was full of distractions: a lawn to be mowed, a hedge to be clipped, weeds to be pulled from the cracks in the sidewalk, laundry to do, a dripping faucet that needed a new washer, a refrigerator stocked with lots of beer and juice, but not a lot of food.

By the time he got to the office, his starched white shirt had wilted and circles of perspiration shone dark beneath the armpits of his lightweight suit.

Al Cuneo and Frank McKinnon were in the reception area by the elevators. Behind them stretched the city, visible through the wall of floor-to-ceiling windows. Grain elevators stood along the city's southern border, and a patchwork quilt of fields lay beyond them.

Frank, who was in his late forties, wore gray trousers and a plaid, short-sleeved shirt. His black knit tie was knotted loosely below his open collar, and in deference to the heat he had not worn a jacket. He sat in the receptionist's swivel chair, his hands laced behind his head.

Al Cuneo, six or seven years younger than Frank, sat on a desk top. He wore cuffed white shorts, a sports shirt, and Timberland topsiders without socks. His legs were black with thick, curly hair, and only a few wisps of downy hair were on his pate.

"Cecil," Frank said, too obviously surprised too see him on a Saturday. Had it been so long?

"Frank," he said. "Al."

Al said, "We were just going to lunch. Want to come?"

Cecil glanced at his watch. It was almost two o'clock. He shook his head. "Got some things to check on," he said.

"For a client?"

"Leonard Nash."

"Ah. He got you, then. He tried here this morning."

"He got me. And I think I may have uncovered that stash everybody thinks he has."

Frank's chair gave a hard squeak as he sat forward. "Oh, boy."

"Yeah."

"How much?" Al said.

Cecil shrugged. "It's in a safety deposit box. I'll find out Monday."

Frank said, "Do you two remember all his earnest assurances that nothing was left? All those real estate scams . . ."

"That solar energy thing . . ."

". . . the chain of convenience stores."

"But you could almost believe all of it was gone," Al said. "All six, seven million. You know, he bought a new sports car every year. For a couple of years he had that chauffeured limo. Who else do you know with an indoor swimming pool? Who else flew to Vegas every other weekend in a privately chartered jet?"

"I may be wrong. It may be nothing, or nothing much," Cecil said. "He wants into this lock box. He wouldn't say what was in it."

Between the three of them, they had diligently defended Leonard in lawsuit after lawsuit, and had duly lost each one. Had filed a bankruptcy petition for him when it became inevitable, had stayed with him after his attempted flight. His was a no-asset bankruptcy case, meaning that after the secured creditors took their collateral, and Leonard claimed his personal exemption, there would be no assets left to pay any unsecured or undersecured creditors—including those he swindled, defrauded, or embezzled from. Under Texas law the property exempt from the claims of Leonard's creditors included his half-million-dollar home, his home furnishings, and two of his cars. Naturally, Leonard's victims were highly incensed about all of it.

"You know he wasn't fleeing the country with nothing," Al said.

"It was just a matter of knowing where it was," Frank said. "I wonder, though, why he would tell you."

"He has to know we're going to turn it over to the bankruptcy court," Al said.

"It may be nothing," Cecil repeated, and, waving them silent, he went back to his office.

So many people Leonard had fleeced. Several years ago Leonard had bought a handful of abandoned 7-11's and leased them to another convenience store chain (an undercapitalized corporation Leonard controlled) at a rent more than double the fair market value, thereby cheating the other shareholders. The favorable leases increased the value of Leonard's buildings—in fact, nearly doubled their value. Leonard then sold the buildings at the inflated value for roughly six hundred thousand dollars to a limited partnership he set up, a limited partnership consisting primarily of doctors at the Baptist hospital. Since Leonard kept a twenty-five percent interest in the limited partnership, that put four hundred fifty thousand dollars cash in his pocket.

The linchpin of the ungainly contraption was the convenience store chain. It, after all, brought in the revenues that paid the rent. For more than a year Leonard kept it running by shifting money, real and apparent, from pocket to pocket at a frenetic pace. Finally there was no more cash to shift and the suppliers went unpaid, which choked off the inventory. The convenience stores folded abruptly, all of them, and the shareholders lost everything they had put into them. The corporation defaulted on its leases. Suddenly the renovated 7-11's were empty, no new lessees were forthcoming, and it looked like the stores were worth even less than Leonard himself had paid for them. Hundreds of thousands of dollars had passed into Leonard's hands, never to be seen again.

The setup was typical of more than a dozen others, which was why Leonard was now sitting in the Pepper County Jail awaiting trial on ninety-seven felony counts.

Cecil stopped thinking about it, tired of caring. His elbows were on the desk and his head was braced between the palms of his hands when one of the younger lawyers looked in on him. "Hey, Cecil," he said. "I think they're about ready to go to lunch."

Cecil looked up and made an effort to smile. "I've got some things to clear up here, first. If you're all going to the Steakhouse, I might be along later."

David Loring looked at him a moment, then nodded and went on. David was a fifth-year associate at the firm, too much younger than Cecil to press him, though even Frank or Al might not have bothered. Whatever Cecil said, nobody expected him to show up at the Steakhouse. Gradually, gradually, he was less and less a part of the firm's essential composition.

When everybody else had gone, Cecil went home. Somehow he got through the rest of Saturday.

Then Sunday.

Then . . .

5

Monday. Cecil Armstrong soft-boiled an egg and ate it out of the shell. He drank a small glass of orange juice. He used to read the paper while he ate, but at some point he had let his subscription lapse. He didn't listen to music. They had had a nice stereo system, but Laura had taken it with her when she left. He ate as he always did, in silence, sitting at the small formica table in the kitchen.

A bottle opener with a magnet in it held a picture drawn in crayon to the front of the refrigerator. The picture was drawn on faded construction paper, badly abraded along one edge. The crayon colors, drawn in a heavy, childlike hand, were brown and green and purple. Above the picture, which was obviously meant to represent a man, a child had scrawled "I love you Daddy. Sarah."

He had come across it several weeks before, in a box of papers he was throwing away. When his daughter had given it to him (at age four?), he had smiled and patted her head and told her she was a good girl; it was very, very nice, thank you so much. After it had spent a few days on his dresser, he threw it in a box. The fact that it was a gift, that she had done it for him, had left him untouched. His life had been too full then for him even to notice such bounty.

Now it was sixteen years later; he had come across it and cried.

He finished eating, washed his glass and his dish, and set them in the drain. His cabinets were filled with glasses, mugs, and plates of all sizes, but he lived pretty much on the handful of plates and glasses sitting in his drain.

He pulled on his suit jacket and went out to his car, locking the back door mechanically behind him. Because it was Monday, he drove out to the sandstone cliffs overlooking the eastern part of Lake Merriweather. He spent a lot of time out there, looking out over the blue water. He began every week there, seeking the impetus to start another one.

Sitting on the hood of his Jaguar, he listened to the birds and the crickets and the wind in the tall grasses that grew to the edge of the cliff. Below and to his left was the marina and its cluster of reedlike masts. The water washed against the rocks below him with a peaceful murmur, and the sun cast a glinting yellow streamer across the water.

Here he could think about his wife, whom he had long neglected and who now was gone. She had a career now with a Dallas art firm called Rupert and Holmes. She had a social life. Once, when he had tended to rage about such things, a private detective reported to him that she was seeing a man named Lawson Grindstaff. Whether she was seeing him still or seeing someone else now, he didn't know. Laura was no longer part of his life, though there was last week's phone call to think about.

"Sarah's getting married, Cecil," she had told him. He heard the control in her voice and wondered at the pain he still caused her.

"Cecil? Are you still there?"

"Yes."

"Sarah didn't call you about it?"

"No."

Laura went on to tell him about the man his daughter was marrying. A Ralph Elliot, and Laura had flown up to meet him. "He's terribly distracted all the time, like you were. Half the time he's talking to you, he's thinking about something else. He's—a law student." Her control wavered briefly, and he heard the grief in her voice, grief for the daughter who would marry a man like her father.

He cleared his throat so that when he spoke his own voice would be even. "Does that leave him any good points?"

"Oh, integrity. Brains. Charm, when he cares to use it. He's generous. I expect he'll do well financially."

He cleared his throat again. "Well, that's something."

Which started her crying. He tried to comfort her, as best one could by telephone. When it seemed to him that the tears had become excessive for the circumstances, he asked if something else was wrong.

"He even looks like you," she said finally. She sobbed and hung up on him.

That was midafternoon on Thursday. He got no more work done that day, little done on Friday. Now, though, he could handle it. He could replay the conversation and think out its implications without it getting him down.

A quarter slipped out of his pants pocket and clattered on the long hood of the car. He slipped off the hood of his car to pick it up and hurl it out over the lake. He counted so he could estimate the cliff's height, but he didn't hear the plop, just the gentle washing of the water against the shore, its placidity undisturbed.

His lovely daughter, Sarah, majoring in drama at the University of Alaska, as far from her father and mother as she could possibly get. If she were doing well, it was all right. It wasn't imperative that their lives intersect, just that her life, wherever she lived it, was filled with dignity and meaning. And she was getting married. It was good that she was close enough to Laura to tell her, that Laura cared enough about him to call him and let him know.

He walked for a bit. In time, he was at peace, and he could go on.

Cecil and Mick both got to First National Bank early Monday morning. It wasn't like either had to hunt among the bank's various branches; branch banking did not exist in Texas. Each man was interested in Clark Holland's safety deposit box. Only Cecil had a clear idea of how to get in it, and to do it, he had to make a stop along the way.

At nine-fifteen he carried his largest brief-case—empty—into the First National Bank with him, and he asked the receptionist behind the rail in the lobby for Walt Jeffries, who, when buzzed, came out of his glass-walled office with his hand extended and a broad smile stretching across his face. "Hi, Cecil, how are you?"

They shook hands. Cecil allowed that he was doing fine. On an empty desk in the carpeted part of the lobby, behind the rail, Cecil showed Walt his paperwork, which included a court order that District Judge Alan "Mac" McElroy had executed for him only thirty minutes before. Together they went back to the vault.

"Oops, let me get my keys."

Cecil waited for him, holding the handle of his briefcase in both hands before him. Walt came back, they went in and unlocked drawer number 951. "Here, you can look at it on this table," Walt said, pointing. "I've got a call waiting I've got to take care of. If you could just bring your sched-ule by my office on your way out, I'll sign it for you."

"Hey, Walt . . ." But with a smile and a quick salute Walt was gone. Cecil sighed, looking at the black handles of the zippered gym bag crammed into the drawer. He lifted it out and carried it to the table. The bag was heavy.

It wasn't the way it was done. He had known Walt a long time, and he was aware of Walt's pattern of carelessness in the interests of expedi-ency. Walt took Cecil's faithfulness for granted, which was well and good, but there was protec-tion for both of them in following procedures to the letter.

The gym bag had a Texaco logo on one side and the inscription "Texas Rangers" on the other. It had a soiled look: a large raspberry stain, an odor so faint it could have been all in his imagination.

He could wait until Walt finished with his call and returned. He could carry the bag into Walt's office and open it in the big middle of the man's desk. On the other hand, the thing about Nash— the thing that had cost everyone so dearly—was that *nothing* associated with him had any value, whatever its apparent worth.

With another sigh, Cecil pulled back the zipper.

When Cecil came in to the bank that morning, Mick was already standing by one of the high, round tables in the lobby. The table had its own chained pen, its stacks of blank deposit and withdrawal slips, its brochures on the Christmas Club, high-interest CD's, and car loans. Mick was trying his best to be inconspicuous, but there was a bank teller, a young woman in her mid-twenties, who kept glancing at him. Not with awe or lust, either. He knew what it was; he'd seen it too often before. The fascination of abomination, his legacy from his dear departed, dear decaying, long-since-rotted mother. Another man might draw looks that suggested the woman was interested in going out—a dinner date, perhaps, followed by a playful romp amid the bedclothes. Mick didn't draw such looks, didn't have such dates, though such a prospect with this teller would have appealed to him. As it was he would rather she kept her mind on business.

He had the key to the lock box, but banks didn't work like post offices. A key alone didn't give you access. The thing he had thought of after that knot-head Clark thoughtlessly fell on his own damn knife was that, when you died, your bank froze your accounts and denied everyone access to your lock box until somebody could jump through all the tedious hoops of probate.

He had no plan to get around that. He was hanging around to get the feel of things, to assimilate facts, however trivial, to sort things out in his mind. He had thought of approaching the receptionist, presenting himself as Clark Holland, but on the desk behind her was a copy of the morning paper. Did it mean she had seen the follow-up article in the inside section and knew that Clark was dead? No, but they were calling Clark's spastic accident with the knife a murder, and he was reluctant to establish any bond between himself and the dead boy. He had been in the apartment twice. Suppose he *had* left a fingerprint somewhere?

So he stood filling out a withdrawal slip for an account that did not exist, studying the brochure on low-interest car loans, watching a score or more of bank customers come and go, until a graying man in a seersucker suit pushed through the swinging section of the rail into the carpeted area and asked for Walt Jeffries. Mick watched the man because he looked familiar, he could not say how he was familiar; more importantly, he watched because the man was getting closer to the bank's vault than he, Mick, was getting.

"Hi, Cecil, how are you?" The smiling banker, the false bonhomie, the two-handed handshake. The two men studied papers on the desk behind the receptionist, pushing the newspaper's morning edition casually aside, saying things like, "Like to get into this lock box," "Court order," "Inventory."

As he watched, Mick crumpled his withdrawal slip and pushed it into the side pocket of his jacket—it had his name on it now—and he pushed the brochure on car loans back into its rack. He was associating the graying man with Leonard, though associated how he couldn't say.

He glanced at the teller and caught her looking at him again. She smiled uncertainly.

He smiled back, patting the breast pocket of his suit. "Forgot my checkbook," he said softly, almost mouthing the words. It was the best he could do to make his lengthy stay in the bank lobby plausible. He didn't bank there.

He felt her eyes on him as he strode confidently to the revolving doors and pushed through. So much for inconspicuous, he thought.

With any luck, it wouldn't matter.

Cecil found himself looking at roughly a dozen stacks of folded documents, rubber-banded together. The gym bag was crammed with them. On the front of the top document in each stack was a sketch of a long suspension bridge, and below it, "City of San Francisco, State of California."

He pulled the rubber band off of one of the stacks. Each of the documents looked the same. He had to pull one out and unfold it to find that it was a twenty-year bond, issued in March 1983. A page of interest coupons was attached. The face amount was five thousand dollars. The bond was made out to Bearer.

He had hit the mother lode.

He slid the municipal bond back inside the rubber band. There had been no bearer bonds issued after 1983. Congress had effectively eliminated their sale, fearful that if securities couldn't be linked to their holder, the holder might not pay taxes on the interest income.

Cecil riffled the stack. About twenty bonds, each identical, from what he could see of them. He pushed the stack back into the gym bag, hefted the bag as if to judge its weight. His mind was multiplying it out: twenty bonds per stack, times a dozen stacks, times five thousand dollars per bond. This was the heft of great wealth, and liquid wealth at that.

He rested the bag on the table to zip it shut.

Wrote, "Texas Rangers gym bag; municipal bonds, 200 or more, $5,000 denominations" on his probate schedule. Signed it.

He levered the gym bag into his briefcase, snapped shut the clasps, and took his schedule into Walt's office to get his signature, thinking, *This is like buying time on TV-10, what with Walt's mouth.* Walt signed without reading, though, still talking on the phone. "Sure, Jim, no problem. I understand." He winked at Cecil, gave him a parting wave.

I'm walking out the door a millionaire, Cecil realized. Nobody knows it but me.

Mick sat in his car in the parking lot, wondering which of the cars belonged to the man inside. Not that it mattered. The man would come out and get into one of them, and Mick would follow.

Alternatively, the man worked in one of the nearby office buildings and would be leaving the bank on foot. He would still come through the revolving glass doors, and Mick would follow.

If the man got in a car, the most likely prospect was a big gray Oldsmobile with a car-phone antenna. The man looked like a lawyer or a high-level executive; the car fit the profile. An Acura Legend was another possibility. A Chrysler K-car and a Chevrolet Chevette weren't even worth considering. A slightly more likely possibility was a dark green Jaguar that looked about five years old. Its windshield was caked with grime beyond the reach of the wipers, and a wash of mud rose up around the right rear tire. Mick was betting on the Oldsmobile.

The man came out finally and went to the Jaguar. He unlocked the front door on the driver's side, pressed a button, and opened the rear door to drop his briefcase in behind the seat. He was handling that briefcase like it weighed something.

Lawyer, not executive, that's what he was. One of the ones who invested in Leonard's oil-field equipment scam? Mick followed the Jaguar into a parking garage across from the Pioneer Building, an office tower that had housed the now-defunct Pioneer Savings Bank on the lower floors. If he remembered right, it was Pioneer Savings that had built an underground tunnel to its parking garage—any way to spend a buck, in those days.

Not the oil-field equipment. Who was representing Leonard now?

The Jaguar pulled into a space two levels down. The McKinnon law firm. McKinnon, Armstrong, and, oh, Cuneo. Mick stopped his car behind the Jaguar to block it in.

Cecil was opening his rear door to get the briefcase when he heard a car door slam and looked up to see someone getting out of a car that was stopped directly behind him, its motor idling. The car was a dark blue BMW, a big one. He didn't know the man.

"How you doing?" the man said in a voice like rending metal, as he came around the car toward him. He was a big guy, broad in the shoulders as well as tall, and he was wearing an expensive-looking suit, though, incongruously, his nose was a squashed vegetable, broken many times, badly reset.

The pug-ugly face, the voice, the hand reaching into the jacket pocket—Cecil's heart broke into a thundering gallop as his adrenal gland dumped its entire contents into his bloodstream. He had thought he was having a panic attack at the traffic light! This was the real thing: instant sweat, all over his body; instant palpitations. "How you doing . . . ," and before the harsh tones had died away, Cecil was slamming the rear door, opening the driver's door again, tossing the heavy briefcase across the driver's seat onto the passenger's side as if it were a toy.

"Hey," the big man shouted, quickening his steps.

Cecil swung into the car, pulling the door shut behind him even as the man outside the car got his hand on the door handle, as the automatic door locks snapped down. Cecil jammed his key at the ignition, and it went in like a spike into soft soil, so perfect was his aim. The Jaguar roared to life, slammed hard into reverse, plowed backward into the big Beemer, sluing it around. There was a metallic shriek as the Jaguar grated along the side of the Beemer, as the big man stumbled back, his face expanding in surprise, the Jaguar's door handle ripped off and in his hand.

The Jag was free of the BMW, headlights facing headlights. Cecil shifted gears, tromped on the accelerator, and the car jumped past the idling BMW as the man's body landed on the car at the windshield's edge, as his fist drove through the window by Cecil's face in a shower of glass. The man fell away.

The suspension screamed as Cecil turned the car onto the next level of the parking garage, the rear tires sliding.

Mick had run to the center of the garage and leaped, catching the sloping rail of the next level, raising himself, throwing himself over.

As Cecil accelerated up the ramp toward the entrance, he saw the big man rising up between two of the cars, a terrible figure of judgment, bleeding hands held together and extended in front of him, in them a dark object that drew in all light and Cecil's gaze with it. Gun, he thought, and threw himself down across the seat as his Plexiglas windshield crumpled in a million fragments stretched in starry white opaqueness across his dash.

The car tore blindly through the exit, taking with it the broken arm of the tollgate. Cecil spun the wheel, his head hanging through his side window, trying to find his lane with the big car. He tugged at a loose edge of his windshield in an effort to peel it back. The car bounced back into the road from a curb, and he was back in control.

He turned right at the first corner he came to. He did not slow down.

Cecil stopped the car finally in the parking lot of the Sheraton, beside the dumpsters in back of the building. As soon as he had the car stopped and the parking brake set, he began to shake. He sought out his eyes in the mirror, seeking reassurance from his own reflection. Finding none.

There was glass everywhere. Tiny fragments seemed to grate in his very pores, cutting, working inward. He touched the spot of blood on his cheek, saw that already his hand was sheathed in bright blood. He turned his head and saw that blood covered his neck, darkened the collar of his shirt and of his suit. He probed at his face, looking for a glass cut deep enough to account for all of the blood. He felt no pain.

When he found the source of the blood, he leaned back against the headrest, holding his ear. The bullet had hit him. He began to giggle.

The bullet had hit him and passed on, taking the great part of his left earlobe with it.

He was afraid to go to his office. The last time he had tried that, he had been shot. It was the visual image of the man who had done it, however, that set the muscles in his abdomen to quivering. That image rushed in on him, and, trembling, he pushed it away only to have it come at him again. In this internal vision, the man was bigger than he could possibly have been in reality, tall as a shadow, impossibly broad of shoulder and narrow of hip. A crimson light was reflected on his face, and his voice was metallic and unearthly. In fact, when he thought what description he could give of the man, he could come up with nothing but his size—oh, and the rumpled nose, a detail too human to be quite forgotten.

He drove because he could not stay forever in a hotel parking lot, and as he drove his giddiness left him and depression settled in. Almost, he began to think of his attacker, not as a person, but as a representation of the chaos that had destroyed his life from without and increasingly threatened it from within.

He drove past his house, and though it looked benign and harmless across his slightly overgrown and bedraggled yard, he did not stop. He circled the block and went past his house again. No dark giant was pressed against the clapboards; no dark BMW was in the driveway. He circled two blocks. Then three.

Four blocks from his house and one street over, a large dark car was parked against the curb. Adorning its trunk was the blue and white shield of the Bavarian Motor Works. Cecil rolled to a stop behind it, his head swiveling back and forth lest Grendel burst forth from the ground and take him.

The car, by all appearances, was empty. No one was in sight, save an elderly lady wearing a pale sweater despite the August heat and walking a diminutive poodle.

Cecil climbed carefully from his car, leaving his car door open, his engine running. He walked around the front of his car and saw that the front panel of the passenger side of the BMW had been crushed. On closer inspection of the damage, he could find traces of his Jaguar's dark green paint. The BMW's presence, so close to his home, suggested, strongly suggested, that his attacker knew where he lived. It suggested only a little less strongly that even now his attacker was inside his house, waiting for his eventual return.

Strangely, he felt no apprehension; perhaps it was just that he had run through his emotional energies for the day. He felt numbness. He had a new vision now, one of pulling into his driveway, walking up to the back door wagging his briefcase, letting himself inside the house. Oblivion.

He stepped back from the car, looking at it a little vacantly because still in the grip of the vision. Five minutes ago, he didn't know about the car and he could have done it, he could have gone home. His fate would have descended on him unknowing. He would have been helpless before it.

Now, he knew. Some premonition had awakened in him and kept him from going home, perhaps the same premonition that had put the fear of the devil in him back at the parking garage. It was not his time. Someday his time would come. His body would fall, wearily, his soul be set free. Someday, not yet.

And deep within his spirit—queerly, even neurotically—what he felt was the faintest twinge of . . . regret.

6

It was Tuesday afternoon, just before four o'clock. David Loring had settled into the long afternoon's paper grind that would end for him sometime between six-thirty and seven o'clock. It was a sleepy afternoon, made more so by the susurrant rush of the air conditioner and the general lack of activity in the hallway outside his office. David's secretary Nancy swept into his office with the answers to interrogatories he had dictated only fifteen minutes before, and he looked up, jaws creaking in a great yawn.

"Goodness," said Nancy.

"Nancy, how am I going to maintain any sense of accomplishment, if the minute I get something off my desk and onto yours, you're bringing it right back?"

"Work harder?"

"Easy enough for you to say, when you move at twice the speed of anyone else."

"Indeed." She marched out with her nose held absurdly high, turning back in the doorway to give him a brief grin. She was, in David's opinion, as smart as any lawyer in the firm, himself included: a secretary because her schooling had stopped with a high school diploma.

As he yawned again, Frank McKinnon, at forty-nine the firm's oldest partner, leaned into his office to say, "Davises are here. I saw them sitting in the lobby."

His voice was unusually sharp, and David stifled his yawn. "It's Cecil's case. I just did a deposition for him once when he had to be in Austin."

"Where is Cecil, do you know?" Frank came in and sat in one of David's client chairs.

"Uh-uh. He isn't here?"

"Nobody's seen him since Saturday." Frank was sitting forward in his chair, grimly setting about the task of cracking each of his knuckles. He seemed alarmed by Cecil's absence, which in turn alarmed David.

"A road trip?" he ventured. "Doesn't anybody know?"

"He missed a court date this morning," Frank said. "It didn't turn out to be any big deal. The judge called, and Al handled it."

"Still, it's not like Cecil."

"No, it's not like Cecil." Frank had finished with his knuckles, but he seemed distracted by one of the diplomas on the wall behind David's head. David did not turn to look; he had never seen Frank so anguished.

"I'm not being straight with you," Frank said, focusing on him finally. "The police called here about noon, a Lieutenant Macklin. They found Cecil's car, abandoned apparently, in the parking lot of the Greyhound bus terminal. Macklin wanted to talk to Cecil."

"Do you mean his car was parked there overnight? What makes it abandoned?"

Frank tilted his head to one side and then the other, too distressed to speak.

"Bullet hole in the windshield, whole thing opaque from all the lines running through it."

David's face became still. "No," he said. "No."

"Greyhound called it in this morning. The car had been there at least twenty-four hours, but maybe longer. It could have been there as early as Saturday, which was the last time anybody saw him. Police called here after they checked it out."

"How do they know it was a bullet hole? Every hole is not a bullet hole."

"It is when there's a .38-caliber bullet embedded in the headrest. And apparently there's some dried blood on the seat—or it looks like blood. They're doing tests. If Cecil doesn't show up, all this is going to be in the papers tomorrow."

"Did they look in the trunk?"

Frank nodded soberly. "No Cecil, thank God."

"In the bushes?"

"Yes, and he isn't in any of the hospitals, either here or in San Antonio. He isn't at home."

David and Frank sat and looked at each other, a numbing lethargy developing between them. When David stood, it took an effort of will. "I'll cover the Davises," he said. His voice cracked. He cleared his throat and said it again.

"Fine." Frank shook his head as if to clear it. "You might want to meet with them in Cecil's office, if the files are in there."

*   *   *

David found the Davises already in Cecil's office. Cecil had one of the firm's four corner offices, and his windows, huge expanses of plate glass, overlooked the town to the south and east. His desk was clear of papers and books, but Cecil was always neat. The dark cherry wood gleamed like a polished coffin.

Regina Davis stood up when David came in. Her husband Bob stayed in his seat and nodded his head. Regina was their spokesperson. After David apologized for Cecil's absence, she said that they were there to quit.

"Quit?"

"We want to drop our suit against Dr. Shackelford. We've gone over and over it together, and we don't think it's right."

Bob's chin came up. "Her mother don't like it. She's a big Baptist from way back, and she says Christians don't sue one another in the courts." His wife looked at him, and his head slid down into his neck ever so slightly.

"Dr. Shackelford's a Christian, I take it."

Bob nodded. Regina said, "He's an elder in the Presbyterian church up in Barton."

"I'm a Presbyterian myself," David said. The subject of the lawsuit was coming back to him. A pregnant Regina had gone into the hospital on a Friday morning when her water broke, and the admissions nurse noted "Water broke, 8:30 A.M." on the admission sheet. Dr. Shackelford spent a minute with Regina on his way to lunch and golfed most of the afternoon, leaving as his only instructions word that one of the nurses should beep him when labor started. The fetus became infected and died. The doctor didn't see Regina again until Monday morning, when all that was left for him to do was induce labor and deliver the stillborn child.

"Has Dr. Shackelford come to you and confessed his carelessness?" David asked. "Has he expressed sorrow and said he'll be just as careful as he knows how to be the next time a pregnant woman places herself and her baby in his care? Has he offered to make it right to you, to make any kind of restitution at all?"

"He damn well hasn't," said Bob with sudden passion. "All he does is go bar-hopping weekends with all his middle-aged lady-friends, same as he always did as far as I can see."

Regina said, "It just feels wrong, this lawsuit does. It makes me feel greedy. All we can get out of this is money. It's like we're making a profit on the death of our daughter."

David remembered his deposition with Dr. Shackelford and one particular run-around.

Question: During Regina's hospital stay, can you say that she and her baby received the optimal medical care?

Dr. Shackelford, pursing his lips, fingers laced around his crossed knee: No, I wouldn't say she received *optimal* care.

Shackelford's lawyer: Off the record. I'd like a short conference with my client, privately.

After a ten-minute session of schmoozing in the hallway, Shackelford came back: I think I misunderstood your last question. In my mind, optimal care includes optimal *results*, and since the baby died, of course, the results weren't optimal here. That's what I meant when I said the care wasn't optimal; I meant the result wasn't optimal, because, of course, the baby died.

David looked at the doctor, whose mouth was drawn tight, who had sweat sitting on his forehead in fine droplets. David looked at Shackelford's lawyer and studied, for a moment, his bland expression. David was outraged. It was all he could do to keep from throwing his papers in the air, slapping everyone around a bit, and stalking out. He was only thirty years old and hadn't been at the game long enough to take such obfuscation in stride.

Now he sighed. "It is true that a lawsuit can't bring your daughter back. The damage has been done, and there's no way to undo it. And your little girl was worth infinitely more to you than any amount of money. I can appreciate that as Christians you feel that revenge is wrong, and you don't want that." Bob muttered something here, but David pressed on. "Lawsuits aren't about revenge, or at least they don't have to be. Dr. Shackelford has disgraced himself, and by sticking with this lawsuit we can make that disgrace public. Maybe as a result of this lawsuit his insurance will be canceled, or the hospital will boot him, or patients won't go to him anymore. If that happens, we'll have protected the next young mother. If none of those things happen, the good doctor will at least be a good sight more careful in the future. And you don't know, maybe we are God's instruments for bringing Dr. Shackelford to confession and repentance."

Both Regina and Bob were nodding, Bob with conviction, Regina more uncertainly. David was feeling uncertain himself, having just declared himself the instrument of God without His say-so, him a Presbyterian whose last regular church attendance had been in childhood, whose last foray into the Bible had been in college, whose last prayer had been the last time he was in trouble.

"You really think it's the right thing to do?" Regina said in a meek voice.

"I really do. Of course, it's your conscience, and it's going to have to be your decision."

She stood up. "Thank you, Mr. Loring. I'm glad Mr. Armstrong wasn't here to see us."

David stepped around the desk to shake the hand she extended toward him. It was cool and delicate in his grasp.

When they had gone, David sank into the client chair Bob had vacated and with the sleeve of his jacket wiped the perspiration from his brow. He wondered if he had changed their minds for more than the moment, if he had accomplished anything at all.

Frank appeared in the doorway. "They wanted to give up on it, didn't they?" he said.

"Yeah. Heard from Cecil?"

Frank shook his head. "But I heard your speech. Someday you could make one hell of a lawyer."

David nodded, glumly. His worry about Cecil hung like a lead weight in his stomach. He didn't feel like one hell of a lawyer, but like one hell of a manipulative son-of-a-bitch, if he was one hell of anything.

On his way home that evening, he drove by Cecil's house. It was just over a mile from his apartment, at the eastern edge of the town's southwestern residential area. It was one of the older houses, a two-story clapboard, unusual for a Texas suburb.

David pulled against the curb in front of the house, noted that the lawn needed mowing, that one of the shutters hung crooked. He got out of his car, squinting into the westering sun. The asphalt driveway was uneven, he noticed as he walked up it, cracked in places, and grass and clover grew in the cracks. Cecil had not maintained the place well in the last few years.

The back door was locked, though. All the windows were closed. The front door was locked as well. David peered through a window into the empty living room, almost devoid of furniture. He sat in the porch swing, which groaned beneath him. Cecil had been his mentor when he had first come to the firm. It was Cecil who had kept tabs on David's first case, who had told him at nine-thirty one Monday morning that in Texas filing deadlines were ten in the morning instead of five in the afternoon as in the rest of the country; Cecil who had stood and grinned as David scrambled around to get his answer together and to get out the door with it to go to the courthouse. It was Cecil who had coached him on the eve of his first trial.

David got up and went to his car.

The houses between Cecil's clapboard home and David's apartment complex were typical of any Texas suburb: square, one-story houses of tan brick set on square, slab foundations. Hip roofs, with gutters running along all four sides of the house.

It was hard for David to believe that Cecil was dead.

Surely he wasn't.

At home David sat for several minutes in his car, in his assigned parking space, thinking of Cecil and trying to muster the energy to get out of his car and go inside.

7

The dark-haired woman who lived below him was sitting in a wrought-iron lounge chair by her front door.

"Hi," she said brightly. She closed her paperback on her index finger, marking her place in the book.

David paused at the foot of the stairs that led up to his apartment. "Hi," he said.

"Diana Puller," she said.

"David Loring."

"I remember."

It was a hot evening, exceptionally muggy, and Diana was dressed for the weather, wearing a matching knit pullover and miniskirt, with horizontal stripes of pastel colors. Like the short terry-cloth robe he had last seen her wearing, this outfit accented the lean, brown legs, now crossed at the ankles. She got too much sun, and it was quickly aging her, but she retained enough smoldering beauty for David to wonder what she must have looked like at twenty.

She had found her place in her book again and had resumed reading. David gave his shoulders a small shake as he started up the stairs to his apartment.

When he was halfway up, she called to him, "Have you read this? It's pretty good." He leaned over the rail to look, and she held up the book.

On the dark cover was the hazy picture of a pickup parked in a hayfield, with a disproportionately large ax in the foreground. The title, displayed in elongated, raised red letters that stretched across the top of the front cover, was *Forty Whacks*.

"It's the true story of those murders up near Tulsa a couple of years back," she said.

"Little Johnny took his ax and gave his mommy forty whacks."

She smiled. "That's 'Lizzie Borden took her ax.' That was another true-crime story, a long time ago."

"I don't read much of that true crime stuff. Actually, I don't guess I've read any."

"You read fiction?"

"Almost exclusively."

"I remember when I was little, our mother would read to us, and the first question I always had for her was, 'Is it true?' "

"What did she say?"

" 'Yes, in a sense.' And I'd say, 'No, not in a sense. Is it true? Did it really happen?' "

"How young our lives are shaped."

"Is that a quote from something?"

"Not that I know of. If I'm going to speak, I guess, why not speak in stilted language? In a way it's what I do for a living."

She had found her place in her book again. "Bye, David."

"Bye."

He had his tie off and his shirt unbuttoned when the doorbell rang. Diana was sitting on the rail in front of his apartment.

"This is the second time I've seen your chest, and I hardly know you," she said.

"Just wait till we've been formally introduced."

She had a deep, throaty laugh. *If she weren't ten years older than I am,* David was thinking, *I'd think she was a real sexy woman.*

Diana hopped off the railing. "I was fixing to make fajitas and I thought maybe I should double the recipe. What do you think?"

"Is this a dinner invitation?"

"No, I just wanted the benefit of your culinary expertise."

"I'll take it as a dinner invitation. I accept."

"Great. Give me thirty minutes, then come on down. Okay?"

"Gotcha."

When he came down, her door was open, and the slightly greasy smell of frying meat wafted through the doorway on a current of air conditioning.

"Are you determined to cool off all of south Texas," he called, "or shall I shut the door?"

"Hi," she said from the kitchen doorway. "Come on back. I just wanted you to feel welcome." She eyed him. "You sure look preppie."

"Thanks. I guess."

"Oh, you look fine. It's just that you'd be wearing jeans and cowboy boots if you were from around here."

"What makes you think I'm not from around here?"

"Look at yourself, you look like a flag!"

He looked down at himself. He was wearing cuffed blue shorts, topsiders with no socks, and a tennis shirt with broad, horizontal red and white stripes. "You have flags in Texas," he said defensively.

"Yes, but we don't wear them." Seeing that he was taken aback, she said, "Oh, I'm sorry. Five minutes, and already I'm criticizing your clothes. And, really, it's your Yankee accent that gives you away."

"You're not going to tell me I have an accent. I'm the only one around here who doesn't have an accent." He picked a tortilla chip out of the yellow glass bowl on the counter and dipped it in the guacamole.

"Shame on you, you'll spoil your appetite."

"That's what I'm here for."

"Not yet, you're not. Would you like wine with dinner? It's French, but that's not too much of a culture clash, do you think?"

"I'm not much of a drinker, anyway. Water will do me." He selected another chip and this time dipped it in the hot sauce.

"Stop that. Here, help me carry this stuff to the table. I set it up on the back patio. It's not air conditioned, but it shouldn't be too hot out there, I don't think."

"Mm." The hot sauce was working on him, and his mouth was on fire. He helped her get the food from the counter to the wicker patio furniture he remembered from his last visit.

Plain stoneware was set on a white linen table cloth, and the wine glasses were crystal.

"Say, this is nice," he said, trying to work moisture back into his seared mouth. "Could I have some water?"

"There's a gallon jug of spring water in the refrigerator. Could you help yourself? I need to step into the bathroom a minute before we eat."

"Fair enough." In a cupboard he found plastic glasses imprinted with pictures of lemons. Since the water was refrigerated, he didn't bother with ice. He drank deeply, refilled his glass and left it on the counter.

He stepped past the closed door of the bathroom and leaned into Diana's bedroom for a moment to see what it was like. She had a big four-poster bed and an antique chest of drawers that was missing its mirror—a rose and mint-green afghan was folded over the wooden rod around which the mirror would have swiveled.

Near the door was an art deco dressing table with its round mirror still intact. A picture lay facedown in front of the mirror. He stepped into the room and lifted the picture, noting that the frame was scrolled silver and the glass inside the frame was broken. A few jagged pieces were still wedged between the photograph and the frame; the rest of the glass was missing. A rough hole was torn from the center of the photograph, as if it had been stabbed out with repeated jabs of a sharp instrument. The many jagging lines of ink suggested that the sharp instrument had been a ballpoint pen.

In the bathroom the toilet flushed. Water began to run in the sink.

David recognized the man in the photograph. It was Leonard Nash, a local wheeler-dealer who had gone bust and was now cooling his heels in the courthouse jail on multiple charges of fraud, racketeering, and embezzlement. Cecil represented him—had represented him. Diana had distracted David from thoughts of Cecil, but the sudden association brought his worries back with enough force to kill his appetite. It was a small world.

As Diana opened the door and came out of the bathroom, David laid the photograph back on its face. He turned toward her, his hands in his pockets.

"I didn't mean to be giving myself the nickel tour," he said. "It's a nice place you have here."

She raised an eyebrow at him. He had the definite feeling that she was not pleased. "Ready to eat?" she said.

He winced as if she had scolded him. On his way back to the table he picked up his water from the counter and sipped at it. The hot sauce had burned itself out, but had left his lips and his tongue feeling dry as old parchment.

At last they were at the table, looking across at each other, the food between them. She opened her mouth to speak, and for a moment he thought she would say grace. Instead she closed her mouth and smiled. It was a pretty smile, he was beginning to think. "Dig in," she said.

They dug, putting flour tortillas on their plates, filling them with the pan-fried combination of chicken, onions, and peppers, ladling in the guacamole, the sour cream, the hot sauce.

David folded his tortilla around it all and lifted the dripping fajita to his mouth. "Good," he said.

It was good, but hotter—which is to say spicier—than he had expected, and he thought that next time he would forgo the hot sauce. "Hot," he said, and drained his water. The water didn't have enough bite to it to kill the fire, and he poured himself a glass of the burgundy.

"Oh, come on. The food's not that hot."

David nodded vigorously. "Good, though." He sipped his wine, which was cool but not chilled. It had more bite than the water, but still it did little to cool his lips or his tongue or the lining of his mouth, all undergoing spontaneous combustion.

When they had settled into the rhythm of eating, Diana asked David to tell her about himself. "You said you spoke stilted speech for a living," she said. "Does that mean you write greeting cards?"

"Uh-uh. Lawyer," he said through his food. "You?"

"Unemployed."

"Looking?"

"No."

"Good work if you can get it," he said.

"A long time ago, I was the cosmetics manager at a Dillard's department store." He had drained his wine glass, and Diana refilled it for him. Perspiration had beaded on David's forehead, and he could feel a cold line of sweat roll between his shoulder blades.

"Just a minute," he said. He got up and got the jug of water from the refrigerator. When he had refilled his glass, he sat down, leaving the jug on the table. He took another bite of fajita.

"You know, they don't eat food this hot in Chicago," he said.

"Chicago," she said, nodding as if the mention of Chicago made everything clear to her. "And now you're here. Where do you work?"

"McKinnon, Armstrong and Cuneo. They were going to work my name in there, but it just seemed like too much, you know?"

"Would your name be the next one?"

"Well, no. They say I'll be a partner come January, but there're several more people ahead of me on the letterhead."

David made his second fajita without the red hot sauce. What he had not yet realized was that the white stuff that looked like sour cream was the even-hotter sauce. As he continued to eat, sweat trickled into his eyebrows. He mopped his forehead with his bare forearm.

"You're suffering, aren't you?" Diana asked.

"Well, yes." He drained his water glass, paused, and drained his wine glass.

"Wait right here."

He was sweating like a pig—did pigs sweat, or was it just an expression? His cheeks were wet with perspiration, and his shirt was sticking to him. When Diana came back, his eyes were tearing. He seemed to be leaking moisture from every pore of his body. "This hot stuff really cleans out the system," he said. "How come you're not sweating?"

"I'm a Texas girl. This food isn't hot. Here." She held out a vegetable. "Eat a bite of this."

"Diana, I'm having enough trouble."

"Do it. Trust me."

"But . . . it's a radish."

"Let me guess, you're a weekend botanist. I know it's a radish. Are you going to take a bite or aren't you?"

Feeling trapped, he bit into the radish. As he chewed, it cooled his mouth. He swallowed and sipped some water, and the spice-fires were gone.

"That's incredible," he said.

"Isn't it?"

He held the radish. "I can eat anything with this."

"Maybe you can. Don't get carried away."

He laughed and took the last bite of his fajita, then he made himself another one. Gradually the sweat on his forehead dried. When the fajita was gone, he finished the radish, and he sat back contentedly.

She smiled at him. He looked back at her with affection.

"You know," he said. "You have the most striking brown eyes." And he thought, *I said that? I had more of the wine than I thought.*

"David, look at my eyes. Closer."

"Oh. They're blue."

"Yes."

"Huh. I don't know how I could have made such a mistake."

"Perhaps if you spent more time looking into my eyes and a little less glancing down at my boobs."

There was a silence. He laughed awkwardly, eyes cutting downward despite his best intentions. "They're *dark* blue," he said, defensively.

"My boobs?"

He laughed again, more awkwardly. "It's the uncertain light," he said. "Your eyes *looked* brown, reflected there in your boobs."

And she laughed. The tension between them dissipated. He smiled back at her, relieved.

"Can we go inside now?" he said.

"Sure." So they went in to the sofa, where they sat with legs outstretched and on the coffee table. They might have been two small children.

On one wall of the living room hung a large, dark tapestry that stretched from floor to ceiling. Silver threads sketched in the form of an armored man on horseback, lance tipped forward.

"Is that from Europe?" David asked, inclining his head toward the tapestry.

"Spain. It's supposed to represent Don Quixote."

He was frowning, still thinking of his mistake about her eyes.

"What?" she said, looking back at him.

"Was I really spending excessive time out there admiring your morphology, or were you just jerking my chain?"

"My morphology?"

"Your, ah, form."

"No, I was just jerking your chain."

His face cleared. "Really?"

"Yeah."

Their faces were very close. He was thinking about kissing her; thoughts of the butchered photograph in her bedroom made him wary.

"So are you going to kiss me or look at me?" she said.

He took a breath and crossed the inch-wide

chasm. Inclining his head fractionally, he put his mouth on hers. He found himself staring at her staring at him, eyeball to eyeball.

"One of us is going to have to close his eyes," she said, her mouth moving against his.

He closed his eyes and in the darkness focused on the texture of the lips against his own, the softness of a woman's mouth. Passion launched a blitzkrieg on the citadel of reason, and reason promptly capitulated. His arms closed about her, and he pulled her across him, feeling her hips roll outward into space, pulling them back onto the couch beside him. She was lying across him, her face upturned.

He pulled back and opened his mouth to say something stupid, opened his eyes at the same time and saw tears on her face.

"Diana?"

She began to cry in earnest.

She said, "I'm sorry. I don't know what. I, oh . . ."

He held her against him and stroked her shoulder.

"I'm sorry, but you've got to go." Her nose had stopped up, distorting her speech.

"No," he said. "I . . ."

"Yes. Go. I'm so, so horribly embarrassed."

"You don't need to be, just . . ."

"Go. Now." He found himself on his feet, being bumped and pushed toward the door.

In the doorway she stopped him, holding his face between both of her hands. "Please forgive me," she said.

"There's nothing to for—" She pulled his face down to hers and kissed him with electrifying if somewhat salty fervor. Then he was through the door, and she was closing it, and he heard a wail begin inside her apartment.

He stood stock still on her doormat, feeling tremendous agitation.

"She isn't over Leonard," he said aloud.

"She's sure over Leonard," Mick was saying. "She's sure over Leonard now." He was in Otto's apartment, binoculars pressed hard against his eyes, watching Diana's patio and what he could see of her living room through the sliding glass doors. He had been watching until his hands were cramping, so long had he been there, so hard was his grip on the binoculars. David's and Diana's Mexican dinner was a torment to him.

Otto was out at the time, which was good. The last thing Mick needed were a lot of smart-ass comments from a chowderhead. "Whoa, Mick, someone bird-dogging your chick. What's he got, you think, that you ain't got? Look at her smile there, I think she likes him. Look, she's laughing now."

He could see her smile. He could see her laugh. And before they went inside, he memorized every feature of the prick's face, with and without the magnification of the binoculars. Things could happen to a man's looks, he was thinking, and the prick might not look that way forever. Unconsciously, Mick stroked his own warped nose between thumb and forefinger. Things could happen to a man's looks.

Diana's face received equal attention. She smiled, though not at him; laughed, but not with him, and his guts burned. The swell of her breast caused his hands to shake too much for him to control the focus of the binoculars.

They went inside, and all he could see through the gauzy curtains were their legs, side by side on the coffee table. He knew they were kissing. He imagined the feel of her lips against his own, the feel of her skin beneath his barbell-calloused hands.

Oh, they were kissing. He jumped up and danced in his rage, his knees pistoning up against his chest, his feet driving down into the floor. He put the binoculars to his eyes again. When David and Diana got up and left his field of vision, it was more than he could stand. He knew where they were going: to the bedroom, to the bedroom. He bounced from one foot to the other, unable to control himself. It was too much. He threw the binoculars into Otto's recliner, went to the door and jerked it open.

He stood for a moment, chest heaving, hauling in the humid air through flaring nostrils. He ran. Slamming the door behind him, taking the stairs to the ground floor three and four at a time, blasting out into the night.

David went into his own apartment and closed the door as Mick came around the corner, and Diana's door was closed already. Mick ran past, moving faster and faster, into the neighborhood of curving streets. *Into the bedroom!* He slapped a mailbox as he passed it and knocked it from its post to the street where it clanged and scraped. A light came on. When he came upon a car parked by the curb in front of him, he didn't slow down and didn't swerve. He leaped, and his left foot came down on the car's trunk, his right foot came down on the roof—which began to collapse even as he passed over it—and his left foot came down on the hood. He staggered slightly as he hit the road.

His voice started low, building gradually into a scream. "Eeeeee," he cried as he ran. A cat darted out of a driveway just in front of him, and he adjusted his stride to kick it into the air, where it somersaulted once, shrieking, and landed on its feet again directly in his path. He stepped on its tail, left it screaming and spitting behind him.

David still felt shaken. Somehow he had crossed some boundary too quickly; somehow Diana's outburst was his fault, he knew it was. How was he ever going to face her again after this? He got a glass of water and put on some Mozart to steady himself. The phonograph arm swung out over the record and dropped. A moment's static gave way to the building rush of violins.

David settled into his wing chair with a sigh. He found himself staring at the dim reflection of his lampshade in the glass door of his antique bookshelves. Mozart's measured discipline asserted control over the violins' exuberance, and that control brought a certain peace to him. What he needed was a book, an old book, and he had plenty of those. He went to the bookshelves, slid back the top shelf's glass door, and mulled over the possibilities.

Old books were his favorite books, books that were old in any sense: books written enough years before his birth to open to him the world as it was before he got there; old volumes, musty with age; most especially, familiar books, books that he had read before. He pulled out a volume of Shakespeare, finally, then found that he couldn't concentrate.

If it weren't necessary to pass the door of Diana's apartment to do so, he would go out for a run. As it was, he felt trapped.

At last he took his jumprope into the carpeted living room, and he ran in place, twirling the rope about him. Then he hopped, still twirling. Then he spun the rope so fast that it passed twice beneath his feet on each hop, then three times. He couldn't make four.

He sat collapsed against the seat of his wing chair, heaving for breath but on the whole feeling better.

Draping the rope over the bathroom doorknob, he went in to shower. A cleansing shower and then bed, he thought; he would be born anew in the morning.

Mick drove toward home on the long straight highway lined on both sides with street lamps. Beyond the lamps, twisted, straggly mesquite trees crouched low to the ground in shadow. His radio was off, his side was hurting, and suddenly the night was too quiet.

The night was always too quiet, too free of distractions. It was at night that Mick always felt most alone, most trapped within himself like a wild animal caught in a pitfall. By the time he got home, his sweat had dried on him in a sour perfume, and he drew a bath as hot as he could stand it.

Easing down into it, he thought unexpectedly

of his mother, which in turn made him wish for a few of his long-standing defenses: gin over ice, freezing cold, in a tall glass beside the tub; a book, especially a novel, with its world of retreat where none could follow.

He settled back in the tub, feeling it was too much trouble to climb out and track water into his library and down into his kitchen. Had he known he would need them, he would have gotten his gin and a fat hardback before getting wet. Now, for a few minutes, he was alone with his thoughts. Indeed, how bad could they be? His mother, that terror of ages, had been dead twenty-five years, stricken dead by the cancer he had for so long lain awake and prayed for.

He stroked his nose. Pliers. He had gone to Clark with pliers after swearing he would never use any human being so. He felt some guilt over that, but he had, at least, left the boy's nose alone.

"Mother," he muttered. And felt black dread.

Later that night he lay paralyzed in his bed, listening to the creak of stairs and that familiar tread. He saw in the doorway the glint of a broad-bladed knife, gripped by its steel-and-hardwood handle. No pliers this time, the knife.

She plunged it into his throat and twisted as the blood spurted around it. He felt his bowels give way. He smelled that smell. Mother!

He was sitting upright in bed, sucking hot air back and forth through his burning throat. A dream, a dream.

He hated, oh, he hated to dream.

8

Pounding, going on and on without getting louder, without diminishing. David lying awake, listening to it. Someone at the door. Red glowing numerals at the side of his bed read three-fifteen. The pounding continues. In a dreamlike state, he lifts his bathrobe from the post at one end of the bed's footboard. He slips the robe on as he moves to the door. Outside his bedroom his bare feet pad on the linoleum floor.

He stands by the door, his hand resting against it, feeling the vibrations of the knocking. Beyond the pounding he hears wind. Above him, rain drums on the roof. His skin prickles with the premonition of who is out there.

He opens the door a crack, and through the crack a hot breeze blows, carrying rain. There is the low rumble of distant thunder. He swings the door wide, standing in the darkness of the entrance hall.

She is there, visible under the outdoor lights. She wears a beige trench coat, buttoned to the throat. The belt is not buckled, but tied about her waist.

Her hair is wet, her bangs plastered to her

forehead. Raindrops have spattered the raincoat and turned the shoulders dark. Beyond the sheltered porch, rain drubs the sidewalks, the lawns, the asphalt tennis courts.

She steps into the apartment, and her arms go around his waist. Her hands are cold through the thin fabric of his robe. He puts his arms around her. Her cold, wet head rests against his shoulder as warm air sweeps through the doorway to swirl around them.

Outside a long streak of lightning touches down on the tennis courts, and thunder crashes down at once, reverberating through the two clinging bodies.

She steps away from him, pushing the door shut with her back. She pauses there, her face a shadow in the sudden darkness. Beside her shadowed face the door's peephole glints with light.

Her elbows move as she unties the belt, unbuttons the coat. The trench coat slips from her shoulders and drops to the floor, a puddle of fabric at her feet.

His mouth opens, soundlessly. He is not breathing. When she comes forward against him, her flesh is hot. His breath comes back raggedly.

He is on fire.

David Loring opened his eyes. Sunlight was baking him through the window at the head of his bed. His bed was empty, except that he was in it.

The sheet was drawn up smoothly to his shoulders, and it was tucked in at the foot of his bed. The spread was on the floor.

Throwing back the sheets, he sat up, clad in

the briefs that were his customary nightwear. His head pounded. His tongue felt wrapped in cotton. He sat for several minutes, hunched forward, his hands against his face.

When he could do anything, he stuck his fingers between two slats in the miniblinds and blinked into the sunlight that stabbed through the opening. The sky was blue, completely cloudless. Leaning forward he saw that the sidewalks were dry as chalk.

So it hadn't rained last night. It had all been a dream. His heart rate slowed. A dream.

He felt relief.

Disappointment.

He stood, finally, to go back to his bathroom, and his skin felt funny, like it didn't really belong to him.

When David left for work, there were people on one of the tennis courts, a couple of women getting in their exercise before the heat of the day descended. He paid little attention to them on his way down the stairs; there were often people on the courts in the morning. As he started down the sidewalk toward his car, though, his peripheral vision picked up one of the women gesturing in his direction with the head of her tennis racket. She was at the far end of the court, but when he stopped to look, he realized that the woman was Rhonda Hazelhoff.

The other woman turned toward him, following the direction of the tennis racket. That woman was Marie.

He had woken up that morning with a sense of dislocation, and now that sense of dislocation

was stronger. Marie waved a hand at him, casually, and turned back to the court, crouching to
receive serve, pointing her white cotton panties
at him. Rhonda looked at him, shrugged, and hit
her serve. It went into the net.

"Hey," David said. "What is this?"

Rhonda's second serve was a patty-cake serve;
the ball went in, but there was no speed on it.
Marie walked around it so she could hit it with
a forehand stroke, but her shot sailed long.

"You're not even supposed to be here," David
called to Rhonda. "You're supposed to be in
Oklahoma City, or Amarillo, or someplace."

"I live here."

"Where?"

"Same building as me," Marie said, glancing
over her shoulder. "Do you mind? We're trying
to play."

"How long have you known each other?"

"Since Saturday. You weren't there to intro-
duce us, but we managed it ourselves."

He walked out onto the tennis court, waving
his arms vaguely. "*When* did Rhonda move into
your apartment building? Was the whole situation Saturday a setup?"

"Don't flatter yourself," Marie said.

"I moved in Saturday afternoon."

"What, did you have your furniture with
you?"

"I don't have any furniture. I bought a mattress Monday."

"Oh."

Marie tapped him on the shoulder with her
racket. "We're playing a game here. Do you
mind?"

*   *   *

David had seen it on the bargain tables the last time he was in Walden's: *Men Who Fear Commitment, and the Women Who Love Them.* He picked it up and looked at it, because he recognized the man in the title: It was himself, good old David Loring. When he got home that day, he sat and tried to list all the girls and women he had had at least two dates with. To have two dates with one girl was to make a legitimate stab at developing something.

He couldn't remember all the names. "Mark's sister," "Beth's friend," "That girl I met at that dorm party," was sometimes the best he could do. But the list came to thirty-nine people, and he had the sense that he had forgotten some.

Commitment was a problem; okay, he was pretty sure of that. To solve it, he guessed, you had to pick somebody and commit—but to whom do you commit? He had lots of good reasons to let Rhonda go. Marie obviously hated his guts, and so was an unlikely candidate. There was Diana—he had kind of a crush on her. It wasn't every night you had a dream like the one he had had. A crush wasn't enough on which to base heavy commitment, but he could run with it. If he fell in love, surely that was a basis for commitment.

David turned into the firm's parking garage and walked through the tunnel to the office building, listening to the echo of his footsteps in the tunnel. Eros! Romantic love! He had been deep in love a dozen times. Might as well build a house on a beach as to base lifelong commitment on that.

*   *   *

He sat at his desk, tapping his pen. He thought alternately about Diana, about his problem with commitment, about Diana again. He didn't know Diana, of course. She was pretty, had a presence about her.

"But is she a nice person?" he said aloud.

Nancy came in with a small stack of papers. She stopped to make a production of looking all around her. "Is who a nice person?" she said.

The right side of his face rested in his open hand. He stopped tapping his pen. "You heard that."

"My mother heard that, and she lives in Cincinnati."

"Oh."

"Here's the brief you gave me yesterday. I finished it." She laid the papers on his desk and put the tiny cassette tape on top of them.

"Thank you."

"What's her name?" Nancy said.

"Diana."

"It's a nice name."

"Yeah," he said. "But is she a nice person?"

Nancy shrugged and smiled at him, and she shut the door behind her.

He didn't really wonder whether Diana was a nice person; he didn't know why he said that. What he really wondered was this: *Is she too old for me?*

Though he knew the answer to that one, didn't he? Too old, too old. For several minutes he stared at nothing in particular, then pulled his mail over to him. Today it consisted of six brochures describing various legal seminars on tax law, real estate law, domestic relations, and more, all offering credits toward Mandatory Continuing Legal Education. He filed them one by one in the trash can, glancing at each long enough for any strong interest to register. They all made it to the trash can.

He looked at his calendar and saw that the MacLeods were supposed to have filed their answer to his lawsuit on Monday. When they filed, they were supposed to send him a copy, and he hadn't gotten one.

He called the clerk's office. The MacLeods hadn't filed.

He swiveled in his chair to look out the window, where several blocks away gray clouds obscured the top of the Texas American Bank Building, the shell of another defunct institution. A storm was coming.

The hair stirred at the nape of his neck, as he saw again the fantastic storm of the night before, Diana in the foreground. He felt her hands at his waist.

He shook himself. The MacLeods. The MacLeods hadn't filed their answer.

Maybe his dream was a premonition of events to come. Maybe the dream storm presaged the coming storm of passion that would arrive tonight.

The MacLeods. The MacLeods had a lawyer, was the thing. Their lawyer was an old geezer named Abner DePuy, who practiced alone. Somehow Abner had dropped the ball on this one.

David's client, Dick Shumaker, had built a room onto the MacLeods' house and had not been paid. There was not a lot at stake.

Well, there was twelve thousand dollars at

stake. It seemed like a lot, but it dwindled against the expenses of pursuing a lawsuit to judgment and of collecting on that judgment, especially considering that success was seldom certain. David himself tried to avoid any case with less than twenty thousand dollars at stake, but Cecil Armstrong had taken this one.

Cecil gave it to David with instructions to keep costs down. He had to, going for just twelve thousand dollars, and taking a judgment by default fit right in with those instructions. Dick Shumaker could use what cash he had to try and collect on the judgment.

David dictated the default judgment and took it out to Nancy. "Rush job," he said.

"How long is it?"

"A page, two pages."

"Ten minutes."

So at ten-thirty he was headed down the hall on his way to track down the judge, a middle-aged woman named Naomi Wasserman with a preference for pantsuits in shades of green. David had seen her sentencing men to life imprisonment, leaning across the bench above them in an outfit of lime green with yellow stitching.

In Texas they elected their judges. Anyone with a law degree and sufficient popularity could be a judge for as long as he or she felt like it. The judges had to register by party, too, and so were subject to the vagaries of politics on the national level. In 1984 so many supporters of Ronald Reagan had voted a straight ticket that every sitting judge in Houston had lost his seat to the Republican candidate just lucky enough to be on the ticket that year. The only exception was a case where the Republicans had failed to field a candidate at all.

Hence Naomi and her pantsuits. Everybody loved Naomi—not necessarily the lawyers, but certainly everybody else. She was a local institution and was likely to remain one for years to come.

Frank McKinnon stopped him just before he reached the elevators. He looked unusually frazzled. "Haven't seen Cecil, have you?" Frank's collar was unbuttoned, his tie was crooked, and the hair on top of his head stood up in a kind of rooster's crest.

"No. Has he turned up?" Despite the distraction of Diana, Cecil had never been far from David's thoughts, his absence a cause of barely suppressed dread.

"No, just checking. I keep thinking he'll show up. Even though his car was shot all to hell, despite that, I keep thinking he's got to be all right. I just can't believe something bad has happened to him. I mean something really bad, like somebody killed him." He ran his fingers back through his hair, causing it to stand up even more prominently.

David nodded.

Frank grimaced. "Maybe he's buried deep, out there in a cow pasture somewhere, and they haven't found him yet." He shook his head. "I wish he'd just call." Frank and Cecil had been best friends and law partners for twenty-some-odd years. Though David had known Cecil only five years, they had once been close and even he had a hard time believing that disaster could have befallen Cecil. Frank's denial, he saw, was stronger, and far more desperate.

"I'll call Laura," Frank said. "I should have already, but I've been putting it off." Frank shook his head, moving on. David punched the button for the elevator.

Frank turned back. "Where're you off to? You're not in trial, are you? I may have to talk to you about taking over some of Cecil's stuff." Trials didn't come along nearly as often as David had anticipated in his law school days. Even though trial lawyers talked like they were always in trial, a small percentage of lawsuits got to that stage. In five years, David had been on his own in ten trials. So far, he was six for ten: a respectable record, though perhaps not one Perry Mason would have been proud of. But then, Mason's usual opponent was a prosecutor named Ham Burger.

"Default judgment," David said. "Should take thirty minutes."

"Collection case?"

"Yes, against Richard and Annette MacLeod for Dick Shumaker. Friend of Cecil's."

"Didn't they have a lawyer, Abner DePuy?"

"Uh-huh." Without any apparent effort, Frank somehow managed to know something about every piece of work going on anywhere in the office.

"When was the answer date?"

"Monday. Two days ago."

"Just getting to it?"

"I knew there was a lawyer on it, so there was no reason to expect a default. I just noticed that I never got a copy of their answer."

Joe Bob Raymond trundled past, burdened with a stack of *Southwestern Reporters* that came up to his chin. He was in shirtsleeves, rolled to the elbow. On his feet he wore rattlesnake cowboy boots, the diamond pattern running back from the toes of the boots. Joe Bob was the most flamboyantly Texan lawyer in the firm, as perhaps he had to be—a name like Joe Bob took some living up to. By contrast, Frank McKinnon, the senior partner, was wearing a gray suit with understated pin stripes invisible from four steps away and wing-tip shoes. David wore a blue suit and black penny loafers.

After Joe Bob passed, Frank said, returning to the subject, "Abner's getting old, probably just forgot the answer date."

"Yeah, probably."

"Why don't you give him a call and remind him?"

"Huh?"

"Give him a call," Frank said patiently. "Tell him he needs to get his answer in by tomorrow noon, or you'll have to take a default judgment against him."

"But if I do that, he'll file his answer."

"Very likely."

"Dick Shumaker can't afford for him to file his answer. It'll cost him months and another thousand bucks or more."

"Suppose the circumstances were reversed, David. Would you want Abner to take a default judgment against you, or would you want him to call to remind you of the answer date?"

Never happen, David thought. He said, "That's

hardly the point. What I would like and what I'd expect are two different things."

"It's professional courtesy, David. Give him a call." It was bad medicine for David to take, and, apparently sensing that, Frank smiled and winked and patted his shoulder before moving on down the hall.

So much for the one thing David had hoped to accomplish today. Abner didn't take his call, and he was forced to leave the ultimatum with Abner's secretary. Not a lot of satisfaction there.

Cecil would have taken the judgment, David thought, and Cecil carried enough weight to do it whatever Frank's objections. It's what David should have done as well, despite what Frank had said. As a lawyer, he had a duty to use his independent judgment in representing his client's best interests—though Frank was a lawyer as well as his boss. The Rules of Professional Conduct provided for following a senior lawyer's instructions.

"Cecil!" David said. "Where the hell are you?"

It was just after lunch when a peremptory female voice barked his name from the doorway: "David!" The pause that followed was designed to force him to look at her, which he resisted doing.

"Yes, Ellen," he said.

"Frank's holding a meeting in the library. All lawyers."

"Yes, Ellen."

"Well? Are you or are you not one of the lawyers of this firm?"

"I would answer that, but I assume the question is rhetorical. I'll be right along."

She came in and sat in one of his client chairs, crossing her legs. His eyes followed the thin legs in dark stockings to the navy skirt and the red, double-breasted blazer and finally to the face, narrow and pale with dark slashes of blush across the cheekbones. "I'll wait and walk along with you," she said in a friendly tone that he distrusted. Ellen Uhlan, at thirty-nine, was seven years a partner and the only woman in the firm.

He sighed and closed his appointment book. "Let's go, then."

His phone buzzed twice, and he picked it up. Ellen stopped inside the door with her arms folded across her chest, clearly peeved at the delay.

"Yes," he said into the receiver.

"A Madison Whitney for you."

"Fine." As the phone clicked he placed the name. Madison Whitney was the bland-faced lawyer who'd had the pow-wow with Dr. Shackelford in the hallway. The health care was not optimal because the result was not optimal. "David Loring," he said.

"Hello, David? Madison Whitney here. You remember me, I represent Dr. Bernard Shackelford and his insurer, Gibraltar Financial. I asked for Cecil Armstrong, but your receptionist said he was out of town this week. Can I talk to you about that malpractice case?"

"Sure."

"Well, as you know, it's set for trial in two weeks. I don't want to play games with you, so

I'll go straight to it. Gibraltar Financial has authorized me to offer one hundred fifty thousand dollars in settlement of all claims—wrongful death, the mother's action for the miscarriage, the whole schmear."

"One hundred fifty thousand dollars."

"That's right. One-fifty, the whole schmear."

"I'll have to talk to my clients." Who had wanted to drop the whole thing yesterday, one hundred fifty thousand dollars poorer.

"Of course. Sure. Just let me know Monday, if you can. If we're going to go to trial on this thing, I've got to get humping."

"I'll get to you Monday." He hung up. Some cases you slugged out deposition by deposition, interrogatory by interrogatory, and, at trial, witness by witness. Some dropped hefty settlements on your head like ripened fruit.

Ellen said, "Who was that?"

"Settlement offer."

"A good one? What is it?"

"Don't we have a meeting to go to?"

"You can tell me while we walk. Who was that on the phone? Give me a name."

"Madison Whitney."

"Hmm. Oh, Dallas lawyer. White, Babcock . . ."

She knew the firm. Sometimes he thought he worked in a firm of raving geniuses. "Yeah, yeah," he said. "White, Babcock, Berkeley, and Moore."

"You can't refuse to talk to me about this."

"No, of course not. I did hope I could string it out a bit."

There were nine lawyers in the firm, but only two of them were in the library. There was

Frank at the head of the long conference table and Al halfway along one side, feet on the table and ankles crossed. Al was wearing a seersucker suit and a bow tie, deep maroon with tiny points of white. The light from the overhead fluorescents reflected dully through the downy hair on top of his head, but still he could have been a model with his neatly trimmed dark hair, his tanned face and hands, his starched white shirt.

"David!" Al said as he entered the room. "And Ellen."

"This the firm meeting?" David said, looking around dubiously.

Al said, "This is everybody who counts."

"And David," Ellen said behind him.

Al winked at him. "She has a crush on you, kid. I can tell."

Ellen glared at Al, her black eyes glittering.

"Actually," Frank said, "I think this is everyone who could make it. If we don't have enough, I'll send you down to pry Joe Bob out of his office, but he starts the Petrella trial tomorrow. We need some systematic way of dealing with Cecil's caseload—as it turns up or as we can figure it out. Partners don't file caseload reports, though they probably should, so it's hard to tell exactly what all Cecil was involved in."

Al said, "You know Leonard Nash? He was Cecil's. Been calling from jail every couple hours wanting to talk to his attorney." Nash, of course, was the big real estate syndicator whose savaged photograph lay facedown on Diana's dressing table. Though David had never met the man, had never done an hour's work on any of his myriad legal problems, he listened now with heightened interest. He had no insider knowledge. He knew only what the world knew, that Leonard Nash had swindled half the people in town, blown the whole wad, then filed bankruptcy to stall everyone. The details of many of his transactions had become common knowledge through nine months of newspaper and T.V. coverage. Just over a week ago the man had been picked up at Dallas-Fort Worth trying to board a plane to South America; south Texas gloated.

"I've been talking to him, and I'm tired of him," Frank said. "On Saturday Cecil told Al and me that Leonard had put him onto a lock box at First National. We all thought it might represent some of Leonard's supposedly evaporated wealth, but Cecil disappeared sometime that weekend without saying anything else about it. I don't know what's going on there. I don't trust Leonard, and I don't like him, and I don't want to mess with him, so somebody else has got to."

"David should have some free time. He just got a settlement offer on a big case he's working on. Didn't you, David?" Ellen said.

David was flipping through a fat volume of Martindale-Hubbell, looking for White, Babcock, Berkeley and Moore. "Yeah, I may have more time than I might have, depends on what you guys think of the offer."

"I'm one of the *guys*, am I, David?" Ellen said.

"Oh, I'm sorry. Was I leaving you out?" He had found the White, Babcock listing, and within it Madison Whitney, born in Tyler, Texas, 1944. Princeton, B.A. 1965. University of Texas, J.D. 1968. "Grand Chancellor, Order of the Coif," he read aloud. "Would that mean he graduated first in his class?"

"It would," Frank said. "Who are we talking about?"

"Madison Whitney. Board certified, personal injury law, Texas Board of Legal Specialization. Board certified, civil trial law, Texas Board of Legal Specialization." David closed the book. "He just called with an offer on the Davis malpractice case. One hundred fifty grand, he says. For the whole schmear."

"One-fifty," Frank said, sitting back.

Sounding incredulous, Al said, "The whole schmear?"

"Madison Whitney seemed to think it was important. He kept repeating it."

"He's the Coif lawyer," Al said. He said it mockingly, but he was kidding. Ding-a-lings did not graduate first in their class at Texas.

"The case is up in Cruz County," David said. "Maybe worth, what, three hundred thousand if we win?"

Frank said, "Yeah, maybe. Weren't there some problems with that case?"

"Still are. First, some problems with the cause of death. All the tissue samples from the still-born have been lost, and all that's left are five slides. Our expert, the man who made the slides, got his medical degree in Mexico. He's white, but he couldn't get into any med schools here. He's an assistant M.E. in Houston now, but he just got back word on his pathology boards, and he flunked them."

"Ouch," Frank said.

"He's willing to testify that it's malpractice to

let a mother go twenty-four hours after her water breaks. What we don't have is an obstetrician who will testify to that."

"Makes you wonder why we're getting the one-fifty offer," Al said. "You think he sees something we don't?"

"Also, it's Cecil's case," David said. "I haven't even finished reading the file."

Frank said, "Sounds like you want to take the offer."

"Well, there's a problem. You remember the Davises were in here just yesterday, wanting to drop their lawsuit. The reason was that Christians aren't supposed to sue Christians in court, at least according to Regina's mother."

Al held out a hand, palm up. "This is perfect then. It gets them out of court."

"And Regina didn't want to be making a profit on the death of her daughter. I held onto them by saying that the lawsuit wasn't just about money. It was going to disgrace the doctor publicly, put pressure on his insurance company, and protect other young women who otherwise might not know better than to trust him."

Frank was frowning. "You shouldn't have said that. We can't be in the revenge business. We bring lawsuits to win money judgments. It's all we can do."

"That's not what you said yesterday. Yesterday I was one hell of a lawyer. And I don't think I put it in terms of revenge. I think I portrayed it as more of a public service."

"Well, we can't be in the public-service business either. We hope we do serve the public good, of course, but that can be only incidental to serving our clients. And in cases like this one, the only thing we can hope to win for our clients is money."

"You might have pointed this out yesterday."

"We didn't have a decent settlement offer yesterday."

Al was waving his hands. "Hey," he said. "Hey. I heard about this speech of David's, and it was fine. It was what he had to say to hold the clients."

"And I meant what I said," David said.

"Of course you did! You had to mean what you said to be convincing—and you had to be convincing, because keeping them in the lawsuit was in their own best interests. Now, though, the situation has changed. Now, taking this settlement offer is in their best interests." He looked around. "It's up to David to deliver a new speech that makes it obvious this offer is in their best interests and that makes them feel good about taking it."

"I agree with Al," Ellen said.

David looked at Frank, who slowly nodded.

"Do any of you guys ever feel like a manipulative S.O.B.?" David asked.

"Certainly," Al said, adjusting his bow tie and looking smug.

"I'll tell you what," Frank said. "Just be up front about it. Tell the Davises we got the settlement offer and see what they say. Tell them if they take it, it will get them out of court, and the money can be their daughter's contribution to the family or the church or whatever special cause they want. Why should the insurance company keep it? Disgracing Dr. Shackelford, protecting future patients—that's a public benefit that might or might not come about if we go to trial. Even if we win. If we lose, the doctor and his insurance company will be publicly exonerated."

"But it's their decision?"

"It's their decision. It's their cause of action, and if they want to take it to trial, we'll do our damnedest by them."

David looked at Al, who shrugged and said, "We could win a slice of three, four hundred grand."

"Okay," Frank said to David. "Call the Davises, see if they'll go for it. If they will, it will free you up for more of Cecil's stuff. For now, let's say this. You take your office, you take his office. Everything that comes in for either one of you goes to you. If you get swamped, holler, and we'll see what we can do."

"Okay. But before I talk to the Davises, one more thing: We have the Davises on a forty percent contract. Suppose we just take a third and give them a full hundred grand?"

Frank sighed. "How many hours have we got on the case?"

"I don't know."

"Find out."

"It's a difference of ten thousand dollars to us, Frank," Al said.

"Find out," Frank repeated. "And, David, go see Leonard Nash this afternoon. Get him off my butt."

"Okay." David looked at Al and Ellen. "It looks like, small as it was, this meeting about Cecil's caseload was bigger than it needed to be."

Al said, "I picked up two hearings for Cecil this week. I'm involved."

Ellen, who didn't do trial work anyway, said, "Don't look at me. I just heard they called a meeting."

9

To get to the jail on the seventh floor of the courthouse, a person had to take one of the three main elevators to the sixth floor, then change to a tiny, ancient, long unrenovated elevator cage for the trip up to the top floor. The county law library was on the sixth floor; Mick couldn't watch the little elevator from there.

What he did do, he sat on one of the wooden benches in the courthouse lobby, and he read his newspaper. From there he could see who got on the elevators, and he could see the numbers light up above the elevator doors to tell him where the people went.

By that Wednesday he knew by sight the librarian and the judge's clerks and the legal assistants who spent a good part of their day on the sixth floor. He knew the deputy sheriffs who had jail duty. He was the master of every article in eight days' worth of *Wall Street Journals, USA Todays,* and local dailies.

What he didn't see was, he didn't see Cecil Armstrong, the son-of-a-bitch who took Leonard's stash from under Mick's very own nose. He didn't see Diana—her little visit to Mick had taken care of that. He didn't see anyone at all he could identify as one of Leonard's friends or lovers or business partners.

Give it until the end of the week, he had told himself, and he planned to finish the week out, but he had given up all hope of accomplishing anything with his mind-numbing vigil when David Loring walked through the main doors of the courthouse, got into the elevator, and took it straight up to the sixth floor. No briefcase, no books, no legal pad—no indication that he was going up to the library to do research.

He didn't know it was David Loring. He knew it was the prick that had been romancing his woman the night before, the prick that lived in the apartment above hers.

It was 3:34 when David went up. Mick threw away his newspaper, no longer interested in what the NASDAQ was doing or what Irving Kristol thought of the President's new tax proposal. He made a quick trip into the men's room to run a comb through his hair and button his collar and push his Windsor knot up against his throat. He settled his blue poplin suit more carefully on his shoulders. He went back into the lobby to lean against the wall directly across from the elevators. One of the cabs was coming down.

It opened and a young woman in a blue skirt and white blouse got out. She glanced at him, then turned into the county clerk's office.

Mick paced across the lobby, hands thrust deep into his trouser pockets.

*   *   *

"Who are you again?" Leonard said, standing, unwilling to commit himself to the conversation.

David, seated at the table, repeated his name. "I'm one of the lawyers at McKinnon Armstrong."

"But not my lawyer." David was beginning to dislike the man, though just to look at him there was nothing to dislike. Leonard had the look and the bearing of a movie star, with a thin nose, thin mouth, and high, delicate cheekbones set in a square face.

"You didn't hire a single lawyer," David said, trying to sound patient. "You hired the firm of McKinnon Armstrong, which has nine lawyers. A number of us have done work for you. Did you ever meet Al Cuneo? Uh-huh, I understand he defended you in a couple of those lawsuits. And you've met Frank McKinnon. I know you've talked to him on the phone."

"Why isn't he here?"

"Frank isn't Cecil Armstrong, either."

"He's an experienced attorney. He has a reputation."

Irritated at the summary dismissal of his own experience and reputation, David said, "I like to think that what I lack in experience and reputation, I make up for in good looks and a warm smile."

Still on his feet, Leonard leaned across the table above David. "Just who the hell do you think you're talking to?" he said in a voice of icy calm.

David stood up himself, forcing Leonard to move back or be bopped in the nose by the top of David's head. David hated all this jockeying for dominance, but that didn't mean he was going to let himself be out-jockeyed. He said, "Who the hell do you think *you're* talking to? I may have graduated from law school last week, and other lawyers may laugh at me behind my back, but I've got enough experience and reputation to walk out on you. You want Cecil? Too bad, he's out of town. You want Frank? Too bad, he's tied up and can't be here. What you've got for about ten seconds more is me. You don't want McKinnon Armstrong anymore, fine. You fire me. You want McKinnon Armstrong, you apologize, and I'll sit here and continue to talk to you." Several seconds passed in silence while David concentrated on returning Leonard's stare. Finally David smiled. "Fine," he said. "Have a nice life."

"Wait." Leonard swallowed. "I apologize. I didn't mean to insult you. I don't have anything against you personally. I was just upset, understandably upset, I think, that the lawyer I've been dealing with isn't here. That's all. I'm just upset that Cecil isn't here." His tone had become congenial, placating. The only sign of the upset to which he admitted was the flaring of his nostrils on each intake of breath.

"Cecil can't be here."

"I accept that."

"Okay." David sat down. Leonard sat down.

"What it is, I asked Cecil to probate the estate of a Clark Holland. I directed him to a will, in his own files ..." Leonard recounted the substance of his interview with Cecil. He concluded, "Since then, I haven't heard from Cecil. What I want to know is this: What about the contents of that lock box? Are they safe?"

"What were the contents of the lock box?"

"Ask Cecil."

"I can't."

"Well, call him or something."

"Cecil's disappeared. Nobody's seen him since Saturday afternoon, shortly after he talked to you. As far as I know he never saw this lock box." It's what he had assumed, what Frank and Al had assumed, too.

Leonard's nostrils were flaring rhythmically.

David told him about the abandoned car with the bullet and the bullet hole. "Did that have anything to do with you and your lock box, do you think?"

"Huh? No, couldn't have."

"What was in the lock box?"

"Nothing much. Some documents."

"Or money maybe? Lots of it?" David felt on the verge of understanding something.

Leonard's gaze came back to David's. "What makes you ask that?"

"That's not an answer."

"No, it's not."

"I want an answer."

"Don't we all."

David reached across the table and grabbed Leonard by the front of his starched polo shirt. He pulled him forward, against the table. "Cecil Armstrong is a friend of mine. If you've set him up . . ." He could see it clearly: Cecil getting Leonard's cash out of the death-sealed lock box, getting hit on his way to the firm by one of Leonard's accomplices; Leonard regaining control of his illicit cash.

Leonard's face had gone red. David shoved

him back into his seat. "I'm sorry," he said. "But you've got to talk to me."

Leonard was looking down at the creases David's hand had left in his starched shirt. He looked up, his face still flushed. "You bastard," he said.

"I know. I'm sorry."

Leonard came over the table at him. David's wooden chair flipped, and he sprawled on his back, his hair brushing the wall behind him, Leonard clinging to his tie and a jacket lapel, coming down on top of him. Leonard's head impacted the metal wall that David's head had just missed, and Leonard's body went limp on top of David's. His eyes were glassy, his voice a whisper borne on cloying, perfumed breath. "Don't you ever put your hands on me, don't ever touch me, you misbegotten son of a . . ." He seemed to run out of breath just as he got to the good part.

David rolled Leonard off of him. In the metal door's small, reinforced window, he saw the back of the deputy sheriff's head, bobbing gently. The man was wearing a Walkman.

"Look," David said, turning his head toward Leonard. "I said I'm sorry, and I really am. Let's just forget it, okay?" He was thinking that none of the victims of Leonard's swindles could have ever laid hands on him—Leonard wouldn't have retained the poise necessary to close the transaction.

"I'm sorry, too," Leonard said, struggling onto his hands and knees. His breathing was coming slowly under control. "It's just something about being touched. I don't think I've been grabbed

by my shirt front in maybe twenty-five years."
He put out a hand and helped David to his feet.

All right, Leonard, David was thinking. *Nice recovery. I was beginning to think I should have paid more attention to that psychiatric evaluation I saw attached to the arrest report.*

"I didn't have anything to do with what happened to Cecil. I'm as concerned about it as you are. It wasn't cash in that lock box. I'm not even sure what it was." Leonard fixed David with his guileless yellow eyes. "From something Clark told me once, I thought he might have been keeping some municipal bonds there. Nothing to give me any motivation to take out Cecil." Leonard bent down to brush the dust off his knees, worked to bring back the crease in his chinos with thumb and forefinger.

David knew he was being conned. He didn't know how he was being conned, but he knew he wasn't getting the straight story. If any wealth the lock box contained was in the form of bonds, then it couldn't have had anything to do with Cecil's disappearance. All bonds were registered these days, had been for years. No one would have had any motivation to shoot Cecil to get them. He brushed the dust off the shoulders of his jacket, felt of the back of his head.

"I can't believe you attacked me," David said, musing aloud.

"Pardon?"

"What, did it give you time to think?"

"Why did you grab hold of my shirt front? We were both upset, it was understandable."

"Okay." There was something mighty slick

about Leonard. "Do you know a Diana Puller?" David said suddenly.

"Sure I do. I've been seeing her for years." Leonard nodded, smiling easily.

"It turns out she has the apartment below mine. Kind of a coincidence, thought I'd mention it."

"Say hi to her for me, if you get a chance. Tell her I'd like to see her."

He had hoped for more of a reaction. "She keeps your picture on her dresser. But somebody's smashed the glass and slashed up the photograph."

Leonard was shaking his head, still smiling. "Poor Diana. It must have been this arrest. I think she had quite a glorified image of me."

"Huh." Maybe. David knocked on the door for the deputy to let him out. Leonard was a smooth one.

The back of the deputy's head continued to bob in the window. David knocked harder and finally got a response.

One thing to remember: Leonard sure didn't like to be touched.

At four-ten, an empty elevator cab went up to the sixth floor.

Mick wandered casually into the clerk's office. A young black woman came to the counter to help him. He smiled at her, resting his weight on one elbow and turning back toward the lobby. One set of the elevator doors opened, and David Loring stepped off.

"That man right there," Mick said. "I've seen him around. Is he a lawyer?"

"Yeah. Hey, Debbie," she said to a woman at the desk behind her. "Who's that blond guy you've got the crush on? Is he a lawyer with McKinnon Armstrong?"

Debbie flushed scarlet. Mick smiled at her. "I should know him," he said. "I feel like I've seen him everywhere."

"I think his name is David Loring," she said.

"Thanks. I won't tell him about the crush."

Once he was out of the clerk's office, he put on some speed and pushed through the heavy glass doors, but he need not have hurried. David had stopped in the middle of the courthouse lawn to watch a robin pecking at something in the grass.

David walked the five blocks to his office. It was nothing for Mick to follow him back.

David kept at his paperwork until seven that evening, when he took the elevator to the basement and walked through the tunnel to the parking garage.

He had been having trouble with his concentration. The image of Cecil's immaculate desk would float before him; the images of a starred windshield, of a slug burrowed molelike into a leather-covered headrest, of blood-spattered upholstery ... David would find himself tapping his pen and gazing sightlessly at the papers before him. With an effort of will, he would refocus his attention on the task at hand.

Since his interview with Leonard, he had been feeling a growing dread, for Leonard was connected somehow with Cecil's disappearance. Now that he was in his car, pulling out of the parking garage onto the road, giving his mind free rein, he was increasingly certain of the connection. What he needed to do was call Walt Jeffries or somebody at the First National Bank and follow up on the lock box angle—okay, do it first thing in the morning.

He felt too restless to go home. He had a low-grade headache, and the sun's reflection on the hood of his car was about to blind him. Every evening he traveled west on the expressway, into the blinding sun. Every morning he traveled east on the expressway, into the blinding sun. How unfortunate that the town had grown westward instead of east!

A Chevette slid through the space between David and the minivan two car lengths in front of him just in time to exit the expressway. David touched his brakes to let it pass. Once he would have given the Chevette a blast of his horn, but he had decided some years ago that he disapproved of punitive honking.

What was in the lock box? What kind of papers was he going to need in order to find out? Maybe Cecil had already prepared some of them, and he would find them in that "Lazy Y Ranch" file Leonard had mentioned.

David found himself pulling into the parking lot at Westgate Mall. Funny that he had begun the day so distracted by Diana, when now he could remember what she looked like only with effort. And yesterday he had begun the evening pondering Cecil's disappearance, only to spend the night dreaming of Diana.

There were a lot of people in the food court today; terrible line at the Taco Bell, he wouldn't go there. Chick-fil-a. A lemonade and a chicken sandwich would be nice.

The woman in front of him got three sandwiches and two orders of waffle fries. Her flesh rippled out of control despite the pressures of too-tight polyester stretch pants. David turned and looked around at the crowded food court, feeling for some reason that he was under observation—it was that itch-in-the-middle-of-your-back sensation—but he didn't see anybody he knew. He turned back around, picked up his sandwich and his lemonade.

To get to the tables, he had to wade through a gaggle of high school girls in big, droopy shirts and knee-length shorts. When he was past them, he saw Marie sitting alone with a plate of rice and vegetables from Moon Wok.

He tried to do a quick fade into the pack of high school girls, but his efforts only earned him a couple of disinterested stares from beneath meticulously styled bangs. The crowd at his back forced him forward, past Marie's table, which, as it turned out, didn't seem to matter.

The town was just too damn small, he thought; you couldn't go anywhere without running into people you knew. Sometimes he found himself longing for Chicago's faceless crowds, the chance to go outside your own home and merge into anonymity.

He made it unhailed to a solitary table, where strangers and plants and red brick pillars obstructed his view of almost everybody. He had eaten about half his sandwich when Marie sat down across from him. "Hi," she said, and he cringed, remembering her "Damn it, I liked you" and her annoyance when he spoke to her on the tennis courts.

"You don't look glad to see me," she said.

"It's not that. I just didn't think you'd seen me."

"Ah," she said.

"Ooh. That makes it sound like I was avoiding you."

"Rhonda told me about the situation I walked into Saturday."

"How do you know her, really?"

"Swear to God. Ran into her at the clubhouse that same afternoon when she was renting the apartment. She said, 'I know you,' and somehow after that we hit it off."

David shook his head.

"And I was just razzing you about that woman downstairs. I mean, she's got to be forty-five years old."

"I would have said forty."

"You were just running away from Rhonda and me, weren't you? I think you're scared of women, that's the root of your problem."

"I didn't know I had a problem."

"You run away."

"That's fear of commitment, not fear of women."

"Isn't that a problem? Hey, if I get up to get one of those lemonades, will you still be here when I get back? Or is that asking for too much of a commitment?"

He pulled the lid and the straw off his lemonade and pushed the open cup across to her. "Have the rest of mine. I'm finished with it."

She lifted it to her mouth for a long drink.

"Thanks." She wiped her mouth with one of David's napkins. "You know, Rhonda really cares for you."

"I guessed that when she moved into my apartment complex."

"Where else was she going to move? There are only two or three apartment complexes in town she could have moved into."

"There're a lot of places in Dallas. The city has more to offer, too."

"It doesn't have you."

"Ah."

"No, listen. Rhonda told me all about you two. I think you ought to get back together."

He studied her. She was wearing a simple rose-colored dress that had the lines of a burlap sack, but the casual look set off her long, tawny hair attractively. "What about me and you?" he asked, not sure that he wanted to pursue such a relationship, but wanting to know his options.

"What about you and *Rhonda?*"

He looked away from her. "History," he said.

"You don't have to let the past control you."

"Look, you don't know anything about this. You know how I could get rid of Rhonda, get rid of her tomorrow? Ask her to marry me. Take that ring I got for her the last time out of my sock drawer, hand it to her, and—poof!—no more Rhonda. You talk about afraid of commitment."

"Why don't you do it? You might be surprised."

"I don't want her."

"But you just said it would drive her away."

"I don't have the energy."

"I figured you'd say that. Will you wait here a

minute? I'm going to get some more lemonade. There's nothing here but ice."

David thought immediately of escape, but when Marie moved, he found himself looking into the pale gray eyes of the man behind her. The man was staring straight at him, unblinking as a snake.

David stood slowly, transfixed, but the man—a big man, as broad as the table at which he sat—remained seated.

So David sat down again, still watching the man's eyes, not blinking, though his eyes burned. What could he do? A man was staring at him in a crowded food court, and he was staring back. He was going to stalk over and demand an explanation? Too easily, he could see the man continue to sit there, watching him with cold, reptilian interest, unspeaking, as stolid as a stone hill.

Marie came back and sat in her chair between them, severing their gaze. David shook his head like one dazed, letting out his pent-up breath in a long sigh.

"Is something wrong?" Marie said.

"I don't know."

"You're sweating."

"It's hot."

"Not in here. They're refrigerating this place like they need it to store milk."

Behind Marie, the man got up with his tray and dumped it in a bin marked "Thank You," not even glancing in David's direction. He moved off down the mall.

Marie followed David's gaze, watching the man with David until he was lost in the crowd of shoppers. She looked back at David. "Do you know him?"

He shook his head.

"Is something wrong with him? Is he supposed to be dead or something?"

"Look, you and I are through. I appreciate that. Rhonda and I are through, too, and I ask that you appreciate that. Right now I have to go."

He stood up, but she stopped him with a hand on his wrist. "You're right, David, I'm sorry." She cut her eyes in the direction Mick had gone. "But really. What is it about that guy?"

"I don't know. I've never seen him before."

"Then you're weird."

10

David walked from his car toward the tennis courts, which shimmered in the heat. Around the corner of his apartment building, Diana reclined in her wrought-iron lounge chair. She was still reading her crisp paperback edition of *Forty Whacks*, but she was nearing the end and the last hundred pages or so were curled in her right hand.

"Hi," she said, looking up. "I've been expecting you."

"Man, you look good," David said with a tired smile. "Feeling better now?"

"Yes. I'm sorry about last night, I really am."

"Forget it."

"I'll try. Come on out when you've changed into something more comfortable. I've got a fresh pitcher of margaritas here." She nodded toward the small, wrought-iron table with its pitcher, its ice bucket, its two glasses. "Or if you'd rather, I'll bring out another pitcher with nothing but ice water. I remember you said you weren't much of a drinker."

"Thanks."

He came back wearing shorts and a tennis

shirt. True to her word, Diana had brought out another pitcher filled with water. David poured from it, and ice tinkled against the glass sides of the pitcher. Diana already had a margarita, still half full. They tipped their glasses toward each other and sipped their drinks. They smiled at each other, a little awkwardly.

"I guess I'm still a little shy after my crying jag."

"No need to be." There was a wood and canvas lounge chair folded up and leaning against the brick by the front door. He unfolded it and sat down.

"I know it must have been . . . unsettling."

"Well, it was. But I've had plenty of time now to resettle."

She smiled at him. He found himself wanting to ask her about Leonard Nash, but could think of no delicate way to approach the subject. He drank his water in silence, then put the glass back on the table.

"No margarita?" Diana asked him.

"Not for me. I don't want to interrupt your reading."

"It's all right."

"And I've had a day like you wouldn't believe. I need a little time to vegetate."

She smiled as if she understood. He bent to kiss her forehead, kissed her upturned mouth instead. Her lips were cold from her drink.

He went upstairs, the feel of those lips still on his own.

Otto's apartment was no good for watching Diana's front door. Mick had to walk around to the clubhouse, beyond the tennis courts, and then he couldn't see anything through his own reflection in the glass doors. He stepped outside in time to see David go upstairs.

Mick clenched and unclenched his fists, smiling faintly as he crossed the tennis courts.

"Mick!" Diana said, looking up when his shadow fell across her page.

"Hey, baby." He smiled, but Diana didn't find it reassuring. Above his smiling lips, his nose was a broken turnip. Leonard had never told her what happened to his nose.

"Scare you?" he said.

"Startled me."

"People always think it important to make that distinction." He settled in the chair David had just vacated, and it cracked and groaned beneath him.

"Did you just happen by, or do you have more smut about Leonard to peddle?"

"I just came to see you, baby."

Which gave her a chill.

"I can tell you one thing about Leonard you might not know. He's got a new lawyer." Mick cut his eyes upward in the general direction of David's apartment.

"Who?"

Again Mick rolled his eyes upward.

"God? Leonard is now represented by God Almighty?"

Mick's eyes narrowed. "By David Loring."

"David? You're kidding."

"Very good. I could almost believe that's news to you." He poured from the pitcher of margaritas into David's glass. "Mmm, tart," he said.

"Might have been sitting too long, though. Most of the ice has melted, diluted it."

"If I'd known you were coming, I'd have made a fresh batch." The sarcastic edge she had intended wasn't there. She sounded, she realized, submissive, eager to please. Scared.

Which she was.

Mick nodded, taking the apology as his due. He said, "Anything Loverboy tells you about Leonard's case, I'd like to know. I'm not saying you need to be seeing a lot of him. Just whatever he tells you. You know, it's kind of hot out here. Why don't we go inside?"

"My apartment?" She shook her head. "I come out here on purpose, to soak up the heat."

"Ah, but you're dressed for it. I'm wearing a suit." He got up, causing the chair to emit another tortured creak. Still holding his glass, now empty, he picked up the pitcher of margaritas with his free hand. "Come on." He pushed the door open with his knee and went inside.

He beckoned with his head, standing inside the shadowed hall. "Come on." His voice was soft, encouraging.

Diana stood, slowly, her eyes fixed on Mick's face. She placed her book face down in her chair.

Mick turned away, clearly expecting her to follow.

She turned and ran up the steps to David's apartment, taking them two at a time. David's door was unlocked, and she went straight in.

He came out of the living room, holding a tiny brown book in one hand. She was turning the deadbolt, fastening the chain. She turned to face him, breathing hard.

"Bogeyman?" he said.

"Mick Rothgut." Seeing no enlightenment in his face, she added, "Friend of Leonard Nash. He's in my apartment."

David glanced at his page number, closed the book, and set it on his end table. "Shall we call the police?" he said.

Diana took the phone from him and gave them the information herself. "Stay put," the dispatcher told her. "We're sending a patrol car by."

David got his baseball bat, a Louisville Slugger, out of his hall closet.

"You're not going down there," Diana told him.

He smiled. "No, I'm not. This is just in case," he said.

"This is Shakespeare, isn't it?" Diana said, holding up the book he had been reading. *"Much Ado About Nothing."*

He looked embarrassed. "It's a Cambridge edition, my great-grandfather's copy," he said. "Published in 1864."

"Yes, but why are you reading it now?"

He shrugged. "It's good."

"I love these bookshelves." They were mahogany bookshelves with glass doors. Each shelf was detachable and could be lifted off the shelf below it.

"Me, too," he said. "I use them for my first editions." He opened one of the shelves. "I don't collect scholarly books, except for the Shakespeare, just stuff I read and liked growing up. This one, for example. *Pebble in the Sky,* published by Doubleday in 1950. It was Isaac Asimov's first book. This one's the first book edition of *Tarzan of the Apes*, A. C. McClurg and Company, 1914.''

"Wow."

"That's what I think, every time I look at them."

Somebody rang his doorbell. Diana looked at him. David picked up his baseball bat and went to answer it.

"Mick's not a policeman, is he?" he asked, looking through the peephole.

For a while Mick waited, hoping that the prick would come down to investigate, but the prick didn't show. He left the apartment and walked over to Otto's apartment building, going all the way around Diana's building rather than cross in front of the prick's balcony and his sliding-glass doors.

He was in Otto's living room, watching through the balcony doors, when the police arrived. Otto was in the bedroom, grunting and breathing heavily, and from time to time Mick heard the sound of a woman's voice—though the words were indistinguishable. He didn't like Otto, but at least the guy was a man's man, unlike some.

There were two patrolmen. Diana and David both went down to walk through her apartment with them. There was no one there. "We'll go by and talk to him," one of the patrolmen told them. "At this point, that's about all we can do."

Mick had left the door standing open. He had left his glass and the pitcher on the kitchen counter. "Do you want to take these and dust them for prints?" Diana asked the patrolman.

"What for?" The patrolman was young, probably only in his mid-twenties, though he had a saucer-sized bald spot at the crown of his head.

"I don't know," she said.

David said, "In case something happens later, and you have prints to compare these to."

The patrolman looked at his partner, then back at them, shrugging, smiling. "We don't do that."

Mick watched the policemen leave a few minutes after they had arrived, walking down the sidewalk directly below him, the sound of their voices carrying clearly on the humid air.

"Are we really going to go talk to him?" one said.

"Do you want to?"

"Not really, but I kind of think we gotta."

Mick slipped the door shut, closing the two-inch gap. He wouldn't go home right away. "I kind of think we gotta" did not sound like untiring enthusiasm for the task. They would give up.

"I used to date Leonard Nash," Diana said after the police had gone. "Mick told me you're representing him now."

David nodded. "I saw the picture." He jerked his head toward her bedroom.

Her eyes narrowed, and David remembered that Leonard's picture had been facedown when he saw it. Though he wanted to ask a few questions about Leonard Nash, in the circumstances he didn't see how he could. He left about thirty minutes later.

"Sure you'll be all right?" he said.

"My locks are as good as your locks," she said. "I don't have a baseball bat, but I do have something just as good. Maybe better."

"You don't have a handgun, do you?"

She would only smile.

Night came. The moaning and heavy breathing coming from Otto's bedroom subsided. As darkness closed down, the outside lights flared on in concert. The bad thing about his vantage point was that he could not see Diana's front door and could not tell whether the prick was still with her. If Diana herself left the apartment, and went the long way around the building as he had done—but she had no reason to do that—he would never know it.

At midnight he left Otto's apartment. It seemed dark inside Diana's apartment, though the reflected light of the outdoor lamps in the windows made it hard to be sure. After looking in both directions with his hands in his pockets, he vaulted over Diana's privacy fence and stood listening at her balcony doors.

Nothing but the buzz of the outdoor lights and the sound of the crickets.

A broomstick lay in the track of the sliding door. He was defeated.

Unless . . .

He slipped back over the fence and trotted down the sidewalk to his car. Leonard Nash's ring of keys was in the glove box. He took it out.

After looking at the locks on Diana's front

door, he retreated with the keys to one of the lampposts to sort out the most likely prospects.

In painstaking silence he let himself into the dark apartment. He went down the short hall to her bedroom, putting each foot down carefully, slowly allowing his weight to settle on it.

Her bedroom was black. It took minutes for his eyes to adjust, for her to take dark shape against the white sheets. He moved close enough to hear her breathing.

The sight of her sleeping face was almost unbearably poignant, sending a shaft of pain beneath his breastbone, making it difficult for him to draw breath. He imagined that he would strip naked and slide beneath the sheets with her, feel her rub comfortably against him, still in sleep, feel her nuzzle against his throat. His breathing deepened. In his imagination, he could feel the warmth of her body against his, feel the warmth of her breath against his cheek, smell the fragrance of her hair.

His throat tightened. No. It could never be that way, not tonight. She would come rigidly awake, try to scream; his hand would be on her mouth; widened eyes would stare frightened into his . . . He had seen the way she bolted up the stairs. He knew she was scared of him. Gently, gently—he had to approach her as he would a trembling fawn, win her trust in little things. Win her love.

He stood looking down at her for what seemed a long time. Once she started in her sleep and for a time thrashed restively, but she quieted. The poignant feeling came back, even stronger than before, a painful longing that demanded satisfaction.

But he resisted. He stood smiling down at her, and he resisted. Late, late in the night, he slipped wraithlike from the apartment, pausing outside the door just long enough to lock it again behind him. The harsh caw of a nearby mockingbird startled him and set his heart to racing.

He looked in all directions, but he was unobserved by human eyes.

11

David talked to Walt Jeffries at nine o'clock the next morning. "I was just fixing to call Frank about this," Walt told David. "I didn't know Cecil was even gone before I read about it in the paper last night."

"It was in the afternoon paper?"

"Front page. I thought I'd talk to Frank before I called the police, because Cecil was in here. He didn't disappear over the weekend like the paper said. He was here on Monday."

"And he had a court order?"

"Signed that morning."

"So what was in the lock box?"

"Ah. Cecil left me a carbon. Let's see . . ." There was the sound of some paper shuffling. "Texas Rangers gym bag; municipal bonds, two hundred or more, five thousand-dollar-denominations. Wow."

"Wow," David repeated. "What kind of municipal bonds were they?"

"Ah. Well." It turned out Walt didn't know any more than was written on his form. That was one of the reasons he wanted to talk to Frank before calling the police.

Frank was in San Antonio, taking a deposition. Al and Joe Bob were in trial. Not only could David not put Walt through to Frank, he didn't have anyone to tell about his newest suspicions: that Cecil's disappearance was connected with Leonard Nash and roughly one million dollars in municipal bonds.

Left to himself, David spent the day in Cecil's office, going through the Leonard Nash files. At six o'clock, he was sitting with his elbows on the desk, his hands buried in his hair. The Nash files were all over the place: in stacks on the floor, fanned out over the desktop, in accordion folders leaning against a leg of the desk. Fourteen lawsuits had been filed against Leonard before he sought refuge in bankruptcy; the pleadings were all there. The bankruptcy petition was there, with deeds and contracts and notes and other evidences of Leonard's assets and liabilities. A copy of Clark Holland's will was there; a copy of a power of attorney made out in blank.

The available documents gave a clear picture of the development of the case up through Monday. Then there was nothing except for indications that there should be something: Cecil missing; Leonard talking about a lock box. Somehow, there was a tie-in with that kid murdered last week.

What did Frank know about this Clark Holland? Frank still hadn't come in, but David tried him at home. Frank answered the phone.

"I thought you were in San Antonio," David said.

"I was. Just got back, and it was late enough, I thought, to let the office go for the day."

"Huh. Well, the reason I called was to ask what you know about a seventeen-year-old named Clark Holland."

Frank, it turned out, did not know anything about Clark Holland, except—wait—wasn't he the kid who was murdered in that studio apartment last week? The very one. What has he got to do with Cecil? David told him about his conversation with Leonard, and about Cecil's visit to the First National Bank on Monday morning.

There was a long silence. "I should have thought about a possible connection with Leonard's lock box," Frank said. "I was assuming that Cecil disappeared some time over the weekend when all the banks were closed."

"Do you think Leonard could have set him up?" David told Frank his theory that Leonard could have used Cecil to get cash or cash equivalents from the lock box, then had an accomplice take the cash away from him.

"But Walt said the lock box contained municipal bonds."

"Quite a lot of municipal bonds."

"Those bonds are all registered these days. I'm not sure it would do somebody any good just to steal the certificates."

"And maybe forge the necessary endorsements or whatever and have them reregistered?"

"But when the forgery was discovered . . ."

"The thief could have already sold the securities to a BFP." Or bona fide purchaser.

"Be a pretty trusting BFP. But, tell you what, I'll call this Macklin fellow at the police department and suggest he talk to Walt. If Cecil was ever at the bus station with a Texas Ranger gym bag, somebody might remember it—especially if Cecil had just been shot."

David hung up. It hadn't occurred to him that the location of Cecil's car when the police found it could be significant. That it was at the bus station opened the possibility that Cecil had left it there himself, and that he had gone somewhere voluntarily—though, of course, that theory left the blood and the bullet unexplained. A million dollars in bonds: The guy who had them is missing, and his car is at the bus station. What did that suggest? David wondered if anyone had talked to Cecil's ex-wife.

In Cecil's rolodex he found Laura Armstrong's home and office numbers, but no one answered at either place. David sat back, considering.

Flipping through the rolodex had made him think that maybe he should just call all the names there to see if anyone knew the whereabouts of Cecil. He might come up with another Walt Jeffries. "Oh, yes, I saw Cecil at the bus station. He said he was there to meet . . ."

David called Frank back. "What's the name of the place that Laura works?" he asked.

"You're not thinking of calling Laura, are you? I did it just last night, and I can't say it was a positive experience."

"She hadn't seen Cecil?"

"No. She was sure as hell upset, though, to hear that he was missing."

"Oh."

"She cried. I had the idea that she might have been drinking."

"Suggesting she already knew about Cecil?"

"Well, it was in yesterday's paper, maybe not the Dallas paper. I'd say it was news to her, though."

"Oh."

"To answer your original question, when Laura left Cecil she went to work for a pair of art dealers. I think the company was called Rupert and Holmes. Dallas, of course. I think I've heard somewhere that Holmes is dead, which would leave Rupert. Jack Rupert."

Directory assistance had a listing for only one Jack Rupert. After thinking about it some more, David called Jack Rupert at home.

"Hello?"

Rupert was old, and he had an old, dusty voice that creaked faintly with age. David tried to explain who he was. "I'm trying to reach Laura Armstrong," he concluded. "She does still work for you?"

"Yeah, she does work for me. Doesn't live with me, though. I'm wondering why you'd call here."

"Was she at work today?"

"Can't say that she was."

"Can you say that she wasn't?"

The question elicited a dry, dusty chuckle. "I reckon I can say that."

"Can you tell me the last time you saw her?"

"Well, I reckon I *can*. I'm not sure I understand yet why a law associate of her ex-husband is trying to get ahold of Laura."

David sighed. "He's missing."

"I think I saw something about that in this morning's paper. Been missing for nearly a week now, has he?"

"The story was in the Dallas paper?"

"Yep. Buried somewhere in the front section of the *Dallas Morning News*. I probably wouldn't have seen it, but I was looking for it. Last night a Frank-somebody called Laura from down your way. You know him?"

"He's one of the lawyers here. Did Laura seem upset?"

"Well, now, what do you think?"

"Does that mean yes?"

"Yes, she was upset."

"And when did she tell you Cecil was missing?"

"Yesterday evening."

"She called you on the telephone."

"Can't say that she did." He laughed another wheezing chuckle. "Yes, and I can say that she didn't. You lawyers. All of you talk like that? Precise as a damn Masterlock."

"Maybe too precise. I get the idea I'm poking all around what I want to know, and I just haven't hit the right spot yet. To save a lot more question-and-answer, could you just speak generally to how you came to know about Cecil's disappearance?"

"Laura told me, as I said, and it was right here in my living room. She just found out, I guess, and she came over all upset. Left this morning— no, not what you think, I'm old enough to be her daddy. She didn't want to be alone, is all. Left this morning to go by her apartment and get gussied up a bit before coming into work, and that's the last I saw of her."

"So she didn't come into work. Did you try to call her?"

"Well, no. She looked kind of wore out. I was

thinking she could use the time to herself, and I didn't want to bother her if she was napping or something."

"Well, as I said, she doesn't answer her phone now."

"So you said."

"You're not worried."

"I guess not very."

"Okay. Well, thanks for talking to me."

"Nothing else you were wanting to ask about?"

"Should there be?"

"I take it what you're really looking for is Cecil, and you were hoping Laura might have heard from him?"

"Yes."

"That Frank-somebody that called her last night, didn't Laura tell him she hadn't heard from Cecil? Did Frank think she was holding out on him?"

"Well, I don't know. I'm just poking around."

"I know you've felt like you've had to drag information out of me, but you're not very forthcoming with details yourself, young man."

"I don't have any details to come forth with."

"I see. Well, nice talking to you."

"Wait, what is it you were thinking I should ask about?"

But Jack Rupert had hung up. David stared at the receiver in his hand, brooding, feeling that somehow there was more he should have gotten out of that conversation.

When he came around the corner of his apartment building, he saw that Diana's door was standing open. Before he could think any alarming thoughts, though, Diana came through the door, and she put her arms around his neck, and she kissed his mouth with evident passion. David dropped his briefcase on the sidewalk, and he stepped back on it and very nearly tripped over it and took Diana with him. But he held onto her with both arms about her waist, and it steadied him just enough to save them.

"Wha," he said, when the kiss was over—or not quite over, because she was kissing him again.

"Thank you for the roses," she said between kisses. "And the chocolates. I love Godiva chocolates."

He held her by the shoulders. "Diana, you've got to believe me when I tell you this . . ."

"But you didn't send them. I know." She kissed him again. He held her away.

"But I didn't send them. That's right. I didn't send them. That means somebody else did."

"You didn't write 'Sweets for my sweet'?"

"Ugh. No." He shook his head.

"Or 'Roses for my rose petal'?"

"Double ugh."

"But . . . Mick. It was Mick." She pushed away from him. "Damn you. Why *didn't* you send the roses and the chocolates?"

He smiled reflexively, unsure of himself, and she punched his shoulder. Hard.

The evening did not end with passion and bliss. Hours later David stood alone on his balcony, staring out across the apartment complex. There was a heavy mist, and the light from the lampposts formed fuzzy spheres of light at the top of the iron poles. Most of the grounds were left in darkness.

Five-thousand-dollar bonds, two hundred or more: one million dollars. Cecil had taken it from the bank, and he had disappeared. David had begun to suspect him of embezzling the money and disappearing to South America—though Cecil was so scrupulously honest. And, of course, there was the bullet and the blood.

The crickets sang their night song, and the song was mingled with the croaking of frogs. In the apartment directly across from David's the curtains were open, and he became aware of a man standing inside the apartment, standing alone in the darkness, looking out. A big man? But the light was too vague for David even to discern an outline.

David's eyes strained in the darkness, and he became convinced that what he was looking at was a shadow, just a shadow, and not a man at all.

It was later still. Cecil's house gleamed faintly in the soft rain, which had been falling for just over an hour. Cecil's was a white frame house, gables covered with a wood shingle that was painted to match. The lawn still needed mowing; the weeds stood taller than the grass and had gone to seed.

David parked his car across from the house, killed the engine, and sat. The night got darker. The rain fell harder, drumming steadily on the roof of his car. On the radio, Mick Jagger sang that time, time, time was on his side.

David let his car seat back a couple of notches.

On Monday Cecil had left the house for work as he had on a thousand mornings, and he had not come back. Something had happened, and he had not come back. David was beginning to believe he was decomposing in a shallow grave out in the mesquite somewhere.

He didn't know, and not knowing was making him restless.

The radio played something by Eric Clapton. David didn't know what he hoped to accomplish by staking out Cecil's house for an hour or two in the middle of the night, but he couldn't bear to stay in his apartment. He had to do something; not knowing what only made his inactivity more difficult to bear.

Eventually he got out of his car and pushed the door shut behind him. He carried his Louisville Slugger in his right hand, though for no particular reason—no rational reason, anyway. There was no denying that Cecil's house spooked him.

As he stood by his car, looking at the house, the rain worked through his hair and ran cool along his scalp. For a moment, moonlight broke through the clouds and glinted off an upstairs window before the night closed down again.

"Sheesh, this is creepy," he said, and the sound of his own voice, harsh against the patter of rain, was creepier still. He put his head down and slogged through the wet grass to the porch, where the swing creaked softly in the shifting breeze. From there he could see what he hadn't expected to see—that inside the screen, the front door stood ajar. The gap was less than an inch, but it was there.

It had not been there on Tuesday.

He turned the knob on the screen door and found that it was not locked. He didn't pull the door open. Goose bumps rose all over him suddenly, and the hair on his neck bristled. He whirled, gripping his baseball bat in both hands, but nobody was there. The branch of an oak tree beside the road crashed to the sidewalk between David and his car, splintering into fragments.

David's insides convulsed, and his heart beat out a fast cadence.

Stepping off the porch, his eyes strained upward in the darkness. Bare tree limbs were dark against the slightly lighter background of the cloudy night. One of the limbs was broken off, maybe sixty feet above the ground.

It was a dead tree. The limb had fallen because it was dead and its time had come to fall. David said these things silently to reassure himself, and he began to concentrate on slow, deep breathing. A rodent or a cat or something ran through the shrubbery behind him. He bolted for his car and made it, and he swung into the driver's seat and slammed the door and gunned the ignition more or less simultaneously.

He called the police from a 7-11 on the expressway. He asked for the Lieutenant Macklin who had talked to Frank, but ended up talking to a Sergeant Larry Jenkins.

"We'll send a car around," he said.

"Thank you."

"Will you be there to meet them?"

It was something he hadn't counted on, but he said okay.

And when he got back to the house, the patrol

car was there, its siren off, but its blue dome-light flashing. As David got out of his car, one of the policemen shone a flashlight in his face. "David Loring?" The beam of light sparkled on myriad streaks of water coming down between them.

"Yes."

"Wait out here, please."

So they left him alone while they went in to check the house. David got his baseball bat from the car and stood holding it, leaning back against the wet car. His head and his clothes were soaked. Water dripped in droplets from his nose.

The policemen came out. "You familiar with the house?"

David nodded.

"Why don't you come inside with us a minute." He eyed the bat. "Expecting trouble?"

"No," David said, but when he went with them inside the house, he took the bat with him.

They had a floor lamp on in the living room. It did little to illuminate the corners and edges of the room, but it seemed to be the only source of light available. There were several paintings on the walls, scattered randomly in an arrangement that was vaguely disquieting. Below the paintings, dark furniture hunched against the walls. The center of the room was bare; no carpet covered the scuffed oak flooring. There was no coffee table. David thought of a warehouse.

"This the way you remember it?" The patrolman stood at David's shoulder. He had closely cropped blond hair, an inadequate moustache not quite reaching to the corners of his mouth. The other cop had dark hair and a thin, pale face. He stood some distance away, his eyes warily on David's baseball bat.

David nodded. The house had been like this for a couple of years now. Before that, in the days when Cecil had had a wife and family, the house had been different.

The dining room table, made of dark, gleaming mahogany, was about twelve feet long and half that distance across; it looked sturdy enough to support a midsized car. The patter of rain sounded softly against the dining room's bay windows.

In the kitchen, they flipped a light switch, and an overhead fluorescent guttered on. The floor was covered with twelve-inch tiles. The refrigerator was white, the sink and faucets chrome. Broken dishes, broken glasses, and an overturned drawer of silverware were piled on the floor.

"I don't think he kept it this way," David said. The blond policemen smiled, but the dark one nodded soberly. David bent and picked up a crumpled piece of faded construction paper. He unfolded it carefully. On one side was a rough crayon drawing of a man with brown, scrawling hair, a green suit, and a purple tie. Below it a child had written, "I love you Daddy. Sarah." The other side was blank.

David laid it reverently on the counter. "He has a daughter named Sarah. She's in college now," he said.

A bedroom opened off of the kitchen. It was where Cecil had been living. The double bed was bare; the sheets lay in a pile on the floor. The mattress cover had been cut and peeled from the mattress. Slacks and shirts and about a dozen suits were cut and ripped and lying in a big pile around the door of the closet.

"Someone's been in here, too," David said.

In a ten-gallon aquarium at the foot of the bed, air bubbled to the surface and gently stirred the plastic plant life. The tank held two angel fish, one floating on the surface.

Outside again, he gave the police his address and his daytime phone number. He sat in his car and listened to the rain as they got into their patrol car and drove away.

It was when they were gone that he saw a movement by the side of Cecil's house. It was a shadow, bigger than a man, and then it was nothing. With gooseflesh standing out all over his body, David started his car, and he drove away.

12

David was followed on his way to work the next morning. He didn't notice the car that started off from the curb as he exited the parking lot, didn't notice it tailgating him all the way to the expressway, didn't notice it riding in the left lane, beside him, as he drove into town. When he stopped at a traffic light at the end of the exit ramp, though, the car was behind him and it bumped him. Tapped him, really, bumper barely touching bumper, just hard enough to be felt.

In his rearview mirror, David saw the blue and white shield of the Bavarian Motor Works. Above it, sunlight glinted from the windshield, almost obscuring the car's occupant, a huge bear of a man.

It was the familiar size of the man that sent a shiver along David's spine, that caused him to grip instinctively the end of the baseball bat poking up from the footwell on the other side of the gearshift. Rather than get out of his car to inspect for possible damage to his rear bumper, he touched his automatic door lock, and all four locks thumped down.

The light turned green, and as David started forward, the big BMW came along behind him. At Tenth Street, David turned right, toward the police station, and the BMW went straight, in the direction of the law firm.

David stopped by the curb in front of the police station, trying to think whether the police could help him. He had not remained calm enough to focus on the BMW's license plate—and, when it was behind him, it had been too close to see. He could not even describe the man behind the wheel very definitely. "He was big, Officer. Big. Let me describe for you a big man I saw at Westgate Mall the day before yesterday . . ."

He could ask for an escort to his office. No one would be lurking in the parking garage or around his office building, and he would feel foolish, but there were worse feelings than foolish.

Mick Rothgut. This was the Mick Rothgut about whom Diana had told him. Mick was probably jealous of him, and maniacally obsessed. But then . . . there was the open door at Cecil's place; the wrecked, perhaps the searched, interior. There was the man he had seen, or had thought he'd seen, in the shadows of the house.

And the man in the apartment across from his. Perhaps it was David himself who was deranged, a growing paranoiac.

In the end, he pulled away from the curb without bothering the police. He drove into his parking garage alone and circled down to his parking space. His only concession to his increasing nervousness was to carry his baseball bat with him through the tunnel to the office building. It was only when he saw the startled look of the law firm's receptionist that he realized how much of a concession it was.

Standing in the mail room—without his baseball bat, which he had dropped off at his office—he sorted through his mail in search of Abner DePuy's answer to his petition in the Shumaker–MacLeod lawsuit. It wasn't there. On Wednesday David had delivered his ultimatum. If Abner had filed his answer that day, or even the next, a copy of it should be here now, waiting for him.

Al stuck his head in to ask if he had talked to the Davises yet about the settlement offer.

"Yes. They're going to take it."

"Tell Madison Whitney?"

"Not yet."

"Hey, what do you look so down in the mouth for? You should be ecstatic."

"I know. I guess I feel a little less idealistic than I did."

"You're growing up."

"I guess."

Al stepped in to slap his shoulder, then he went off down the hall.

Ellen Uhlan, standing further down the counter in the mail room, said, "You've got the daftest expression on your face," and David blinked at her in surprise.

Joe Bob Raymond laughed from the doorway. He said, "We men wouldn't know half the things that are wrong with us, we didn't have Ellen to tell us." He moved on.

Ellen glowered. If she had been a cat, she would have spit.

David gathered up his mail and took it back to his office to open.

When it was read and sorted (and filed mostly in the trash can), he called the clerk's office and confirmed that, yes indeed, Abner still had failed to file his answer. David smiled. It was turning out to be a nice day. He whistled as he fished out the Shumaker file and leafed through it for his default judgment, already typed and ready. It seemed incredible, but he would get to use it after all.

"Oh, David," Frank McKinnon said from the doorway.

David closed the Shumaker file and dropped it into his lap where the desk would mostly hide it. "Yes, sir," he said.

Frank smiled. "You reminded me of one of my kids when you did that. You haven't been stealing cookies, have you?"

David grinned broadly, disingenuously.

"I just stopped by to make sure you knew about the thing with Ed Crowell."

David's smile faded. "What thing with Ed Crowell?" He knew about Ed Crowell's lawsuit, of course, since it had already generated fees to the firm of two hundred thousand dollars. Everyone in the firm knew about the lawsuit.

"You knew it settled last month."

"Sure."

"And it was Cecil's baby. I thought maybe the thing today would be in his appointment book."

"I didn't see it." Then again, he hadn't looked for it.

"You need to meet with Ed and Lola at the

Bekins warehouse at ten o'clock. It's only nine-thirty now. You've got plenty of time."

"Time for what?" He knew Frank was dumping on him, and he knew Frank knew he was dumping on him. What he wanted was to get his default judgment and then to get back to work on Cecil's disappearance. Now this. Lola was a rich little old lady whose niece's husband, Charles Bachman, had wound up controlling all her property. She hadn't been married, not then, and other than the niece and an older brother in an insane asylum she had no family. One day she ran into Ed Crowell at the Picadilly and spent most of lunch complaining to him about how her niece and her niece's husband were treating her: never gave her any money, made her ride the bus instead of taking her places or giving her taxi money, treated her like she wasn't there sometimes.

Ed was a belligerent old coot in his seventies. His older brother had gone through school with Lola, and Ed had worshipped her when he was younger and still capable of such sentiments. However much his capacity for worship had atrophied, rage and fierceness were two things he was still good at, and he made her cause his own. Three weeks after the chance meeting at the Picadilly, they were married. The battle for control of a ten-million-dollar fortune was joined.

"What am I meeting Ed and Lola for?" David asked.

"Under the settlement, one of the things Lola gets is half her father's furniture, which I understand is on the main floor of the Bekins warehouse along with a lot of the Bachmans' stuff and a lot of stuff that belonged to Lola's brother—and therefore, now to the Bachmans. The Crowells and the Bachmans are getting together at ten to sort it out, and Ed wants his lawyer there."

"Don't Ed and Lola live in a townhouse?"

"Oh, they're not going to *use* the furniture. They just want to have it. I imagine most of the stuff will just go across the street to the Allied warehouse and stay there until everybody dies."

Ed and Lola, though they did not regain control of the various trusts and businesses, did get a substantial amount of cash: a half-million up front and some kind of six-figure annuity. And reimbursement for all their legal fees. None of it made Ed happy. If he could strip the Bachmans naked and drive them through town with a horsewhip, it still wouldn't make him happy.

David wasn't clear on what his role was supposed to be. He'd only met Ed Crowell once, and he wasn't anxious to repeat the experience. "What does Ed need a lawyer for?"

"Nothing really. Ed won't recognize any of the furniture, because he's never seen any of it. Lola's kind of scatterbrained and won't remember much. It puts them in the weak sort of position that makes Ed mad. He'll be convinced that Bachman is trying to cheat them out of every end table he can. You'll be along mostly to keep them from tearing out each other's throats."

"Heard anything about Cecil?"

Frank turned back at the door. "The police double-checked all the hospital emergency rooms in the area, and they came up with two reports of gunshot wounds."

"Cecil?"

"No. Both Hispanics."

"I was hoping to get by the bus station today to see if anyone saw Cecil hopping a bus."

"You might check with Macklin first, see who they've talked to." Frank looked at his watch. "Better hurry to the warehouse. The sooner you get started . . ."

"Yeah, I know." David came around the desk as Frank walked away down the hall. The Shumaker file, forgotten, fell beneath his desk.

"Where is the Bekins warehouse?" he called.

"Just a few blocks from here. Check the phone book," Frank said, walking backwards.

It was only nine-fifty-five when Mick saw David pull out of his parking garage again. He had been prepared for an all-day wait. He started his car, waited until another car had gone by, then shifted into gear and followed.

He was trailing David for two reasons. One, of course, was that the prick stood between him and Diana. The other was that the prick just might lead him to the money that Cecil had run off with. The two motivations were not entirely compatible.

The first had dominated when he bumped David's bumper on his way to work—frightening David into running for the police. The prick was so nerveless, so spineless, so gutless, it was a pleasure to torment him. Mick smiled as he remembered the morning. He smiled more broadly at the memory of the night before, David swinging about with that ridiculous baseball bat, bolting finally across the yard at the sound of a harmless noise.

This morning David turned into the parking lot of the Bekins warehouse and got out of his car. Mick drove by. He didn't think he had been seen. After a couple of blocks he had an idea and made a U-turn. He parked on the opposite side of the warehouse from David. No doors on this side of the warehouse, but lots of windows, many broken and boarded, a few intact. Lots of ways to get inside.

Again David was unaware of being followed. He had looked for Mick in the parking garage—he was beginning to hate that parking garage—and he looked for a BMW when he first got on the street. But he had other things to think about: for one thing, the upcoming meeting with the infamous, pugnacious, absolutely rancorous Ed Crowell. The thought of it gave him a sick, unsettled feeling in the bottom of his stomach, which meant, of course, that he was soon devoting all of his thought to it.

By the time he pulled onto the packed dirt by the warehouse, he had nearly forgotten about Mick. He didn't see the BMW drive by as he parked his car; rather, he was seeing the thin patches of dark gravel that were the remnants of a parking lot, seeing the warehouse itself. A window was broken high up in the dingy brick of the building, and the window had been boarded on the inside. The Coca-Cola advertisement painted on the side of the building had faded almost beyond legibility.

The parking lot, aside from his own car, was

empty: no client, no adversaries. The big rolling-metal door was closed. The smaller, man-sized door beside it was closed as well, and locked.

He looked around, his hands in his pockets. The hot sun blazed down on him. His armpits felt soggy, and sweat had begun coming through the suit fabric. A bead of sweat nestled in the philtrum atop his upper lip.

At ten-fifteen a dark blue Rolls-Royce pulled into the parking lot. When it stopped, in the space against the warehouse marked "No Parking, Loading Zone," the white dust the car had thrown up hung in the air, drifting almost imperceptibly on the negligible breeze. David stood blinking at the sunlight glinting from the hood ornament as two people got out of the car, a man and a woman.

"Crowells here yet?" the man said, which let David know he was looking at Charles Bachman. Bachman was tall. His face and neck were seamed and dark from years beneath the southern Texas sun. He wore Wrangler blue jeans and a polo shirt—no hat, though the top half of his forehead was paler than the rest of his face.

"You're the first," David told him. Bachman introduced himself and his wife Susie.

"There's Ed and Lola," Susie said, nodding her head at the far corner of the building.

A man and woman stood there, their images shimmering across the white, hot dirt of the parking area. The woman held her purse across her chest, her arms close to her sides. She looked old and frail, all the frailer in contrast to the man standing beside her, his hands on his hips.

The man's medicine-ball torso bulged above and below his belt.

David excused himself to the Bachmans and walked across the hard-packed ground to his clients. Ed Crowell wore checked polyester pants and a shiny, dark blue shirt. His thin fringe of hair was slicked to his scalp.

"You from the law firm?" he said, when David was halfway to him. "Where the devil's Cecil?"

"Nobody knows. He's disappeared."

"Disappeared! The hell does that mean, disappeared?"

"The police suspect foul play."

"Oh, my," said a tiny voice. It took a moment for David to trace the words to Lola, who was withered and shriveled to the point of decomposition. Her eyes were rheumy and unblinking, and her words were the first evidence of life she had exhibited.

Ed Crowell had lost interest. He brushed by David and marched toward the Bachmans. Lola tottered diffidently in his wake.

"You got the key to this place?" Ed boomed as he approached the Bachmans. "We're prepared to go through it with a fine-tooth comb, a fine-tooth comb, I tell you. Don't give us any fuss about what's yours and what's Lola's, because you've already been through it by yourselves—I know that, don't think I don't—and taken out everything you want. I *know* that." Lola punctuated Ed's truculent statement with a high, whining fart.

Bachman rolled his eyes in reaction either to Ed's belligerence or to Lola's contribution, but he seemed resigned to whatever unpleasantness the encounter might bring him. Lola's flatulence rose around them in the August heat, sharp and sour. David stopped using his nose. When he breathed—and, unfortunately, he had to breathe—it was shallowly and through his mouth.

Bachman turned a key, and the large metal door rolled up automatically with a series of ringing clangs. The stale, superheated air of the interior swept over them and engulfed them. David felt his sweat glands cut loose as they pushed into the heat. He kept thinking about Cecil. He wanted to get out of here and on to the bus station.

The building was lit by bare light bulbs, irregularly spaced, insufficient to do more than illuminate the motes of dust hanging on the dense air. There was a sound like a cat crying, far off—David traced the sound to Lola, who seemed to have developed a slow leak. It made him queasy.

"There's not enough light in here," Ed said. "I need a flashlight. Can't see a dern thing."

David was silent. He had no flashlight. The five of them stood together in the stale heat near the bright entrance of the huge, dim warehouse.

"I may have one in my car," Bachman said finally, and he went out to his Rolls. While they waited, Ed and Lola walked a short distance between two long rows of boxes and cloth-draped furniture. David and Susie stood close together, lost in the silence of their own thoughts. Somewhere in the building, there was the clang of metal on metal, and the sound of something rolling.

David looked at Susie, but she seemed oblivious to the sounds. Bachman came back and paused near them while his eyes adjusted to the gloom. When Ed came back, he handed him the flashlight.

"Is this all of it?" Ed said, waving his fat arm at the warehouse.

"Yep."

"Every bit of it?"

Bachman did not reply, perhaps because he had already answered the question. Ed went back to Lola, the circle of light from the flashlight bobbing before him. The light revealed little of the warehouse. The roof was low where they were, but David was vaguely aware of the main floor opening up twenty or thirty feet further inside. He gave Bachman a nod and followed his clients. The flashlight illuminated an old bureau, and Ed said to Lola, "Do you remember that? Was it in your father's house?"

"I . . . I don't know." Her voice was so tentative as to be nearly inaudible. "I've seen one *like* it before . . ."

"We'll take it." The circle of light shifted, and they moved on. Sweat hung in droplets from Ed's nose and chin, and he was surely cooking inside his polyester oven.

Lola paused before what once had been her father's staircase. It was recognizably a staircase, though now it was in pieces. It had been wide enough to accommodate an eighteen-wheeler. The posts that had marked the foot of the stairs were like tree stumps, ten feet high and topped by knobs the size of beachballs. The ruins of the staircase gave David new insight into the extent of the family wealth.

"I remember this," came Lola's voice, softly as the musings of a child.

"Would you like to have it? We'll take it," Ed said.

"Lola has a brother, you know," Bachman said. He had been following Lola at a safe distance. "The brother's stuff is Susie's."

Ed shined the light in Bachman's face. "You've already taken out his share, and more. I know that. You know that. You've been through and looted this place for all the nice stuff, and don't tell me you haven't."

Bachman stood with his head drawn back, blinking slowly in the sudden light. "Take anything you want," he said finally. "I was just telling you." He turned and walked back down the long aisle toward the entrance.

Ed turned on David. "I thought you were here to represent *us*," he said.

"That's right. So far, though, your interests haven't seemed to need much representing."

Ed snorted and slapped the flashlight into David's hand before turning away. David followed meekly, pointing the flashlight at objects Ed expressed an interest in. They were somewhere in the center of the warehouse, and the ceiling was a good fifty feet above them, but circling the perimeter of the warehouse were many dim floors of furniture and junk and crates. David shivered in the heat.

After a bit, Lola started tugging at Ed's sleeve until she got him to lean toward her. "I've got gas," she said in a whisper that reached further than her ordinary speaking voice. "I need to go to the restroom." She looked ill. Even in the uncertain light, perspiration gleamed from the wattles of her throat.

"All right," Ed said decisively. "We'll get you one." He took her arm and marched her back down the long aisle to the entrance, leaving David to follow in their wake. Before he could, something brushed his arm and clanged onto the concrete floor, sliding and rolling away from him. He jumped, clutching at his elbow, which had gone completely numb. The flashlight clattered on the floor, but did not go out.

When he could retrieve the flashlight, finally, pain was coming to his arm. He shone the light along the floor and stopped it on a long rusted crowbar, six feet long. Again he shivered. He turned the flashlight upward and saw high up rows of metal bracing beneath a tin roof.

He hurried down the aisle after Ed and Lola Bachman, still holding his elbow. It throbbed so badly, he thought it might be broken.

Once, long ago, Mick had been good with the javelin—and, in fact, the high school record he had set for the javelin throw remained unbroken. None of that meant that he should have expected to impale a man with a twenty-pound crowbar at a distance of forty or fifty feet. Still, he was disappointed.

As soon as he saw his shot go wide, he slipped from the warehouse by the way he had entered. He wasn't sure that he wanted to kill the prick; that would mean losing his best lead to Cecil. But he had seen the crowbar, had tripped over it, and he had had to try. Feeling the heft of it in his hands, knowing not one man in a thousand could hit a man at that distance, he had had to try.

He removed the license plates from his car, using a screwdriver from the trunk, then moved his car to a place where the prick would see it when he came out. He moved fast, not knowing how much time he had, or whether he had enough.

It was his buoyant spirits that made him sure that, whatever he did, it would work out. Fate was with him. The sight of his car would hold David transfixed, he knew it. He walked back across to the Bekins warehouse and crouched behind the dumpster near David's car to wait for him.

Another sign that fate was with him: A mop handle was there, lying on the gravel beside the dumpster, in just the place Mick would have put it if he had arranged everything carefully in advance. He picked up the wooden dowel, threaded at one end, and he ran his hands along the rough surface. It was only four feet long, extremely light after the weight of the crowbar.

Holding it by one end, he swung it through the air. He smiled in satisfaction at the whistle-sound it made.

"What was that noise?" Susie asked him, referring to the crowbar's clatter. She smacked her gum.

"Lola needs a restroom," Ed was saying. "We'll have to finish this another time."

David shook his head at Susie, too distracted by his throbbing elbow to answer her.

Bachman was looking at Crowell, his hands

clasped behind him. Ed was glaring at him, but
Bachman didn't seem unnerved by it. "Well,
now," he said. "Me and Susie'll be leaving town
tomorrow, gone until sometime the first part of
October. We did set aside all of today to go
through the warehouse with you."

Ed said, "Another time. Our lawyers will call
you to set it up." He looked at David contemptu-
ously. "Huh. You take care of closing up here,
you follow?"

David followed, but he was feeling weak and
sick. Fear, too, was growing in him. The crowbar
had flown at him out of nowhere, planting the
seed of supernatural dread.

"Maybe you all would like to meet back here
after Lola's had her chance at the restroom,"
Bachman said.

"Another time."

The Crowells left. David and the Bachmans
walked out into the sunlight and the relative
coolness of August at midday. "Well, I guess
that's it," Bachman said. "It's a funny thing.
They've been yippin' and hollerin' about getting
in this here warehouse for months now. I did
think Lola was goin' to kill us with that gas of
hers, though."

David was looking down at his suit, which had
turned a shade or two darker from the sweat he
was putting out. He flexed his arm. His elbow
still throbbed, but he thought it was going to be
all right. That heavy bar must have brushed his
elbow, rather than hitting it squarely. He shivered again, involuntarily. "Perhaps you could
give me a call when you do get back to town?"

One-handed, he fished a limp card from his wallet. He was feeling dizzy.

Bachman took the card. "Should be around October fifth, a little after." He went to his car. David felt a surge of panic at the prospect of being left alone.

"Mr. Bachman?"

Bachman turned back from his Rolls. Susie was already sitting in the car on the passenger side.

David said, "I haven't done any work on this case at all and really don't know any of the details. It's settled now, no more danger of the things we say being repeated in a courtroom. I'd really like to know: Did you really mistreat Lola as badly as everyone at the McKinnon firm seems to think you did?"

Bachman looked suddenly sad. He shook his head slowly. "I can't say, son, not really. Lola's a sick old woman, has been for years. Not very interesting to be around. Susie here, and Susie's daddy, are her only kinfolk, and the daddy's in the loony-bin in Florida. I reckon we all should have paid more attention to her." Bachman paused to reflect, squinting up at the sun.

"As for taking over her property, treating it as your own?"

"You have any grandparents still alive, a grandmother maybe? Husband dead, mind a little addled, can't quite manage her own affairs any longer?"

David shook his head.

"I don't guess you'd understand, then." Bachman got in his car, and the Rolls pulled off the lot. A cloud of dust rose white behind it. David stood motionless, watching after it.

The dust settled slowly. Beyond it, parked beside another warehouse on the other side of the street, sat a dark blue BMW. David's fist clenched when he saw it. Mick was playing with him. He wasn't in the car, no one was, but the car was hauntingly familiar.

David opened his car door and reached for his baseball bat with his good arm. His eyes remained fixed on the BMW. He thought he understood a lot of things now.

He started over, baseball bat held across his chest, but then he stopped, heart pounding with a clear premonition of danger. He was only peripherally aware of the dumpster, roughly ten feet behind him, loaded with boxes and bulging Hefty bags.

He heard the swish of clothing behind him and started to turn, but felt a flash of despair even as the pain exploded in his head and dropped him to his knees.

He stared stupidly at the circle of dirt and gravel spotlighted before him. His body was tilting on him, crumpling, and he had no strength to do anything about it. He felt numb.

It took several seconds for his eyes to register the baseball bat lying in front of him. Several more seconds for his mind to recognize the bat as his own. He tried to reach for it, but there was no strength for that either.

He found himself on all fours, then on his face, and then the blackness took him.

Mick stood over him, turning his body with his toe. There was blood in David's hair, and blood dripped slowly into the dirt. Mick knelt and touched David's throat. The pulse was there, though weak and irregular.

Mick had been wrong again. He could not kill a man with a swipe from a mop handle. The crowbar, that would have done it. Not a mop handle. He shrugged.

In large part he had vented his anger at being challenged for Diana's affections; perhaps he had even done something to discourage that challenge. He felt unnaturally calm.

He smiled down at David. The prick might still prove useful to him; there was always that. He smiled more broadly. The prick had seen the dumpster, but it hadn't worried him. He hadn't realized that a man who could run the hundred-yard dash in ten seconds could cover ten feet in one-third of one second.

One-third of one second was not warning enough for anyone.

13

David had no memory of what followed. He lay in direct sunlight through the afternoon, and the dry, white dust soaked up his blood and his sweat. The temperature peaked at ninety-seven degrees at twelve minutes before four in the afternoon.

At some time after four, David's right hand began to clench and unclench, and his eyelids began to flutter. He rolled to hands and knees and lurched unsteadily to his feet. A sticky pool of half-dried blood remained where his head had lain, and he put his foot in it as he started toward the street.

Five-fifteen found him on Polk Street—in Polk Street, actually—shambling northward, in the direction least likely to find him succor. His path angled toward the curb.

Five-seventeen. David staggered away from the curb again, into the path of an old Plymouth Fury, which jumped the curb and smacked down a parking meter before Howard Carney, under a barrage of exclamations and criticisms from his wife Millie, managed to bring the car to a halt.

Thirty minutes later David was in St. Luke's

Hospital with a couple of I.V. drips running into his arm and a catheter up his penis. Howard and Millie spent a good part of the next three days bending over him, loudly debating whether he would live or die, and whether, if he lived, his mind would be permanently impaired like that of Millie's Uncle Jerry, who was kicked in the head by a mule when he was younger. They gave interviews to the press, appeared on TV-8 News, and had their pictures in the paper over the caption "Couple Saves Life." For twenty years they had been going to the diner for their Friday evening meal, and nothing so exciting had ever happened to them.

Or to David. When consciousness returned to him, an old man whose plaid shirt was buttoned to his chin leaned over him, blinking myopically. His head was framed by a harsh fluorescent light in the ceiling. "Dern, Millie," he said, sounding querulous. "He is too looking better."

A feminine voice behind him, cracked and old.

The old man said, "Heck woman, I *know* he ain't opened his eyes in two days, but his head's not swoll up so bad. Dang, we're both wrong now, I do believe his eyes have opened."

The woman's face appeared beside the old man's. She looked exactly like the old man except for a bright blond wig, incongruous with the neck wattles and the prunelike skin. "You're right, Howard, he's looking at us right now. Hey, young man, can you see us? Are you awake now?"

"He don't see us," Howard said. "His eyes ain't tracking. They're just fixed there on one point in space."

"They're fixed on your scaly old nose. That don't mean he ain't seeing it."

The old man grunted. "If you can hear us, young man, you're going to be okay. The first time we saw you, your face was all bloody and swoll up and such. Now it's just a little yeller round one temple."

"It is not. You're looking fine. Don't worry the poor boy," Millie said. She wore a yellow print blouse to match her hair, and it was stretched taut over a distended stomach. The man wore chocolate-colored corduroys pulled halfway up his rib cage.

"There. I seen it. His eyes moved," Howard said, leaning forward on a brightly colored cane. Pipe tobacco was on his breath, and their voices were loud inside David's head.

He was in a hospital room with walls painted the color of guacamole, and the effort of holding his eyes open was giving him a headache. He opened his mouth to say something to the old codgers, but no sound came out. He gagged weakly from the effort, and vomit spurted gently over his chapped lips.

"He still doing that, he can't be doing too good," the old man said. The two faces remained above David, surveying his distress with academic interest. There were chrome rails rising on his right and on his left, trapping him below them. He noticed a gray cable wrapped once around the rail on his right.

"What should we do about it?" Millie asked. "Do you think we should call the nurse?"

"Naw. She'll be in here directly."

David moved his right hand fractionally and

grasped the cable. Unable to muster the energy to move his whole arm, he did manage to rotate his wrist inward until the cable pulled loose. Slowly, breathing deeper from the exertion, he worked the cable through his hand until he came to the end of it. He pushed both buttons. The light came on above his head in response to one of them. His hope was that the other button had summoned a nurse, and that she was on her way.

"Dern," Howard said. "You see what he's doing? It's the first thing that boy's managed to do in two days."

Later that morning—it turned out to be Monday morning—he got an embarrassingly pretty nurse named Elizabeth to pull out the catheter. In the afternoon, he explained to Lieutenant Macklin what he had been doing at the warehouse. At the end of the meeting, he said, the Crowells had driven off, then the Bachmans had driven off . . .

"Isn't it a little unusual that your own clients would be the first to leave, that they wouldn't hang back to have a few words with you?"

"I just met the Crowells that day, they're Cecil Armstrong's clients. Ed Crowell didn't take to me. And Lola was having . . . gastrointestinal difficulties." His head ached, despite the codeine they were giving him. He had to keep blinking his eyes to keep Macklin's face in focus.

"So the Crowells were connected to Cecil Armstrong. I think that's important. Cecil disappears, you take his place, you get hit on the head so hard it sends you into a three-day coma."

"I was taking over all of Cecil's cases, all of

his clients. The Crowells. The Davises, Bob and Regina, on a malpractice case. Leonard Nash."

"Nash? Huh. Tell me about Nash."

Too much about Nash was confidential. Leonard's bonds, though perhaps connected to Cecil's disappearance, couldn't have had anything to do with the attack on David at the warehouse. All he could really tell Macklin, all that seemed relevant, was that he lived above Nash's old girlfriend and he'd been seeing a good bit of her lately.

"Sleeping with her?"

Right above his right eye a sharp, sharp pain was developing. He denied sleeping with Diana. But there seemed to be some nut interested in her, and the nut was *also* connected to Nash in some way, or had been. A blue car, a big BMW, had followed him to work today—no, Friday—and he thought, he wasn't sure but he seemed to remember, that he saw that same blue car parked across the street beside another warehouse just before the lights went out.

"And then?"

"I woke up here."

"Did you walk over to the blue car?"

It felt like a drill. Somebody was boring through his skull with a high-powered drill, going in right above his right eye, boring halfway back into his brains. "I don't remember," he said.

"But it makes sense that you would have walked over."

"Maybe."

Macklin looked sour. "Well, better give me this nut's name."

David did so. "Frank McKinnon said none of the hospitals around here reported Cecil's gunshot wound."

"That's right. They're required to report such things to us, but we called them all anyway."

"How about the bus station? Did he get on a bus?"

"We don't know. The ticket seller on duty Monday morning wouldn't have remembered a two-headed woman in a sequined bathing suit. We showed him Cecil's picture, but all he could say was, 'Are you kidding? You gotta be kidding.' He doesn't look at the customers in the first place."

David slept. Frank and Al woke him up. "Sorry," Frank said. "I thought you might have slipped back into the coma." He let go of David's arm.

"We heard you were up terrorizing the nurses," Al said. He was wearing a floral tie so bright that David had to blink his eyes and focus on something else—Frank's face, for instance, remarkable for deep bruises below his eyes. David put his hand on Frank's, which was resting on the chrome rail.

"Water?" he croaked.

Frank looked anxiously around before noticing the pitcher on the bed-table, which had been pushed against the wall some distance from the bed. Water helped.

"Thanks," David said. "I'm okay. Don't worry so much."

Al said, "Ellen Uhlan wanted to come. Frank wouldn't let her."

David smiled.

"It's true," Frank said. "I thought you'd be too weak to have a lot of people dropping by, waking you up like I did. I said Al and I would represent the firm."

"True!" Al said, sounding incensed. "Who said it wasn't true? Ellen is all torn up about dear David here, all torn up."

"We're not going to have a lot of lawyers left, if this keeps up," Frank said, ignoring Al.

David smiled again. It was the easiest thing he could do.

"Macklin told us about the blue car. That's all you remember? I'm going over now to run Leonard Nash through the wringer."

Al said, "I talked to Madison Whitney about the Davis case. He'll be sending the check and the agreed judgment he wants us to sign."

David nodded, letting himself go limp against the pillows. He was exhausted. Frank stepped away, touching Al's arm as he did so.

"We won't expect you back at the office till Wednesday," Al said.

David did not respond.

He slept a lot and frequently awoke to find people hovering above his bed. Joe Bob Raymond made an appearance, his hat impossibly tall upon his head. Women were there: Diana, for long hours; Rhonda, mute, with tears streaming down her cheeks like rainwater. Never Ellen, despite Al's protestations.

Once when he was awake, when he was sure he was awake, he read the cards standing on his bed-table, and there were cards from everyone, from Marie as well.

Once he came wide, wide awake to find Diana

and Rhonda there at the same time, standing on opposite sides of his bed, focusing on him and ignoring each other. David's eyes began hurting almost immediately, and he blinked in an effort to dispel the graininess.

Rhonda had a hand on his arm, and she squeezed his biceps. "You get well," she said finally, and went out.

Diana remained, her cool hand in his warm, moist one. David let his eyes droop shut. He was conscious of the delicate feel of the bones of her hand. "Was that your girlfriend?" she asked him.

"Long ago," he said. "Far away."

"She's young." Diana sounded wistful.

He opened a tired eye to look at her. "Surely a woman with your blue eyes has no need of envy."

"You must be feeling better. But my eyes are brown."

Both his eyes blinked open. "Didn't we have this argument before? I'd swear you were on the other side of it then."

Diana was smiling. She laughed, and the light silvery sound of it made both of them feel better. "I'll check on you again tomorrow."

"Diana? Before you go, could you help me out of bed? I think I need to go to the bathroom."

Through most of the next few days, he slept like a corpse.

They released him from the hospital on Friday with a bandage wrapped around his head and instructions to return for follow-up in one week. When he asked about returning to work on Monday, Dr. Wood told him he could do anything he felt up to. "Don't tire yourself excessively," he said. And David wondered when you should do anything excessively.

Diana came and got him. "You look okay. You feel okay?" she said as she helped him into her car. It was a Ford Mustang convertible. The top was down.

"When I'm real still," he said, settling gently into the car seat, which was upholstered in white vinyl. "When I don't try to concentrate on anything, yeah, I'm okay. I've been taking a Tylenol 3 with codeine every four hours. Probably that helps."

"I should hope so." She swung into the car on her side, pulled onto the street. Direct sunlight baked his head, and, as the car accelerated, the wind whipped his hair. It nauseated him.

"I hate to sound like an invalid," he said. "Can we put the top up?"

"Sure." The top unfolded above them. When the car stopped in its accustomed space, Diana looked across the seat at him with concern in her face. "You don't look as good as you did at the hospital. You've lost color."

He did not respond. Getting out of the car made him dizzy. He closed his eyes and held onto the door of the car for a moment, and Diana was around the car with one arm around his waist. "Lean on me as much as you need to," she said. "I'm pretty strong."

He did, and she was. She led him into her apartment and settled him on her couch. "We can try those stairs later."

"Thanks."

"You look like you're hurting. Would an ice pack help?"

"It might."

He lay holding it to his temple. For a while Diana sat on the arm of the sofa, watching him. Then she brought out a basket of clothes and set up her ironing board. "You caught me in the middle of laundry," she said, when she realized his eyes were open.

"I'll go on in just a minute."

"Listen, you can spend the night right there if you want to."

"I hope you mean that. I may just do it." They were quiet for a while. Though he kept his eyes shut, he could hear the sounds of her going about her ironing.

"You don't think Mick hit you, do you?" she said eventually.

"Does he drive a blue BMW?"

"Yes."

"I think maybe he did."

"What should we do?"

"I gave his name to the police. I guess it's up to them."

"You didn't see him, did you?"

"No."

"Get the license number?"

"No. I realize there may be nothing they can do."

"You've got a headache, don't you? You keep wincing when I talk."

"It's nothing personal."

"Oh, I know. You don't need to apologize, I'll be quiet. You keep your eyes closed for a minute now. I've got to iron this shirt I'm wearing."

So of course he opened his eyes. She was wearing a white lacy bra with half-cups that left the tops of her breasts exposed. The white material was bright and sexy against her tan, but his head hurt, creating a barrier of apathy that even a lacy bra could not breach.

"You're peeking," she said. "I don't think you're as sick as you make out."

14

The next night, at just past one o'clock, David's phone rang. He knocked the phone to the floor trying to answer it, then leaned off the bed to pick it up. It was Rhonda.

"Hi, David, I just found out today you'd gone home. I wish you'd called me. I could have given you a ride."

"Uh."

"Are you feeling all right, how are you doing?"

"I'm having trouble sleeping."

"I woke you up, didn't I? I'm sorry."

He squinted at his clock. "It's one in the morning."

"I tried not to call. I'm sorry." She sounded so sorry she might start to cry.

"Don't be that sorry. You did wake me up, but I don't think I'll die from it."

She sniffed audibly through a plugged nose.

"Where are you?" he said.

"My apartment."

"Oh. Yeah." Frighteningly close.

"I just watched *It's a Wonderful Life*," she said.

"In August?"

"I rented it. It's so sad."

188

"I know. But uplifting, isn't it?"

"You mean because at the end Jimmy Stewart has his family gathered around him, and all the friends he's made over the course of a lifetime? I guess it's uplifting if you have somebody yourself."

Her recurrent theme. "No," he said. "I mean because good triumphs, goodwill triumphs. Jimmy Stewart has thrown his bread upon the waters and it returns a hundredfold."

"The movie's not the only thing. I was in the laundromat." Her voice broke, and she sniffed a few times, seemingly unable to go on.

David waited. He wondered what was sad about a laundromat.

"There was a guy and a girl in there, washing their clothes together, and they were laughing and chatting and kissing on each other, they were so in love. And I thought, I'm missing all that."

He sighed, not knowing what to say to her. "Everyone feels lost and lonely a good bit of the time. It's part of the human condition," he said.

"In other words, 'That's life, baby. Live with it.' You don't give a rat's ass, do you?"

"I'd give you a rat's ass if I had one, I swear. I'm sorry that a little homespun philosophy is all I have to offer you, but it really is all I have to offer."

"You don't care." She hung up. He stared at the receiver in his hand, dark even against the darkness of the room. Rhonda had shown him uncharacteristic mercy in breaking the connection, cutting him off from the agony pulsing over the phone lines at him. Tonight she was going to bear her sorrows alone. He was thankful.

But when he placed the receiver back in its cradle, it rang again immediately. "She repents herself," he said aloud, but he let it ring. He lay on his back looking up at the ceiling, now that he was awake thinking, not of Rhonda, but of Cecil. And Laura Armstrong, who was proving impossible to get hold of. Laura didn't answer her telephone. All day long he had tried her, and she didn't answer her phone. When he tried Jack Rupert, he got an answering machine. Surely Laura had surfaced again since he last talked to Rupert, but the question nagged at him.

His doorbell rang, in between telephone rings, and he sat bolt upright in the darkness. Someone began hammering on his door. He picked up his telephone. "Hello?" he said. "Hello?"

There was no one there. He banged down the receiver. That sneaky wench. He went out into the hall, moving carefully in the dark. Outside, a girl's voice cried, "David, are you in there? Let me in."

Back in his bedroom he groped around for his pants. He didn't turn on any lights, unwilling to provide even mute testimony that he was inside his apartment.

He grabbed the phone again, dialed Diana.

It was Saturday night, and Mick was watching her sleep. It was stupid, but there he was again, watching her sleep. As he watched her, her sweet face pale in the darkness, feeling swelled in his chest until he thought his chest would burst. If she knew how much he loved her, how much he would do for her! Someday, he thought. Someday she would know.

The apartment was so quiet at night, he could hear the phone when it rang in the apartment overhead. Though the sound was audible, it wasn't loud, and after his first inner lurch, he realized that there was no way it could wake Diana. You had to hold your breath to hear it, really, and two, three rings and the sound was gone. Mick sighed, relaxing.

Then the phone upstairs started ringing again, and it wouldn't stop. Then some asshole started pounding on a door somewhere . . .

Mick was at the door of the bedroom as soon as he heard the pounding. He was in the hall when the phones rang in Diana's apartment, one in her kitchen and one in her bedroom. He damn near left his Nikes there by themselves on the linoleum floor, so startled was he when those telephones went off. He heard Diana's sleepy hello.

To David she sounded drugged, and he felt instant guilt for waking her.

"Hi, Diana, it's David."

"Oh." In a much clearer voice, she said, "What's going on up there?"

"It's complicated. Well, the short answer is that it's Rhonda Hazelhoff, the girl you met at the hospital that day."

"So why call me?"

"I was wondering, would you like to go to Dallas?"

"What, now?"

"Now. I need to go up and talk to somebody, and now seems a convenient time. Considering."

Outside, Rhonda was shouting, "David, I know you're in there. Let me in. Just let me in for five minutes, and I'll go, I swear to God."

Diana heard it. "I see what you mean," she said. "Okay, I'll go. How do we manage it?"

"Remember how we met the first time? I'll come down when I'm ready."

"You can't. You're an invalid now."

"Sure I can. I'm feeling much, much better. Uh, you'll need to unlock your patio door."

"You're a wild man, David. Come on, then."

Mick peered through the peephole, making sure no one was out there to see him as he left the apartment—the pounding was still going on above him, some fool girl shouting something. In the bedroom, Diana said, "Come on, then," and the phone went down, and, damn it, she was *coming*. He could hear slippers brush against the carpeted floor.

For one agonizing, what, tenth of a second?, he stood frozen, hand on the doorknob, asking the question, Did he have time? The thing was, she couldn't see him. If she got to the door of her bedroom in time to catch even a glimpse of him leaving her apartment, it would scare her, and there he'd be starting over again.

He did a quick fade into the living room—and heard her feet on the linoleum floor, realized in horror that she was coming into the living room after him.

She had a dark tapestry there in the living room, a big one, hanging on one wall. The only thing he could do was stand stock still in front of it. It was the only thing. She padded across the living room to her sliding-glass doors—no lights, thank goodness, no lights—and she stooped to lift the stick from the sliding track. There was just enough light against the curtains from the outside for him to see that she wasn't wearing any clothing, or wearing only panties, if anything. His mouth dried up. She stooped, and her form was visible in silhouette—her tiny, tender breasts hung free.

She unlocked the door, pulled it partway open. She went back through the living room, completely oblivious to him, and he found that he could breathe again.

She had given him a way out.

Groping in the darkness on his hands and knees, David found his other running shoe halfway beneath the bed. He sat on the floor to put them on, wearing only an old pair of blue chinos with a hole above the right knee. His socks and his tennis shirts were in their proper drawers.

Rhonda seemed to have collapsed against his door. "Please let me in, David," she was saying. "I won't cause any problems, I'll go away again. If you don't talk to me, I . . . I don't know what I'll do."

He was on the floor, pulling on his socks. He paused, anguished by her pleading. If he let her in, she wouldn't go. It would start a battle of wills that would go on all night: Rhonda crying, pleading, raging for commitment; he, unwilling—unable—to provide it. He tried to harden his heart against her.

Dallas, he was going to Dallas. If he couldn't find Laura Armstrong, then Jack Rupert was a man he was going to talk to. More and more, thinking back, he was convinced that Rupert had started to tell him something and had changed his mind.

Outside the door, Rhonda's sobbing ended abruptly. "You rat!" she screamed. "You. Damn. Rat. You let me in right this minute. I'm not going away until you do."

Just when she had sounded most broken. He brushed his teeth quickly. Shaving would have to wait, there wasn't time. He went out onto the balcony and stepped over the rail.

He nearly hit Mick when he swung down. Mick jumped back, instinctively aware of a dark mass falling toward him. Then he saw David hanging there and realized who it was. The prick had startled him, and that made him mad.

Mick was behind David, so he punched him in the spine. As David fell, having lost his grip on the rails of his balcony, Mick closed an arm around his chest and closed his hand on David's throat.

The prick struggled, but his feet were off the ground and he wasn't getting any air. Mick pushed the glass door open with his foot and threw David into the room, aiming at the far wall.

While David was still in flight, Mick turned and vaulted the fence into anonymity.

David landed on the sofa, head ducked, arms wrapped around it. After a single stunned second, he was able to suck in a chestful of air, though the air hurt his chest. He heard two slaps on the cement patio outside, a thump, and the vibration of the privacy fence.

Then Diana's "Freeze, buster," and he was staring up at her shadowy form above him, the one concrete thing about her the pistol she held in both hands before her.

Even in the dark he could see that the gun was shaking, the barrel dancing in erratic circles.

"Oh, David, it's you," Diana said. She lowered the gun. "I don't know why, I heard the noise and I was thinking Mick."

He sat up slowly, his gaze riveted to the gun. He reached out, and his hand closed on it. Diana released it readily. He started breathing again.

She turned on a lamp. "Hey, are you all right?" she said. "You're trembling."

She was wearing a cotton sweater with blue and white stripes and a pair of panties, nothing else.

"I, uh," he said, looking at her.

"Oh, grow up."

He shook his head. "It was Mick," he said. "Or maybe the bogeyman. As I dropped from the balcony, a giant hit me and grabbed me and tossed me through the sliding-glass doors onto this couch."

"No."

"I didn't see him," David said. "Again, I didn't see him. I'm getting really tired of this."

"Where was he? On my patio? That's scary."

He was looking at her pistol, which was a single-action revolver, probably .22 caliber. The imprint of a hawk was on the grip, identifying the brand, Ruger. She hadn't pulled the hammer back. She could have pulled on the trigger all day long; it wouldn't have mattered.

When he popped out the cylinder, he saw that it contained only five cartridges. The chamber under the hammer was empty, which served as a second safety. He hadn't even come close to having his skull perforated. He felt weak.

"It's Leonard's gun," Diana said. "I was standing by my nightstand when I heard the commotion, and I just . . . pulled it out."

"He didn't show you how to use it."

"I think he gave some kind of demonstration. It was a long time ago."

"But you've never fired it."

She shook her head.

"Maybe I ought to hold onto it for you."

"What, you're saying I'm a girl, I can't be expected to handle a gun?"

David pointed the gun into the ceiling and squeezed the trigger hard enough to make his forearm bulge.

"Why isn't it going off?" Diana asked.

"It isn't cocked."

"It needs to be cocked?"

He nodded. She looked sheepish.

"Maybe I'd better put it back in the nightstand," she said.

She packed a suitcase. When he saw her putting in a curling iron, he said, "I thought your hair was naturally curly."

"Guess again," she said.

"You know, I'm glad we're getting out of here. I don't think either one of us is safe."

"You talking about my man problems, or your girl problems?" She cut her eyes upward.

Rhonda had stopped banging on his door at some point, but so much had been going on he hadn't noticed. "Both," David said. Did the silence mean Rhonda had given up and gone home, or that she was lying in wait? He didn't know.

When they left, they left by the front door, and he didn't see her. They got in his car.

"So who is it we're going to talk to?" Diana asked, when they were on their way.

"Laura Armstrong. She's the ex-wife of Cecil Armstrong, the lawyer in our firm who disappeared."

"I've been following it in the paper. What's the ex-wife got to do with it?"

"I don't know, probably nothing. I can't ever get her on the phone though, and I've got this feeling."

"This feeling?"

"That maybe Laura's disappeared, too." Though he was half in love with Diana, he didn't know how much he should tell her. She had been Leonard Nash's girlfriend, and Nash was a key suspect in Cecil's disappearance, at least in David's mind. Fortunately, Diana didn't ply him with a lot of questions. She turned on the radio and found a station playing rock and roll. He looked at her, wondering at her reticence.

"Doobie Brothers," she said, and let her seat back a little. She rode with her bare feet propped against his dashboard, and after thirty minutes or so she was asleep.

And David drove the car, his eyes following the headlights into darkness.

*   *   *

Laura Armstrong lived in a high-security high-rise. There were three wings of the building radiating off a central hub where the lobby, the manager's office, and the elevators were. It was dawn, and the lobby and the manager's office appeared empty. David pushed the button by Laura's name a few times but got no response. A huge surrealistic painting covered the wall beyond the glass doors, dominating the small space. Though it was impossible to be sure what it was, it might have been a nude man and woman in clumsy embrace.

"Do you think it's a couple of polar bears?" Diana said beside him. She seemed serious.

He looked at the painting some more. "Hell, I guess it could be anything."

Laura Armstrong lived in apartment 422. Since she wasn't answering, he hunted through the alphabetical listings until he found 421 by the name Amelia Clements. He pushed the button.

"Yes?" came a voice from the intercom, remarkably free of static.

David pushed the talk button. "I'm sorry if I woke you," he said.

"Heck, I don't sleep," said the woman. "I guess I've been up since four-thirty, thereabouts."

"My name is David Loring, I'm looking for Laura Armstrong."

"Well you've called the wrong apartment. She's in 422."

"I know. She doesn't answer."

"Then she's not home."

"Well . . . yes. How long has she been gone, do you know?"

"Hasn't been home for a week or more, near as I can tell."

"Can you say where she has been?"

"Nope."

He regretted the form of his question. "Do you mean you don't know, or you won't say?"

"I don't know. I said I didn't."

"Do you know if she'd been planning a trip for some time, or if she left suddenly?"

There was a long pause, and David began to think she had gone away. Finally, she said, "Who did you say you were again?"

"David Loring. I'm . . . Laura's attorney."

"Just a minute." Again, the long silence. He and Diana stood watching the intercom, waiting for it to speak.

"Maybe she died," Diana said after several minutes.

David pushed the talk button again. "Hello? Hello?" he said. The door opened behind them, and they both turned.

An old prune-faced woman with unnatural blue hair stood just inside the glass doors. She had pushed one door open a half-inch and was watching them avidly through the crack.

"Is that your girlfriend?" she said.

He moved his head vaguely. "Diana Puller."

Diana smiled, and the old woman blinked at her owlishly.

"You are Mrs. Clements?" David said.

"*Miss* Clements. You look all right."

He smiled and bobbed his head encouragingly.

"I'd say she left kind of sudden, Laura Armstrong."

"Why?"

"Usually she tells me when she's going somewhere, so I can feed her canary. She has it in a great big cage, huge cage like a parrot's. Hold a lot more canaries if you ask me, but she just has the one."

"She didn't tell you that she was going this time?"

The old woman shook her head. Her lips were pursed slightly and pressed together.

Diana said, "Do you think the canary is all right? It would be terrible if it had starved to death."

"Course it hasn't. She gave me a key for emergencies, and I've been feeding it anyway, asked or no."

"Everything looks all right, inside her apartment?"

The woman sniffed. "Near as I can tell. I don't go poking around. I ain't no snoop."

It was all the information they got. David tried to elicit more from her, but the old woman was offended that he had called her a snoop and she ceased to be forthcoming.

"Thank you, Miss Clements," David said finally. "We do appreciate your talking with us."

It got them another sniff. Since Miss Clements seemed disinclined to say anything else ever again, David took Diana by the elbow, and together they walked to the car.

"She was real helpful until you insulted her," Diana said once they were in the car.

"I did not insult her."

"You called her a snoop."

"The word snoop never crossed my lips. She was the one who said snoop. I never said snoop.

I said, 'Did everything look all right inside the apartment?' I didn't say she was a snoop, I didn't suggest she was a snoop. I didn't begin to suggest it, I didn't begin to begin to suggest it."

"You certainly are defensive."

"Just don't start. You know how easily agitated I am." He put a hand to his temple.

"Ah," said Diana. "The old Be-Nice-To-Me-Can't-You-See-How-My-Head-Hurts ploy."

"Yeah, yeah." He looked up Jack Rupert in a gas station phone book. After locating the address on his map, he decided they could be at Rupert's house by seven-thirty.

"Isn't that a little early for a Sunday morning?" Diana asked him. "Maybe you should call and tell him we're coming."

"I'm too irritated with him for holding out on me when I talked to him the last time."

"What makes you think he held out on you?"

"I don't know. Even if he didn't hold out on me, he made me think he did."

Jack Rupert's house was an enormous brick Georgian with a slate roof. Rupert himself answered the door wearing old-fashioned, striped pajamas and a bathrobe. Thin strands of his graying hair hung down over his left ear, leaving his pate uncovered and completely bald.

"Yes, who is it?" Seeing Diana, he made an effort to comb the hair across his pate with his fingers. "Do I know you folks?" he said in his dusty voice.

"I've spoken to you," David said. "I'm David Loring with the law firm of McKinnon, Armstrong and Cuneo. Cecil Armstrong is a partner there."

"Oh, yes. You called about Laura."

"Is she here?"

He stepped to one side and beckoned them in. "I told you it wasn't like that. Say, nice day, isn't it?"

David glanced up at the sky, blue with just enough clouds to add contrast. It was too early in the day for the heat to have built up, and the slight breeze was cool and pleasant. It was a nice day.

A great staircase wound up from the foyer. A living room opened off one side of the foyer, a formal dining room off the other. The furnishings all looked antique, but the most striking thing about the living room, about the entrance hall, about the dining room, were the hundreds of paintings that covered the walls: big paintings and little ones, in seemingly random arrangement, starting about waist high and going all the way to the ceiling.

"Ooh, I love these paintings," Diana said, turning her head from side to side as Rupert led them back through a swinging door into the kitchen. "Are any of them valuable?"

Rupert nodded. "Some."

They settled around the kitchen table.

"Coffee?" Rupert asked them, getting down three cups.

"Yes, please," Diana said, smiling.

David nodded. "About Laura," he said.

Rupert sighed, pouring the coffee. "Missing," he said.

"What?"

"Been gone a week, last time I saw her was the day I talked to you on the telephone. Thursday. She didn't come in to work on Friday, either, I said, 'Fine, let her take off Friday. She's had a shock.' I couldn't get her at home over the weekend—I tried, satisfy myself she was all right—but I thought, Well, maybe she needs to get away for the weekend. Wednesday, I called the police and reported her missing." He gave them their coffee and sat at the table with them. Though the table had chrome legs and a top of white, speckled formica, the coffee came from a state-of-the-art drip coffee maker. It was delicious.

Rupert stared down into his own cup. He struck David as being unsettled somehow. Diana reached out and patted his liver-spotted hand.

David said, "Any thoughts about where she might have gone?"

"Not if her ex-husband's still missing down your way."

"If he wasn't missing, where might she be?"

"Might be down there visiting with him. You know. They might have gotten back together."

"This is sure good coffee," Diana said.

"It is, isn't it?" the old man said, brightening. "I grind it myself right here every morning. May not make a lot of difference, but it makes enough."

"It certainly does." Watching them beam at each other, David achieved a certain enlightenment: Diana related well to old people, and he didn't. Perhaps if she had been with him, even Ed Crowell would have liked him.

"In the past few years, where has Laura gone for her vacations, do you know?" David asked.

The two turned to look at him over their steaming mugs, and they smiled indulgent smiles.

"You've suggested you were worried about her," David said.

"I guess I can be worried and still enjoy a good cup of coffee," Rupert said. "I don't know about her vacations. One year I think she took a cruise."

"She go with anybody?"

Rupert shook his head. "No idea."

"Why do you suggest she and Cecil might have gotten back together?"

"No reason."

"That night she was here, there wasn't any indication . . ."

Rupert was shaking his head. David sighed. "I think I'm getting discouraged. All of this has to be connected, but I don't know how. None of it makes any sense."

"You have a card on you?" Rupert asked him.

"Huh?"

"A business card. If you do, I'd appreciate you lay it right here on the table, your driver's license, too. You carry some kind of bar card, I'd like to see that."

David laid them out in a row: a vellum card with his name and the name and address of his law firm, the gold State Bar of Texas card with its lone star in the middle of it and his eight-digit number, the driver's license issued by the Texas Department of Public Safety. Rupert passed his eyes over them and tapped the table with a thick, ridged nail. "You can put them up now."

"You're a suspicious coot, you know that?" He

left his business card on the table in case Rupert wanted to call him later. He had plenty of those.

"Too suspicious to trust entirely to those I.D.'s. How hard can it be to get them faked?"

"If it weren't Sunday, you could call directory assistance for the number of the law firm, then call the firm and get them to describe me. As it is, I guess you could get the number for Frank McKinnon and talk to him. He's the senior partner."

"Yeah. I could do that." He took a sip of coffee and looked off into space. "I guess what would really make me comfortable is to have you tell me a story about some bonds."

"What do you know about bonds?" David said sharply.

"That sounds more like a question than a story."

"Municipal bonds," David said.

Rupert looked at him alertly. "Tell me a story about municipal bonds," he said.

David looked back at him. He would far rather Rupert tell what *he* knew about municipal bonds than to go running off his own mouth. On the other hand, Rupert's pale lips were pressed firmly together, and he looked resolute.

"Texas Rangers gym bag," David said. "Municipal bonds, two hundred or more, five-thousand-dollar denominations."

Rupert's head went back. "Ah," he said, nostrils flaring.

"Ah," David said in agreement.

"I've seen those very words on a lock-box inventory," Rupert said.

"Emptying that lock box was the last thing

Cecil did before he disappeared. When you say you've seen the inventory, do you mean to suggest you haven't seen the bonds?"

Rupert shook his head. "I've seen the bonds, though not the gym bag. Federal Express delivered a briefcase full of them to Laura week and a half ago, from Cecil. Drove her frantic. She couldn't get ahold of Cecil, then your Frank McKinnon called and told her he'd disappeared, that his Jaguar had been found shot up and abandoned."

"And she came to you."

"She came to me."

"Where are the bonds now?"

"You'll have to ask Laura."

David studied his pale, rheumy eyes. "You should have told me this last week," he said.

"I had seen Laura just that morning. It seemed premature to be running my mouth. It might be premature right now, you know that?"

"Did she say where the bonds came from?"

"From Cecil."

"Where was Cecil when he sent them?"

"Oh, I get you. Brownsville, Texas." He worked his mouth in a way that let David know he was wearing false teeth.

"This makes less and less sense." David tapped the table. His coffee cup, still half-full of coffee, sat cold and forgotten. "So exactly how many bonds were there, two hundred?"

"Two hundred sixty."

"So you counted them."

Rupert nodded.

"Are the bonds here? Are you holding out on me again?"

"The bonds are not here."

David leaned back in his chair, rubbed his eyes. He was so tired. "Can you tell me anything else about the bonds?"

"They were San Francisco bonds."

"Yeah? Can you tell me what good these bonds are to anybody? They're not like cash."

"The hell they're not."

David sat up. "All bonds are registered these days," he said.

"Not these. These bonds were all made out to bearer."

"Good God."

"Same thing as cash," Rupert said.

"Can you let me use your phone? I need to call Frank McKinnon."

15

The guitar licks of Pete Townshend vibrated the door of the glove compartment as they shot along the two-lane highway at eighty miles per hour. Diana sat partially reclined, her head on the headrest, her eyes nearly closed as the wailing cry of Roger Daltrey cut into the instrumental.

David glanced at her face from time to time, when the road could spare his attention. Her face was relaxed, and dark eyes glinted through her lashes. A semi thundered past them. A piece of gravel cracked hard against the windshield. Roger Daltrey warbled on, building to a final wail. There was more guitar, very rapid. It was virtuoso stuff; nevertheless, David reached out to turn down the volume.

"Are you asleep?"

She shook her head, puckering her lips at him, kissing the air—still in the wasteland of "Baba O'Riley." They had just gone through Childress, Texas on their way to Creede, Colorado. In the miles and miles of cotton, cattle, and mesquite trees, Diana somehow found her way past the ubiquitous hillbilly stations to a constant stream of rock and roll—usually, he had to admit, to great rock and roll. Still, less music and more conversation would have suited him better.

The Who had begun to crackle and fade even before they finished their song, and she set across the radio dial in pursuit of more music. She said, "The big thing I like about you, David, is you do crazy stuff. I like a spur-of-the-moment kind of guy."

"You do?"

"Uh-huh."

"That may be unfortunate. I'm not really a spur-of-the-moment kind of guy."

"You call me in the middle of the night because you're going to Dallas to talk to an old woman and an old man about your missing partner's ex-wife. Tell me that's not spur of the moment."

"It had been building."

"Then you talk on the phone five minutes, and we're off to Colorado."

"That's where Cecil has the vacation house."

"And we have to go and look at it? I mean, right now we have to go and look at it?"

"The vacation house doesn't have a phone. Frank said so."

"You could call the Creede police department, and see if they'd go by and look at the house for you, see if anyone's staying there. In fact, don't the police already know about this place?"

"No. Frank didn't think to tell them. Apparently, Cecil hasn't been up to Creede in ten years. Even before his divorce he never could find the time."

"Which might explain his divorce."

"It might. Anyway, I asked specifically about a vacation house or a time share or something, and Frank thought of this place."

"So why don't you call the Creede police? I'm not complaining, you understand. My point was, I like this. I am glad I brought that suitcase, though."

"I want to go up and look around myself. I have a real uneasy feeling about things—hearing that there's a one-point-three-million-dollar briefcase floating around doesn't do anything to make me feel better—and I'm just going to pursue the matter until I've looked at everything and talked with everybody. We were up in Dallas, anyway, and it's only another—"

"Fourteen hours, maybe twelve at this speed. What are you going to do for a toothbrush?"

"Use yours. Suppose someone other than Cecil and Laura are using that cabin? Could be innocent, could be something sinister. I'm going to get in the middle of this thing and wallow in it until I feel satisfied."

"Well, I'm with you. The two of us can wallow away." They traded places so David could sleep. As he settled back into the reclined seat, Diana found the tail end of something by Guns N Roses.

"Is this okay?" she said. "I don't want to disturb you." Rod Stewart came on, Jeff Beck accompanying him on his screaming, singing electric guitar.

"Crank it," David said.

He was asleep before the end of the song.

*   *   *

By dusk they had made it as far as South Fork, Colorado, just a few miles short of their goal. David, who had been able to sleep not quite four hours, was at the wheel again. He pulled into a cedar-sided motel set on a hillside overlooking the Rio Grande River. A whole row of vehicles was pulled up in front of it: a dusty station wagon with a bicycle strapped to the rack on top, a recreational vehicle, a Blazer, a Jeep Cherokee with a great dent in the rear door on the driver's side . . . Still, no people in evidence, as if after a hard day of hiking in the mountains, all the people had parked their cars, gone into their rooms, and crashed into exhausted slumber.

There was an outdoor jacuzzi by the office; David noticed it on his way in to rent the rooms. It was empty.

"I just rented one room," he told Diana when he came out.

"You horny?"

"It was all they had."

"We could have gone on."

"As full as this one is, there might not be anything in Creede, and I feel really tired." As well as really defensive.

"Oh, lighten up. I'm not afraid you're going to rape me."

"As tired as I am, I couldn't rape you. It would be like that ninety-eight-year-old man who was arrested for sexual assault."

"Oh?"

"The actual charge was 'assault with a dead weapon.' "

"You're sick."

"I don't know why no one thinks my jokes are

funny. The first time I heard that one, I pretty much had hysterics."

"Maybe there's something wrong with your sense of humor."

"Somebody thought it was funny enough to tell it to me."

"Which tells us a lot about his sense of humor."

The banter got them into the motel room with no further displays of embarrassment, Diana wagging her pink vinyl suitcase in both hands before her, David with just himself. The room had two double beds covered with white spreads and a bright red blanket folded at the foot of each.

David said, "I'll get some clothesline, and we can hang one of those blankets down the center of the room."

"You have clothesline?"

"Well no, not really. I was drawing an allusion to *It Happened One Night*, a movie from about 1932 starring Clark Gable and Claudette Colbert. I used to rent it and show it on the VCR every time I started going out with someone new. It was my traditional second date. It wouldn't be any good for a first date, ask a girl over to your apartment to watch a movie on the tube. For a second date, though, gives you some privacy, some control over the atmosphere . . ."

"I don't remember this date."

"We haven't had it yet."

"Something to look forward to. Who was it who said you were a spur-of-the-moment kind of guy?"

"I believe that was you, Diana."

"Huh."

She wanted to soak in the outdoor jacuzzi a bit before going to bed. She had a pair of shorts and a pink T-shirt that said "Aerobercize" on the left breast, and David found an old pair of gray U of C gym shorts in the trunk of his car.

They changed into their makeshift bathing suits and soaked awhile. Once wet, Diana's T-shirt clung to her body in a gratifying way, and David tried not to look, lest he be gratified.

"This is great country, isn't it?" he said, looking around them at the dark trees and down the rocky slope to the glowing whitecaps of the river just visible below. The moon had come out and lighted up the countryside.

The water jets in the sides of the jacuzzi massaged their backs, and the evening mountain air was cool and dry. David was beyond exhaustion. A mellow contentment had set in.

"Your head's feeling better, isn't it?" Diana said. "No more headaches."

"I don't know why people live anywhere else," he said, probing at his head to check the veracity of her statement. "I'll never know why they live in south Texas."

"You live in south Texas."

"Yes, but I don't know why." She was right; his head didn't hurt.

"How did you end up there, then?" she asked.

"I was talking to firms that visited the law school. Al and Cecil came up, and I liked them both, and I liked the sound of small-town life. I didn't think it really mattered where the small town was."

"Did it?"

He shrugged. "Some. My life would have turned out a lot differently if they'd sent up Ellen Uhlan instead of Cecil and Al."

"She one of the lawyers?"

"Yes. Next on the letterhead after Al and Cecil. Then there're two more, and then there's me."

"And you don't like her much."

He shook his head, making a wry face.

"Don't look so guilty."

"Well, you know. She might be a really nice person, she's just trapped inside with a bitchy personality and can't get out."

"Oh, yes. That makes her sound really nice."

It was cold in the motel room, the radiator having apparently been cut off for the season. Each used the extra blanket.

David fell asleep on his side, his body curled tight against the cold, and he awoke in the night with a warm, feminine body pressed tight against his own. He shifted his position so as to restore the flow of blood to his left arm, and, after the feeling had returned to it, he fell asleep again, breathing in the faint floral scent of Diana's soft hair.

The Creede house was stone, with wooden shingles. Through the front window, David could see a wood floor and a rag rug, a stone fireplace, and a slate hearth. The head of a moose overhung the fireplace.

"There's an open book on the arm of that chair," Diana said beside him, her breath fogging the pane so he could not see beyond it.

"I guess we knock," he said, and went to do it while Diana stayed at the window and stared intently through cupped hands. No one responded to the heavy brass knocker, and the door, as he expected, was locked. "You know, we probably came all this way for nothing," he said. Diana didn't respond, and he looked around at the quaint houses and at the mountains beyond them. He could live here, he thought. Set up a little real estate practice, do some wills and estate work, maybe a little commercial law for some of the local businesses. He could ski all winter.

He took a deep breath and marveled at the difference between this light dry air of a Colorado summer and the hot syrup he had to breathe in Texas.

"Why don't you try around back?" Diana said. "If people are staying here, they might have gone off without locking the back door."

"Okay, but you'd better get away from that window. If I'm inside, I don't want the police dropping by to investigate."

The ground dropped off sharply toward the back of the house. A steep stairway made of pressure-treated wood led up to a deck built around the back door. That door, too, was locked.

The window beside it, though, slid open easily.

David peered through into a kitchen with wood floors and with countertops covered with four-inch tile. He looked back, but the house was built on the side of a hill. The ravine below was overgrown with trees and scrub; no other houses were in view.

The window was over the kitchen sink. His

hands on the sill, David pushed himself up and squirmed through the window on his belly, crawling out over the counter until he could swing his legs to the floor. He didn't feel too bad about the illegal entry. He was, after all, a friend of the owner, and he had cause to be worried.

He found out almost immediately that someone was staying in the house. There was milk in the refrigerator that according to the date would be good for another week. Downstairs was the living room and the kitchen, in which a round table sat with four wooden chairs around it. Upstairs was the master bedroom and the master bath. The bathroom had a tiled shower. Makeup shared the counter with contact rinse, a curling iron, a blow dryer, toothpaste, and two toothbrushes—one of which was wet.

David went back into the bedroom, where a two-person jacuzzi stood just outside the bathroom in the bedroom itself. Clothes were hanging in the walk-in closet, shoes arranged below them. In the corner of the closet was a gym bag, red and white and blue.

David was back in the bedroom when it registered, and he had to go back. Red, white, and blue were the colors of the Texas flag, and they were the colors of the Texas Rangers. Sure enough, he found the inscription "Texas Rangers" on one side of the gym bag, a Texaco logo on the other. The bag itself was empty.

"Cecil," he breathed. How could he? How could Cecil abscond with a million plus in a client's securities? For the first time the likelihood of Cecil's corruption slammed down on him and twisted his heart with grief and dread. Cecil corrupt was worse than Cecil dead.

He went out the front door carrying the gym bag. He exhibited it grimly, standing in the open doorway.

"They're here," Diana said.

David nodded.

"With the bonds, apparently."

"Yes."

A man's voice called out from behind Diana. "Hey!"

Diana whirled, and David looked past her. A young man with his blond hair in dredlocks stood at the bottom of the steps looking up. "You don't live here," he said.

"We're friends of Cecil's," David said.

"And Laura's," Diana added.

The young man studied them for a moment. Then he held up a hand to them in salute. "Rasta Stevie," he said. "I guess I'll be seeing you with the Armstrongs down at the cafe."

"I hope so," Diana said.

Rasta Stevie moved on.

"So they are both here," David said. "With the bonds. You'd think they would have left the country." Down the street he saw four people coming toward them, and he could hear the faint sounds of conversation. "We'd better get out of this doorway before we get arrested," he said.

As they came down the steps, the four people separated, two going into the general store, two continuing toward them. David stopped, and dread settled on him more heavily.

"Oh, gosh," he said. "It's them."

And half a block away, Cecil and Laura stopped.

Then Cecil started forward, and David walked alone to meet him, his shadow bobbing down the center of the graveled street before him.

"David," Cecil said.

For a moment David imagined that they would both drag out six-shooters and start blasting.

But Cecil bounced forward the last few steps, threw his arms about David's shoulders, and hugged him. "David, you old so-and-so. What are you doing in Creede?"

David pulled back and held up the empty gym bag. "Looking for these," he said.

"Leonard's bonds? I don't have them."

David sighed and looked away. "That's not what Jack Rupert says."

Diana had come up and taken David's arm. "Hi, I'm Diana. David said you were here with your ex-wife?"

"She's my ex-ex, actually." Cecil smiled then, and David noticed a slight facial tic on the left side that he had never seen before.

"Was that a stutter?" David asked.

"A double negative." Cecil held out one arm to Laura to wave her on, and his hand trembled faintly. As she approached, Cecil looked quizzically at Diana, then back at David. "The firm hasn't taken on another woman associate since I've been gone?"

"No."

"Laura, you remember David. And this—"

"I'm Diana Puller. I'm so pleased to meet you."

"Diana Puller," Cecil repeated. The bright Colorado sun picked out myriad strands of gray in his hair and highlighted the lines around his mouth and eyes. "You two aren't married, then. Engaged? Well, you should be. Man's a fool, live his life alone. I guess I'm trying to figure out why the two of you are traveling up this way together."

"You left town rather suddenly," David said, ignoring the question. "Frank thinks you're dead. He's about to pull his hair out."

"I . . . had a sort of breakdown."

David flourished the gym bag. "Did it have anything to do with this bag and one-point-three million dollars in bearer bonds?"

Cecil smiled again, his facial tic jumping spastically. "Actually it did. It's a long story."

"Leonard was so cagey about these bonds, I thought maybe he had suckered you into emptying that safety deposit box, then had an accomplice kill you to get the contents."

"But now you suspect me, don't you?"

"Rupert said the bonds were in a briefcase. Where is the briefcase now, Cecil? Do you have it here?"

Laura said, "I left it with Jack Rupert."

David looked at her, then back at Cecil. "He denied having it," he said.

"He has it," Laura said, definitely.

A great weight fell from David. He believed her. "That old toad," he said.

Cecil said softly, "Are you thinking he has, ah, appropriated the securities to his own use?"

"I don't know. You don't have a phone in your place, do you?"

"There's a pay phone at the general store." He pointed.

"I got the bonds several days before I heard

from Cecil," Laura said. "Then when I heard from Frank, I got scared. I thought maybe someone had killed Cecil for the bonds, and I knew I didn't want them. I went to Jack with the briefcase and told him I was scared of it, that he had to keep it for me but that he shouldn't keep it either. I told him—a lot of things. I thought Cecil was dead, I said that, that someone had killed him for these bond-things, and that now he was after me, after Jack, after anyone that might . . ."

Cecil took her hand. "Laura," he said gently, and she quieted.

"Do you think we could all walk down to the general store right now?" David said. "I sure would like to talk to Rupert."

The sweet-voiced receptionist at Rupert and Holmes put him through. "Ah, Mr. Loring," the old man said.

"Ah, yes," David said. "I found Laura. And Cecil. I guess you know what they told me."

"Wonderful," Rupert said. "Wonderful. They're all right. I'm so glad you found them."

" 'The bonds are not here.' Isn't that what you told me?"

"It sounds right."

"So Laura Armstrong's a liar."

"No, no. I wouldn't say that, not at all. Laura's a fine woman, fine woman. She did leave the bonds with me, as I'm sure she told you. What I meant was that I, ah, no longer have them."

"What?"

"Look, if Laura Armstrong is there, could I speak to her a minute?"

"Huh? Oh, sure." He stood to one side while

Laura and Rupert conferred. She said yes a few times, then, "Cecil and I would appreciate it if you and David would handle it." She gave the phone back to David.

"Looks like it's between you and me," Rupert told him. "I think maybe you'd better stop by here on your way back down south. I've got something to show you. Not bonds, exactly, but something better."

"Cash."

"No, not cash exactly. Something even better than that."

"Mr. Rupert, does the phrase 'breach of fiduciary duty' mean anything to you?"

"It does, it does indeed. Come and see me, and we'll talk. I'm at home any night after seven. Please come see me there." And Mr. Rupert hung up his phone.

As David put his own phone back into its cradle, he noticed Cecil staring fixedly at nothing, hands thrust deep into his pockets, his face showing signs of strain.

"It's okay," David said, and Cecil started. "Rupert acknowledges receiving the bonds." David hoped it was okay, that Rupert hadn't taken the bonds and done something stupid with them, but he decided not to burden Cecil with it.

Cecil, for his part, did not ask questions. He merely nodded sharply and smiled a brittle smile.

It seemed to David that his continued presence was making Cecil increasingly agitated. The four of them had lunch at the cafe, where they saw Rasta Stevie behind the bar. Cecil kept glancing back and forth between David and Laura. He would engage only in small talk. He never asked about the firm, never asked about Frank or about any of the things that should have interested him. He did seem to retain his initial curiosity as to why David and Diana were traveling together, and Diana fielded the question gracefully. It was Laura and Diana who made the conversation bearable; it seemed to David that the two had become instant friends.

"You'll have to stay the night," Laura said at one point, causing David instant alarm.

"Oh, no," David began, looking at Cecil. "Rupert said we should try to . . ."

"Nonsense," Laura said. "It's fourteen hours back to Dallas, and you'll have to sleep somewhere. Our downstairs sofa makes out into a big bed. David and Cecil can sleep down there, and Diana and I will take the bedroom."

"Well, that's very nice of you," Diana said. "But . . ."

"Good. It's settled."

David looked at Cecil. "Are you sure it's all right with you?"

Cecil nodded thoughtfully. "Yes. Really, I was hoping we would get a chance to talk."

After nightfall the temperature dropped to the high fifties. Cecil offered David a cigar and suggested they go out on the back deck to smoke them.

"We won't be long," Cecil said to Laura, patting her cheek, and they exchanged shy smiles.

Diana and David saw the smiles and exchanged looks of their own.

It was David's second visit to the back deck, which overhung the gully filled with spruces and cedars and pines. The evergreens gave the whole outdoors a Christmas-tree scent he had been too nervous to notice the first time. "I hadn't smoked a cigar since I was in college," Cecil said. "Until recently." Cecil lit a match. His hands shook as he held his cigar over the flame, rotating it slowly.

David sat on the rail. His eyes on Cecil's trembling hands, he bit off the tip of his cigar and spat it out. He dampened the outer tobacco leaf with his lips, inhaling the odor of the fragrant tobacco.

Cecil was holding his third match to the end of the cigar.

"If you inhale the flame up into the cigar, it lights faster," David said.

"Yes, it does, but it doesn't taste as good." Cecil got his cigar burning to his satisfaction and handed the pack of matches to David.

David lighted a match and, like Cecil, turned his cigar over the flame. "Any particular reason you're regressing to your college days?" he said.

Cecil did not respond.

The insects around them shrilled and clicked, and their noise added texture to the silence. A pair of moths beat themselves against the light globe by the back door, their wings tapping occasionally against the thin, glowing glass.

Finally David said, "You're not going back, are you?"

"No. No, I'm not. I've saved enough, I can live

on it the rest of my time. I have my wife now. I have this place, it's a wonderful little retirement cottage. Everything else, I'm chucking it. I don't need it, and it's all too consuming. I think it could cost me the things I love." Cecil's voice shook, and David was afraid Cecil was going to cry. He didn't, but he lapsed into silence, unable to go on.

"This came on rather suddenly, didn't it?" David said. "And why Brownsville?" Close enough to startle him, an owl cut loose with its deep-throated inquiry.

"Pardon?" A little farther out than the owl, a small animal crashed through the foliage.

"Rupert said you sent the bonds to Laura from Brownsville, Texas."

"Oh." Cecil inhaled smoke from his cigar, tilted his head back to release four tiny smoke rings, in sequence. He sighed. "There's a big fellow that's probably tied up with Leonard Nash in some way," he said. "I'm not saying Leonard set me up. I don't know that. Maybe Leonard had a falling out with one of his cohorts. This big fellow bottled me up in the parking deck outside the firm just after I'd picked up the municipal bonds from the bank. I got out, had to smash up my car to do it, and darned if he didn't shoot at me. Messed up my darn car. Hit my earlobe. Here, see that?"

David looked at his earlobe.

Cecil said, "It didn't require medical attention, just some tape and a lot of pinching to stop the bleeding. Later, I tried to go home. Drove by the house, no sign of any problems, but I circled the block, then two blocks, then three ... There it was, the big BMW this guy had been in, parked against the curb. I could see the damage my car had done to it. The guy was nowhere in sight. I knew where he was, though. In my house, waiting. Waiting for me to come walking in, unawares, wagging a briefcase full of bearer bonds. I couldn't go to the office, I couldn't go home. I do and he shoots me dead, takes the briefcase, and he's off. I'm lying on the floor leaking blood, and it's the last thing I'm ever going to do."

"You could have gone to the police," David said.

"Yeah, I guess I could have. I thought of it, of course, but somehow I just didn't have the energy. You know what I felt, thinking this guy was going to maybe kill me?" Cecil held up a hand. "The question's rhetorical. I know what I should have felt. Ha, should have been pissing my pants, but I wasn't. I wasn't afraid at all. No fear. Peace. Life would go on, but without me. I'd never have to do another thing. Never have to *feel* another thing." A large piece of ash fell from the tip of Cecil's cigar to the deck. The orange coal at the end of his cigar was trembling.

"I guess it was a kind of breakdown," Cecil said, a statement David now believed to be near to the truth.

"Why Brownsville?"

For a time Cecil merely drew on his cigar. "I just walked away," he said at last. "And I had to take the briefcase, couldn't just put it down and leave it. There was blood all over my suit, so I got some casual clothes at K-mart. Took a Greyhound bus down toward Cozumel—Mexico—where I honeymooned with Laura, oh, back in the sixties. Sometime before I got to Brownsville, I decided to send the briefcase back up to Laura until I could think what to do with it. I didn't want to take it out of the country. I could have sent it to the firm, but I didn't want you guys to trace me, not before I was ready for you to. I wasn't trying to abscond with the bonds or anything, I had no criminal intent. I just wanted some time." Criminal intent was a necessary element of any felony. As a rule the law did not prosecute those with innocent intent.

"I rented a car in Brownsville. After a couple days walking on the beach, up and down on the beach for miles until the top of my head was sunburned and scaly beneath my hair, I decided if Laura would go with me, if she'd have me, I could still do this one thing. Give it all up, and just hold onto . . . this."

David's cigar had gone out. He struck a match to relight it.

"You trust Jack Rupert?" David said.

"Yeah, I trust him," Cecil said, and at length David realized he would say no more. Perhaps there was no more to say. Cecil had come to Laura, and neither of them had wanted to mess with the bonds, or with Rupert. Time enough for that later; for once, business came second—whether it should have or not.

"I'll take care of Rupert," David said. "If I can."

Cecil nodded.

"You ought to give Frank a call, though. He's worried sick about you. I mean, he's losing weight. He's been your friend a long time."

Cecil nodded.

David turned away from Cecil, his elbows on the rail, his eyes on the dark trees, silhouetted against the sky. The two of them smoked in silence until their cigars burned down.

The temperature had dropped from chilly to cold. First Cecil, then David bent to stub out the butt of his cigar, and they pushed them off the deck with the toes of their shoes. Without speaking again they went inside.

16

Laura just went upstairs," Diana said to Cecil. "She said to send you up."

Cecil looked from David to Diana with raised eyebrows, then went upstairs obediently. David found that in the living room the sofa had already been opened up into a queen-sized bed. Diana looked ready for it.

"Are you sleeping down here?" David asked her.

"Uh-huh."

"Where am I sleeping?"

She patted the bed.

"How did . . ."

"It was really hurting Laura that she and Cecil were going to be separated. She's pretty worried about him."

"They're sure a lot more affectionate than they used to be."

"She told me about some of that. I suggested that I sleep down here with you, but she wouldn't hear of it. I had to tell her we were already intimate."

"Good gosh. We're not, are we?"

She gave him a look.

"Right. I sleep in my street clothes."

Later, long after he thought Diana was asleep, she said, "It's sweet how they need each other."

"Cecil and Laura? It gives me the willies."

"Not very romantic of you."

"Maybe not." He gazed up into the darkness beneath the vaulted ceiling. "I was engaged once, or almost engaged. One image that kept coming to me was that of a long dark tunnel. You can only see the mouth of the tunnel and maybe a yard or two inside, but you know that once you drift into it you're stuck. You grow old in there, and by the time you come out into the sunshine again you're in a pine box. I'm not saying it's not nice in there—it's hard to know how it's going to be in there—but in any case you're stuck."

"Now I've got the willies," Diana said.

"It's not just me. I read something like that in Shakespeare once, though I've never been able to find it again. It's been like that for Cecil: He gets married, he's in the tunnel; his wife leaves him, he's still in the tunnel; they get a divorce, she has an affair . . ."

"Okay, okay, they're still in the tunnel."

"Eventually they acknowledge the reality, and they get back together."

"It's not always like your tunnel. I was married once. And divorced."

"Ah."

"What do you mean, 'Ah'? You sanctimonious bastard." She kicked at him under the covers.

"Ow. Ow! Hey, I'm sorry. I didn't mean to be sanctimonious. Really."

"Okay."

They lay in silence for a while before Diana said, "Anyhow, I can see why your engagement didn't work out."

"She's the one who broke it off."

"And you were relieved, weren't you?"

The observation stung him—because, of course, it was true. He didn't say anything. He lay on his back, staring upward, thinking.

Diana's breathing changed as she crossed into sleep. Sleep didn't come so easily to David.

They drove out of town on the narrow ribbon of asphalt that wound southward through the mountains, where snow glinted in the sunlight on the highest peaks.

Sometime in the afternoon, David said, "You didn't bring that pistol with you, did you?"

"I put it back in my nightstand."

"Oh."

"Why? It's not Jack Rupert, is it? You don't think that nice old man would try to hurt us."

"Suppose Cecil had been dead, that something had happened to both him and Laura. Do you think we'd have heard another word from Rupert about the bonds? 'Oh, here's one-point-three million dollars you might like to have.' We'd have heard diddly squat."

"He has his own art brokerage, which even I've heard of. This isn't such big money to him."

He looked at her, sitting back, as usual, with a foot on the dash. "The heck it's not," he said. "I'm a lawyer. I have decent earning power, and I'm young enough that I'm going to have decent earning power for a while. If I were Rupert's slave—let's say I agreed to work hard and turn over to him everything I made for the rest of my life—do you think that would be worth a lot to him? This briefcase full of bonds is worth more."

She snorted. "You're going to earn a lot more than one-point-three million dollars over the course of your lifetime."

"Yes, but it will be years before I've earned everything I'm going to earn. The bonds are already accumulated. Let's say I make one hundred thousand dollars a year . . ."

"Do you?"

"Let's say I do. And that I can be counted on to make one hundred thousand dollars a year for the rest of my life; to make it simple, for all eternity. If we assume a ten percent interest rate, I'm worth one million dollars."

"Huh?"

"Well, you could have me, which under our assumptions would get you a hundred grand a year. Or you could have a million dollars, put it in the bank at our assumed rate of ten percent, and you'd have a hundred grand a year forever and never touch your principal."

She looked at him, forehead creased, and then she nodded. "I get it," she said.

"I was just thinking about how much money that was, and how convenient it would be for Rupert if we disappeared ourselves. Of course, there're Cecil and Laura, but who knows when they'll decide to come down out of the mountains? I just can't help thinking our disappearance might be . . . convenient."

"Ooh, Springsteen." She reached for the volume control.

So Springsteen thundered, and David mused, and the highway rolled beneath them.

It was just after eight o'clock, Tuesday evening, when they pulled into Rupert's driveway. He was sitting on his front stoop as if waiting for them. A brown-glassed bottle was in his hand.

He took a long pull from it as they walked up. "Get you a root beer?" he said. "This is the best that's made."

"No, thank you," David said.

"That sounds wonderful," Diana said, and she and the old man exchanged smiles. Again, David found himself looking from one to the other of them.

They were inside, among the host of paintings that cluttered the walls in ill-formed ranks. Rupert came out of the kitchen, and Diana had her root beer.

"Come on into the living room," Rupert said. "I'd like to show you something."

"The bonds? You got them back?" David asked.

"Just hold your horses on the bonds, okay? I've got something to show you, and then we'll talk about your gosh-dern bonds."

The living room was fairly dark when they entered it, because of shades drawn over the windows. Rupert flipped a switch, and a row of track lighting illuminated the paintings along one of the inside walls. "Direct sunlight never touches this wall," he said.

"Ooh," Diana said. "That picture in the middle, the Monet, I love it." It was powerful. A multitude of tiny dabs of primary color blended for the overall effect of sailboat and the sun and sea.

"Le Bateau à Voiles," Rupert said. " 'The Sailboat.' It's an early work, not one of his famous ones, and it's not part of any of his series. Pretty good, though."

Diana, who had eased closer to the painting in religious awe, turned to look at him. "You don't mean it's *real.*"

"Well, I don't mean it's imaginary."

"But it's a reproduction."

"Oh. By real, you mean did Monet really paint it. Yes, yes he did."

Diana didn't say anything. She was looking at the painting. David walked up to it as well, peered with interest at the "Claude Monet" printed with brush strokes in the bottom corner. He stepped back, and the million tiny marks of color resolved and became a sailboat on a lake. Some kind of vegetation was in the foreground, some houses and maybe a pier or something in the background. "It is fantastic," David said, his evaluation of Rupert's place in the world having just been revised into the stratosphere.

Rupert said, "It's alive, isn't it? It reaches out to you and transports you—in time a hundred years, in space a continent. And now." He coughed. "Now I have to talk to you about those bonds."

David's head turned slowly. "You're kidding," he said.

Rupert smiled, but nervously.

*   *   *

It was later, much later, and they were at the kitchen table. "You know, when Laura left that briefcase with you, you became its custodian and as such became obligated to exercise reasonable care," David told Rupert.

"I exercised extreme care."

"You transformed readily marketable securities, with a clear market value, into art. Art! With all the risks and illiquidity that entails. You radically changed the form of the property—what kind of care is that? What am I supposed to do with a Monet?"

"You could have it appraised."

"By whom? You?"

"Impressionism is the hottest thing out there right now. You've heard of the Impressionists, and you're an ignoramus. It was Monet's *Rising Sun, An Impression*, you know, that gave the movement its name. Rembrandt or another of the Old Masters—yawn. Oh, I don't mean that, I'd be happy to handle one. But Monet . . ."

"Monet," Diana repeated.

David took a breath, much needed. "Are you really qualified to appraise it?" he asked Rupert.

"I am. Of course, you're right in that this isn't a stock that we can look up the price of in the *Wall Street Journal*. It isn't even a bit of residential real estate, where a half-dozen comparable properties have been sold in the area in the past six months. This is a one-of-a-kind piece of art, and it would require special handling."

"What could we get for it? Give me a range."

"Between five and ten million. Six-point-five, kind of be the area I'd keep my eye on." Humor entered his voice. "Less a commission." He smiled. "The painting never really hit the market last week. It came to me indirectly that its owner was making discreet inquiries, was in some kind of financial difficulty and was pretty anxious to get his hands on some cash. I had that briefcase full of cash equivalents that Laura Armstrong was desperate to hide, that she thought was dangerous, even, and I thought what better place to hide it than in a painting? I'm seventy-three years old. This is the first Monet I've ever handled, and I got it for nothing, a fraction of its value."

David was quiet for a while, thinking. "It's hard for me to believe there are really private transactions in Monets," he said, slowly.

"You want to take another look at the one in the living room?" Rupert asked him.

David focused on Rupert's watery eyes. "Aren't about the only famous paintings that are sold this way a bit on the hot side?"

"Not at all. For example, Van Gogh's *Irises.* An Australian businessman named Alan Bond bought it at auction for fifty-three million in 1987. When he had to sell it two years later, he did it privately. The Getty Museum paid some undisclosed amount for it, rumored to be a lot less. Of course, there were special circumstances. There always are."

"You're not the Getty Museum."

"No, but I stay in touch with things."

"You're not a fence?"

"Oh, no." Rupert shook his head with vigor. "No such thing. What it came down to—there was the Monet. There was the briefcase."

"I think it's wonderful," Diana said, and David looked at her sourly.

"On behalf of Leonard Nash, the putative owner of those bonds—perhaps on behalf of the bankruptcy trustee—I'm going to have to take that painting."

Rupert nodded. "Oh, I know I can't *keep* it."

"I mean, I'm going to take the painting back with me now," David said.

"Think again. You're going to carry a six-million-dollar painting in your backseat? Get real, fella."

"I've got to talk to some people before I know what we're going to want to do with it. But in the meantime—I just don't trust you."

Rupert held his hands up. "What's not to trust?"

"Look, Mr. Rupert. A private residence is no place for a Monet, either."

"You think that Monet is the only valuable painting here? I'm set up for it. I've got a security system like you wouldn't believe. Four security systems, all separate."

David sighed. Finally, he said, "If I write out a receipt for you, will you sign it?"

"So what are you going to do with the painting?" Diana said, later. The car's headlights were twin spears in the night. It was about three in the morning, and they were thirty minutes away from home.

"I guess I turn it over to the bankruptcy trustee, and then we fight like hell with all Leonard's creditors in a heroic effort to get it back for him."

"You wouldn't."

He eyed her, knowing the terrain here to be treacherous. "You sound hostile," he said.

She sighed. "I'm not so much hostile as tired. I'm sad I wasted so much time with Leonard. Now, it sounds like it's your turn to waste time with him."

"I'm his lawyer. That is, unless he's called up Frank McKinnon in my absence and fired us."

"Why turn the painting over to the bankruptcy trustee at all then? Why not ask Leonard what he'd like done with it, and do what he tells you?"

"I said I was his lawyer, not his accomplice."

"What's the difference?"

"More than you think. I'm not happy about being the man's lawyer, you understand, but there's not a lot I can do about it. That decision was made some time ago by Frank and Al and Cecil, who as we see has just retired to the good life."

"You can't really hold it against him. The two of them seemed so happy together."

He blinked his grainy eyes. "No, I don't begrudge him the good life. Why should he drive himself into another breakdown on behalf of somebody like Leonard? It does leave it in my lap, though. I'm too young to retire."

Diana gave him a sympathetic smile. She said, "Will Leonard get to keep the painting? I know some people who will hate you if he does."

"Oh, the whole town will hate us. But for us to win, a judge will have to decide that the source of those bearer bonds wasn't Leonard—or that if it was Leonard, that he didn't actually retain ownership of the bonds when they passed into Clark's possession. And that he didn't give the things to Clark in an effort to defraud his creditors. Leonard's an infamous guy. You think a bankruptcy judge is going to let him walk away with that much money, all the people that are hurting?"

"Good."

"We'll have to try, regardless."

"I hope you lose."

"Leonard would be better able to pay his legal fees if we won."

"So you hope you'll win?"

He sighed. "Not really. Mostly, I'm just unhappy that I'm representing Leonard."

It was not yet light when he pulled into his parking space at the apartment complex. He carried Diana's big pink suitcase down the long sidewalk and around the corner to her door.

"Come in for coffee?" she asked him.

He shook his head. "A quick cold shower and bed," he said.

"A cold shower?" She raised her eyebrows in an arch look.

He smiled. "I'm concerned, though, that you're not quite safe. Maybe you'd better come up."

"Now that's an excuse to get me up there. You could forego the cold shower."

"With that guy hanging around outside your door and all."

"And that girl hanging around outside yours."

"Good point."

He shucked his clothes in his own bathroom, ridiculously glad to be there. The linoleum was cool on his bare feet, as he turned on the water and adjusted the temperature. He climbed into the tub.

The fine spray of water stung his face, then his neck, then his chest, and he made vague scrubbing motions. For a time, he sat in the bathtub and let the water beat on his skull.

When he came out, he dried and stumbled across his bedroom and fell into bed. His own bed. It felt nice, so nice.

He didn't hear a thing that went on in the apartment below him.

17

Her door was unlocked. David had already rung the doorbell a couple of times, and knocked on the door. Turning the knob all the way to the right, he pushed the door inward. And found himself wishing for his baseball bat.

"Diana?" he said. He had just stopped by on his way to work, but now he was thoroughly alarmed.

The air conditioner came on, nearly precipitating a coronary.

He closed the door behind him and stood silently in the hallway, listening. The rush of the air conditioning might have covered some slight sound, but he heard nothing frightening. He smoothed his tie nervously against his shirt.

Half-expecting at any moment to be clubbed to the ground, he walked through the apartment. He peeked through doorways before walking through them, peeked around corners before turning them, stayed away from the bed and the partially open closet door—both haunts of the bogeyman that were well known from childhood. He called Diana's name a few times, softly.

In the end he had to peer under the bed. Had

to open the door of the walk-in closet and grope for the light switch. Had to sweep aside the shower curtain, jumping back. But a careful search of the apartment turned up neither Diana's corpse nor her corpus.

He followed the sidewalk out to the parking lot, where Diana's red Mustang convertible sat in its accustomed spot. Its hood was hot, but then, the morning sun was beating on it. He raised the hood—no need to release a dashboard latch in these older models—and found that the radiator and the engine block were cool. He got grease on his hands.

He washed them inside Diana's apartment. Again he checked beneath the bed, behind the clothes in the closet, beneath the sofa. Standing in the bedroom, thinking, he noted that Leonard's picture in its silver frame was no longer in evidence, mutilated or otherwise, but he didn't look for it.

Instead he sat in the wrought-iron lounge chair by Diana's door to wait. There was a 7-11 within walking distance; a Whataburger and a Grandy's. He had no reason, really, to fear the worst, but by noon his suit jacket was sweated through and still she had not returned.

He called the police from his own apartment and talked to a Sergeant Margaret Cain. "I want to report a missing person?"

"Who?"

He told her.

"How old?"

He guessed.

"Missing how long?"

"I don't know, I last saw her about four A.M. today."

There was a long silence. "Honey," said the sergeant. "Is this some kind of a *joke*?"

He told her about Mick Rothgut, who had been hanging around her, sending her flowers, scaring her.

"Somebody sends me a dozen roses, they're not going to scare *me*," Sergeant Cain said.

"Could you send somebody by to talk to him? I think Diana said he lived in Pheasant Run."

"Number?"

"I don't remember."

They would see what they could do. He waited another hour by the door to Diana's apartment. She still had not shown up, but he had to get to work. He had been out forever.

Diana was lying on the floor of Mick's bedroom, panting for breath, and Mick sat beside her. In the relative quiet, she could still hear a whistling noise, sharp but very faint.

In broad daylight Mick had entered her bedroom, turned her onto her stomach and held her, knee in her back, while he brought one hand and then the other to the small of her back where he tied them with cord. She struggled, but her face was buried in the pillow, cutting off her air and her strength for resistance.

"You shouldn't have done it, baby. You shouldn't have run off with him like that," he was saying, though she picked up only a little of it.

He stuffed her in a duffel bag and carried her out, bag hanging from his shoulder. She was blind in the duffel bag, and the air was stifling and hot. She concentrated on breathing shallowly, on remaining still, but she drifted nearer and nearer unconsciousness.

She had ceased to be aware of time when he dumped her onto his bedroom floor at the foot of an enormous four-poster bed. He ripped the surgical tape from her mouth. Pulling off his shirt, he posed for her—flexing his biceps and his huge plates of pectoral muscles. All the time he was saying, "Why? Why, baby, why him? Why not me?"

She shook her head groggily.

"I've wanted you so much. I tried being nice to you, sending you things, being real careful so as not to scare you. *Kindness and gentleness will win her*, I told myself. *You can win her*. And then you ran off with him, the prick. He's a prick, baby, can't you see that? But I knew you'd come back—you had to come back, you live here, all your stuff was here. I sat there in the midst of it all. I waited for you, baby. I kept a vigil."

Diana tried to say something, but her mouth was as dry as if it were stuffed with cotton balls. Mick leaned closer, and she whispered, "What happened to kind and gentle?"

He shook his head, and his eyes were sad. "It didn't work," he said. "What I want, I have to take. It's always been that way." He shook himself, and through his sorrow his eyes gleamed hard.

"Take—" She had to stop and clear her dry throat. "Taking won't work, either."

"Oh, yes it will, baby, you'll submit to me. You'll come to love me. Everyone submits in time." He picked her off the floor, one arm beneath her knees, one behind her shoulders, and she didn't resist him. There would have been no point. He carried her out of his bedroom and across the landing at the head of the stairs into a windowless bathroom. He laid her in the bathtub.

And he closed the door.

If he was going to rape her, it would be easier on that big bed, she thought, but she said nothing. She didn't want to be raped—and didn't want to say anything for fear it might set him off.

He closed the drain and turned on the cold water.

She was lying on her hands, and they hurt her. The cold water creeping around her fingers made them hurt worse. The water level rose. Diana was still wearing her clothes, and she was conscious of her clothes' increasing weight as the water soaked into them.

Her fear rose with the water level. Her heart was beating fast, and her breath began to come in quick, cold gasps. Fear was closing its icy fingers around her.

When the water had risen to within an inch of the top of the tub, Mick placed his huge, calloused hand on the top of her head. "Everybody submits," he said. His voice sounded sad.

She nodded, terrified. "I understand."

"No," he said. "No, I don't think you do."

Tightening his mouth, he pushed downward on her head. She pushed back, her feet against the end of the tub.

He slid his arm beneath her knees again and

jerked them up. She had time for one quick intake of breath before her head went under. She
held her breath.

Who can hold his breath forever? Time passed,
and her body began to thrash in a mindless effort
to get her head out of the water to take in new
air. She had no leverage to work with, and the
weight of Mick's huge body was above her. She
felt his hands and his elbows on her, his knee
against her chest. Her efforts became frenzied,
and involuntarily she began to gulp water, to
snort it in through her nose, and to suck it in
through her ears. Her ears started to hum. Her
head seemed to be blowing up like a balloon.
Then came a sharp whistling, very loud.

Her struggle took on a dreamy quality. Her
body seemed to be something apart from her,
something tormenting her, something hated. Her
struggles to breathe, which increased with each
swallow of water, seemed to be a struggle more
against her own body than against any outside
power.

Eventually, he took her out and laid her on the
bedroom floor. He put his knee on her stomach,
and water poured out of her mouth and nose,
spurting like a jet from a hose, soaking him, soaking his carpeting, soaking everything. He sat
above her like a bronzed idol, his wet skin
gleaming.

He told Frank that Cecil Armstrong was alive
and well and living in Creede, Colorado. David
was inside Frank's office, leaning against the
door, which was closed behind him. Frank sat at
his desk, body upright, his expression pained.

"I think he's had some kind of nervous breakdown, Frank. He wasn't exactly the old Cecil—tremor in his hands, hard time keeping eye contact. And he's done some foolish stuff. You know the stash of money Leonard Nash is rumored to have somewhere?"

"Yes."

He told Frank the story.

"He should have sent the briefcase to me," Frank said.

"Yes. I think he was scared of you, though. You were part of the career millstone that was drowning him. Maybe he was ashamed, too, of having to break away like he did. I think it was a close one for him. It was cut and run and salvage what he could, or it was suicide."

"I knew he hadn't been happy for a long time, but I thought he was working through it."

David shrugged. "In a way he did. He's past the crisis now. He's got his wife back, and he's rebuilding. Still weak, like he's been sick a long time, but rebuilding."

Frank was silent a long while. He waved his hand at David, motioning toward the door. David took the hint and left him there.

Mick Rothgut wasn't in the phone book. David shoved the book back into his desk drawer and sat looking at his mail, piled in a great mound upon his desk. For the ninth or tenth time he dialed Diana's number and let it ring.

What he needed to do was go to the courthouse, talk to Leonard. Before he did, though . . . He sorted through his mail, looking again for something from Abner DePuy, the old fart who was supposed to be filing an answer in the Shumaker case. There wasn't anything from Abner there. He had a theory now for why Abner hadn't responded to his ultimatum. David was suing the MacLeods, Abner's clients, because they were deadbeats. They had had work done on their house, and they hadn't paid for it. It might be that they were no better about paying their legal fees. Old Abner hadn't filed, and he wasn't going to.

David called Judge Wasserman's office and found that Naomi was there, in the courthouse. He grabbed Shumaker's file and went over to get his judgment.

She gave it to him. "Thank you, Judge," he said, shoving the file back into his briefcase. She smiled at him, black eyes glittering. He left her and went up to talk to Leonard.

"Has Cecil turned up?" Leonard asked him.

"Yes."

"Then why isn't he here?"

The same old thing again. "He's in Colorado right now and can't get back," David said.

"The bonds? Did he have them?"

"He had to hide them. He left them with a firm of art dealers up in Dallas. Rupert and Holmes. It means we'll be dealing with the bonds publicly, but I think that was true as soon as our firm came into it." He hesitated. "The art dealer misunderstood his instructions to bury the bonds. He used them to buy a painting."

"What?"

"A painting that, according to Jack Rupert, is worth several times the one-point-three million we had in bonds."

"What kind of—"

"It was painted by Claude Monet."

A slow grin spread over Leonard's face. "I own a Monet?" he said, looking delighted.

"For now. Unless the bankruptcy court takes it away from us. I really came up here to ask you about something else. What can you tell me about Mick Rothgut?"

"Who? Mick ... Oh, Mick! Mick and I went to high school together. He played football. Holy hell, I haven't thought about Mick Rothgut in years."

The guilelessness was well done; in fact, too well done. "That's not what Diana said about the two of you," David said.

"Well if Diana knows anything recent about Mick, she knows him a whole lot better than I do."

"You wouldn't know his current address."

Leonard shook his head decisively. "Would not," he said. David looked hard into Leonard's pale, yellow eyes, and he knew the man was lying.

"It was Mick, you know, who was responsible for all this. It was Mick who forced Cecil to disappear."

"Tell the police, then," Leonard said. "It's all news to me."

"Tell me about the last three days," Mick said. "Tell me everything."

Diana lay quivering before him. She said nothing.

"That tub in there is still full of water, baby," he told her.

"I'm not your baby."

He rolled her onto her stomach and picked her up by her tied hands, sending spasms of pain up into her shoulders. Only her toes touched the carpet, dragging and bouncing on the way to the bathroom. The pain was terrific.

She would tell him everything.

He didn't give her that chance. Using her arms as leverage, he pushed her face beneath the cold water. She dislocated both of her shoulders in her effort to get her face high enough for her to breathe. Again there was the sharp whistling. Very loud.

Afterward she told him everything, lying on her back, talking too rapidly even to organize her words. She got it all out and lay panting, an empty gourd. Mick dried her hair, stroked her face. He pulled on one arm and then the other, his foot in her side, and her shoulders popped painfully back into place. The pain was separate from her, distant.

He removed her wet clothes and dried her body. His hands were gentle. He left her there.

She remembered the distant sound of him talking, of other voices, and she remembered going downstairs in a bathrobe where two men were standing with him. She remembered *being* downstairs, actually; she didn't remember the going. "Someone reported you missing, baby," Mick said to her. "Isn't that funny?"

She smiled quickly at him, studying his face for approval. He smiled back at her, and she felt relief.

"Are you all right?" Mick asked her.

She nodded.

"Here of your own free will?"

She nodded again.

"Now go back upstairs, baby."

And, feeling relief, she went.

David found a Michael Rothgut in the Grantee's Index in the county clerk's office on the first floor. In 1987 he had purchased 11 Pheasant Run from Southside Realty, Inc. by a deed of bargain and sale.

On his way back to the office David began to wonder how the police had ever managed to talk to Mick if his address was so hard to come by. He called and asked to speak with Sergeant Margaret Cain.

"Oh, it's you," she said when he had identified himself. "We found your Diana Puller."

"You have? Where?"

"She was visiting Mick Rothgut, as you yourself suggested. But two of our officers talked to her. She's there of her own free will."

"She is not."

"She said she was."

The statement was so outrageous, he hardly knew how to respond.

"Good-bye, Mr. Loring," Sergeant Cain told him, and she hung up on him.

It was not yet four o'clock when he turned off the expressway onto Caldwell Avenue and headed north. He had been out to Pheasant Run once or twice before, though now he couldn't have said why. The condominiums were built around the recreational facilities, which included pools and tennis courts. An asphalt road circled the complex, with diagonal parking on both sides.

David drove past Mick's unit, number eleven, and parked several units away on the outside of the asphalt circle. The dark blue BMW that had haunted him the day that someone brained him, the same BMW Cecil had described, though now repaired, was parked in front of Mick's unit. For half an hour, in the building heat of late afternoon, David watched the unit in his rearview mirror, but no one came or went.

It was hot enough that he had to keep the car running and the air conditioner on, and, with the car sitting still, even that was hardly enough. He drummed his fingers on his steering wheel. Finally, he shut off his engine and got out, pocketing the keys. The back of his shirt was sticking to him.

He walked down the sidewalk that ran between two of the buildings. He was casing the place. Inside the circle of condominiums he saw three people. A pale, bloated man in his early twenties ate from a large package of Lay's potato chips and swigged cola from a two-liter bottle of Diet Coke as he flipped the pages of a magazine. On the opposite side of the pool were a man and a woman. The woman, who had dark skin and a mass of dark hair, lay prone on a lounge chair, her back bare and the straps of a black bikini hanging loose at her sides. Her face was turned away from David, toward her hulking companion.

"Oh, boy," David muttered. The man sat sideways on his lounge chair, facing the woman who could be Diana. He was huge, powerfully muscled, and nearly naked, his face, like his body, bronzed and handsome . . . but for his nose.

There was something about the nose. David felt his heart beating in his throat. The man was talking at length, saying things to the woman in a droning voice that was loud enough to hear, but too low for David to distinguish the words spoken.

As the man spoke, his gaze passed up and down the woman's body. His expression was intense, his droning voice hypnotic.

Cold in the August heat, David watched them from the walkway. He stood with hands in his pockets while inside his suit cold sweat dripped like melting ice against his sides.

The young man by the pool finished his potato chips, gurgled the last of his Diet Coke, and lay back beneath his reddening mound of belly. On the far side, the big man murmured on to his companion, from time to time reaching out to brush her back or her leg with the tips of his fingers. David looked around, considering, but he could think of nothing to do.

The big man stood finally, and he was wearing a skimpy Speedo bathing suit that emphasized his bulk. "Come on, baby," he said, just loud enough for David to hear. The woman stood up, but she was largely hidden behind the man as the two of them came toward him. Retreating slowly, David squinted across the sun-bright sidewalk and the cemented area that surrounded the pool. It was Diana, walking docilely in the big man's wake with sun-dazed eyes.

Looking again at the man's face, David recognized the same man who had been watching him at the food court so long before. It was Mick.

David turned and ran from them.

As soon as he and Diana had returned from their trip, Diana had gone to Mick. It was almost more than he could stand.

18

Diana was surprised when he tied her again, and taped her mouth, and put her in the closet. In the long, long silence, she became conscious again of the whistling. "I know you're not going anywhere, baby," he had said, winking. "But this way I *know* you're not going anywhere."

She endured the darkness stoically, for she had no emotional energy left.

David faced his own surprises, though of a more mundane sort. When he got back to his apartment, he found Rhonda sitting cross-legged on his living room floor, sorting laundry—his laundry. On either side of her was a small pile of it, one consisting of whites, one of colors. She was squirting the collar of one of his dress shirts with Fantastic bathroom cleaner.

"Hi, David," she said when she saw him.

He was nonplussed. His anger flared, but was exhausted almost immediately. He sank down on his sofa and sat watching her. "Shouldn't you be using Shout or Spray 'n' Wash or something like that?" he asked finally. "I use that stuff to clean the tub."

"It's all the same thing." She tossed the shirt into the laundry basket and picked out another one.

He coughed. "I don't mean to sound ungrateful, entirely, but what are you doing here? How did you get in?"

"I needed to do my laundry. I thought I might as well do yours while I was at it. Did you know you only had one clean pair of panties in your drawer?"

"Men don't wear panties," he said in a pained voice. "They wear underwear."

"Look at it," she said, holding up a pair. "Panties."

"So how did you get in?"

She shrugged, eyeing the pair of underwear she was holding. She gave it a squirt with the Fantastic.

"And what's in this case?" He touched the hard, square Samsonite case with his foot.

"Cosmetics, curling iron, toothbrush."

"Rhonda—"

"I know what you're going to say. Just don't. You look tired. Let me get you a beer." She got up and went into his kitchen.

"I don't have any beer," he called.

She came out of the kitchen with a bottle of Lowenbrau.

"This isn't going to work," he said. She thrust the bottle at him, and he took it, noticing her legs. They were more muscular than they used to be, and she had gotten a lot of sun on them recently.

She saw him notice them. "Marie and I have been playing a lot of tennis," she said.

"Ah." He felt drugged, but he shook himself and struggled out of the sofa. She pressed against him, her hands on his chest. He pushed past her to the front door. He opened it and tossed his beer bottle over the rail. They both heard it thonk on the grass below.

"Hey," Rhonda said.

He walked past her to the kitchen and got the six-pack of Lowenbrau from the refrigerator. She tried to block his way, but he pushed past her to the door and tossed the six-pack over the rail as well. His aim was less fortunate. He heard glass shatter on the sidewalk below.

"Hey," Rhonda said again.

He got her travel case, handed it to her at the door and pushed her through. "Rhonda, force does not work, okay? Trust me. Force just does not work." He closed the door.

He didn't sleep that night, but lay staring up at the ceiling. Diana sat trussed in the closet, passing into and out of unconsciousness. Mick spent a good part of the night in his car, driving northward.

Jack Rupert was sleeping deeply. He always slept deeply these days, slept far harder than he used to. The ringing of his door chimes, rather than waking him, made its way into the chaos of his dreams, where the ringing became a flute played by a twisted little man with crazy, rolling eyes.

Rupert sat up in bed, suddenly awake. His breathing was shallow and rapid, and his heart fluttered in his chest. The chimes sounded again.

"Good God Almighty," Rupert said, throwing

back his covers and swinging his legs out of bed. The mustard-yellow walls of his bedroom looked black in the night. With two twisted, arthritic fingers, he fished for his teeth in the glass on the nightstand. He stood up, making the faces necessary to work his teeth into their proper place. He pulled his bathrobe on over his brown-and-yellow-striped pajamas.

Before he could go downstairs, he had to turn off one of his alarm systems, the one sensitive to vibration.

His caller had abandoned the doorbell and started to pound on the door by the time he reached it. Rupert peered through the peephole. A huge man was out there, shoulders too wide to fit within the scope of the fisheye lens. The outside lights, always on after dark, made him well illuminated. His fist fell on the door with the boom of a cannon.

Rupert stepped back quickly. He pulled a huge nickel-plated, pearl-handled Colt revolver from the drawer of a nearby table and, with it and the tiny key to the door's alarm system, went to the door again. The booming stopped as he put the key in the chrome receptacle and turned it. The red light switched off, and a green light came on. He jerked open the door.

There was no one there. Light glinted from the moths crowding the globe that hung from the porch roof. Rupert stepped backward, unwilling to lean out and make a target of himself. How could a man be there one moment and not be there the next? A chill shook Rupert's old frame. His mouth was dry, and he smacked his lips in an unconscious effort to conjure up some moisture.

He shut the door and locked it. Reached for the key to turn on the alarm. As he touched it, another alarm went off, sounding from the back of the house.

His hand fell away from the front door's alarm key, without activating the system. Two systems were currently activated, the back door system and the one that guarded the windows. Both were connected to the police department. From the apparent direction of the ringing, he guessed that a window had been forced.

He backed up against the front door, aware now of the intruder's plan: get him to deactivate the alarm system long enough to enter the house somewhere in the back. It was a plan that required speed and a preplanned point of entry. It also required a single alarm system protecting both doors and windows, and for that reason it had failed. Rupert's home had multiple alarm systems. Chalk one point for his defenses.

He crouched in the corner by the front door to await the intruder.

Thirty seconds passed. The wild alarm bells were jarringly loud, and they had his heart pounding in his throat. Somehow, through the jangling cacophony, he heard a crash from the living room. It was not loud, just a sound, its volume muted by the din.

He thought of the *Sailboat*, by far his most valuable possession. Of how the intruder could take it and go and still be minutes ahead of the police.

The painting was insured.

But priceless.

Rupert cocked his gun and advanced behind it, finger white on the trigger, his grip so tight as to be painful. Carefully he advanced, approaching the archway into the living room so as to give him the maximum angle of sight.

Nothing hit him as he passed through the archway. The light in the living room was dim, but bright enough to identify his paintings. Certainly bright enough to identify the blank square of wall where his *Sailboat* had been.

He angled his revolver back and forth across the room, seeking a target. His mind was reeling, though not so much that he failed to realize that the thief had known what he was looking for and had known exactly where to find it. The extraction of the painting had been as swift and as deft as a surgical procedure.

Though unnaturally alert to everything, he was unaware of the shadow that rose up silently behind him. It came over the sofa at him like a winged thing, enveloping him with strong pinions, trapping his arms against his sides. He fired his gun into the floor reflexively, not once but six times, and the sixth time the slug passed through his own foot on its way into the floor. The pain never registered. He was off his feet, hurtling forward with increasing speed, still unable to free his arms from the force that pinned them. The top of his old head drove into the blank square of plaster wall where the *Sailboat* had hung. The plaster cracked, and Rupert collapsed to the floor. Large pieces of the plaster fell away from the wall, showering down on Rupert's broken head, the largest pieces shattering and sending up a rising cloud of dust.

*   *   *

Morning. David blinked his eyes in the sunlight falling on his pillow. Just when he had
given up on sleep, it had come to him. He sat
up, feeling an ache in his bones and in his head
that told him his sleep had not rested him. It
was morning. Yet another day.

His mouth tasted like sawdust, as if he had a
hangover.

The thought of breakfast made him nauseous.
After showering and shaving and putting on a
suit, he took a long pull of orange juice from the
carton in his refrigerator, finishing it. The juice
had an old taste to it. He left the empty carton
on the counter.

"David Loring," Nancy said as he passed her
desk, and he nodded his greetings.

"I am so glad to see you," Ellen Uhlan said,
when he passed her in the hall.

He stopped. She did sound glad to see him.
"Is your pleasure personal or professional?" he
called after her.

She turned and smiled. "Check the files on
your desk, then you tell me."

"Uh-oh."

On his desk didn't describe it. The files were
in three stacks on his desktop, in a pile in his
chair, in a meter-high pile on the floor. It could
only be—and it was—the S and L case, which
had long been in a document-intensive discovery
process he had until now avoided.

Discovery processes inevitably ended in the
filing of lawsuits, his specialty rather than Ellen's, and this case had evidently arrived at that
point. He poked at the top files gingerly, unwill-

ing to probe too deeply. His phone rang and he picked it up.

"Someone from the Dallas police," the receptionist told him.

"Okay."

He didn't catch the officer's name. The gist of the message was that John L. Rupert of Highland Park, Dallas, had died violently. David's business card had been by the kitchen phone.

"What time did this happen?" David asked, numbed.

"Well, now, we're more interested in getting information at this point than giving it, you see."

"I see. Motive? Was the house robbed?"

"Perhaps you could speak generally to your relationship with Jack Rupert, Mr. Loring."

"I don't know what to say."

"Perhaps you could start with when you saw him last."

David haltingly told of the times he had seen Jack Rupert, the times he had talked to him on the phone, the general subject matter of each conversation. At the end, belatedly, he got the policeman's name and badge number. He tried to confirm his instant suspicion, that the Monet had been the murderer's target, but, at this point, they couldn't say what if anything was missing.

If Diana had indeed thrown in with Mick, this was what he might expect. She would tell Mick what he needed to know, and Mick would go up and kill Jack Rupert to get the painting.

"I'm going out," he said to Nancy on his way back past her desk. He took the elevator to the basement, the tunnel to the parking garage.

Halfway to Pheasant Run he stopped his car against the curb. Mick was dangerous; he had learned that the hard way. And Diana—who knew what to think about her anymore?

He had to face it. Diana was the reason he felt compelled to go out there. His hope was to get to her before Mick could get back from Dallas— if it had been Mick in Dallas—and to confront her with what she had done, though even now he could not believe that she had done it.

He went first to Diana's apartment and entered through the front door, still unlocked. Diana had not returned, but her Ruger single-action revolver was in the drawer of her nightstand. He took it out and put it in the side pocket of his suit coat.

It was insurance, in case Mick was there, in case he proved hard—proved impossible—to deal with.

Ten minutes later he was pulling into one of the angled spaces in front of Mick's condominium. The big BMW was not in sight, which so far fit into his theory of Mick in Dallas, perhaps trying to fence his stolen painting. He turned off his car and got out, his eyes scanning the windows.

He walked up the sidewalk, up the four steps to the stoop. The door was stained wood with a curtained oval window and a lever rather than the conventional doorknob. The lever moved easily, but had no effect on the deadbolt that secured the door.

He rang the bell and stepped back.

Knocked hard and stepped back.

He pounded furiously.

Nothing.

He looked to his left and his right along the long, curving sidewalk. There was no one in sight, no one on the sidewalk, no one in the parking lot, no one sitting idly in one of the cars.

He was about to commit a felony. A loud noisy felony. An absence of witnesses was what he would have hoped for. He pulled the pistol from his pocket and stepped away from the door. Shielding his eyes with his left hand, he pointed the gun at the narrow strip of the deadbolt that showed between the door and the frame. He pulled back the hammer with his thumb, rotating the cylinder to bring a chamber with a bullet in it in front of the firing pin. He pulled the trigger.

The sound of the explosion was terrifying. His ears rang with it. The door and the door frame had splintered. The bolt was gone.

David pushed the door open with his foot and stepped inside.

The gun he put back in his pocket. He had committed one crime. At this point, if he shot Mick in his own house it was capital murder. When you broke into another man's house with a gun and shot him, you had a hard time claiming self-defense.

He pushed the door shut behind him. "Hey, Mick," he called. "Diana." But the house was silent as a tomb. He was in a short entrance hall with a staircase on his right, archways ahead of him and on his left. The floor was polished wood, and an Oriental runner went down the middle of it. No one was in sight to mark his entrance.

For now he passed the staircase. He approached

the archway on his left gingerly, staying close to the wall, wanting to see before being seen. The archway opened into a formal living room with a cathedral ceiling. The room contained an Oriental carpet, white upholstered furniture, and a baby-grand piano in the far corner. Art deco prints hung above the sofa: line drawings of jazz musicians filled in with red and yellow water color. Beyond the living room he could see a dining room, and on its far wall a mirror that held his own reflection, tiny and far away.

No point in going that way. He stepped across the archway, moving quietly to the end of the entrance hall. Why he was moving quietly after the blast of gunshot, he couldn't say, except that he was terribly frightened, more frightened than he would have believed possible. Though it might not be true, he had to assume that the police were on their way, called by an alarmed neighbor.

Around each corner, he expected to find Diana's corpse, a useless husk cast aside after being emptied of information. He wasn't sure that his expectation was rational; certainly it contradicted his sure sense that Diana had deliberately betrayed him, had betrayed Jack Rupert to his death.

He stepped down into a large carpeted den, maybe twenty feet by twenty, that had an L-shaped couch and a projection television. The part of the den outside the couch was in use as a small gymnasium, about ten feet square. A weight bench stood in the center of the area, supporting a York barbell bending under several hundred pounds of weight. The squat rack behind it held a second York barbell, bending under the pressure of even greater weight. On the wall by the window, pulleys held metal cords that ran down to plates on the floor, and along another wall was a rack of dumbbells.

An entire wall of the den was lined with books. On one shelf squatted Black's *Law Dictionary*, and beside it Gray's *Anatomy*. On the shelf above them were hardback editions of Dickens, Balzac, and Thomas Hardy; on other shelves, numerous volumes of best-selling fiction, current and past.

From somewhere in the house there was a sound. He froze, eyes darting madly.

A picture of ducks on a lake hung above a crumbling-brick mantle. The artist's name, printed in the lower right-hand corner, was Michael Rothgut.

The sound David had heard was not repeated. "A real Renaissance man," he said aloud in an effort to reassure himself. It didn't work.

He went through the den to the kitchen, done in gray tile with maroon accents; through the kitchen to the dining room; back through the living room to the entrance hall, completing the circle. Already he had convinced himself that he had not heard the sound he thought he had heard.

And then, from upstairs he heard it again, a muffled thump of unknown origins. His heartbeat, which had gradually subsided to normal levels during his tour of the downstairs, started pounding again, a ticking time bomb nearing the point of detonation. He started quickly up the stairs, anxious to get this search behind him, anxious to get out of the house.

At the square landing at the top of the stairs were three doors, all of them open: through one, a small, square bathroom, dark and empty; through another, some kind of library, its walls covered with books. In the center of the library was a leather recliner with a modern black floor lamp angled over it and a small, leather-topped table beside it. The lamp was on, casting a circle of light around the recliner, but the chair was empty. It looked to David as if the huge but erudite Mr. Rothgut had just stood up from his reading and would be back at any moment.

David realized that he was holding his breath. He let it go and drew in another one.

He had to step onto the landing to see through the third door. Looking in at the massive posts of a king-sized bed, he heard the thump again and a muffled sob, and he realized that the sounds were coming from the closet.

He went to it, paused with his hand on the doorknob, and took a last deep breath. Then he opened the door.

19

Diana lay curled on the floor, eyes squeezed shut against the sudden light, surgical tape wrapped twice around her head, covering her mouth.

"Oh, God," he said, looking down at her. She was clad only in panties. Her breasts were bare, a startling white against the dark, dry skin of her upper chest and abdomen.

He knelt and lifted her into sitting position. When he unwound the tape from her head, her hair stuck to the tape, and he knew that he was pulling it, hurting her, but she made no sound.

"Diana?" he said, touching the adhesive still stuck to her cheek. Her eyes were unfocused, not tracking him. Tears welled up in his eyes. He pulled frantically at the tape that bound her legs together, wound around and around, from her knees to her ankles. It pulled smoothly from her close-shaved skin.

He looked again at her face, into her vacant eyes. "Diana? Say something, will you? You're scaring me." With his forearm, then, he swiped at the tears that were obscuring his vision.

Her hands were behind her, and he had to roll

her onto her side to get to them. Mick had tied her hands, using a thin, white cord rather than tape. The cord was wound tightly about her wrists. Where it cut into the inside of her right wrist, blood stained the cord. The knots were drawn too tightly for him. He gave up on them and slid his arm around Diana's waist, hoping to get her on her feet.

Her weight was leaden.

"Oh, God." He laid her again on the floor. He hesitated, irresolute on the landing. Still he heard no sound of police sirens in the distance, drawing closer, though now he would welcome it. The front door was shut; no one had burst through it bearing weapons.

In the bathroom, he looked in the cabinet for scissors, and he found single-edged razor blades instead. He pushed one from the package and left the package on the counter by the sink.

By stroking the rope with the razor, he was able to cut through it, and Diana's hands were free in less than a minute. He held her wrists, rubbing them, knowing they must be dead and numb, devoid of feeling.

His right hand holding her arm about his shoulders, his left arm about her waist, he pulled her up. As he moved her forward, her own legs began to take some of her weight.

"Thank you, God, oh, thank you," he said.

Downstairs the front door opened.

He froze in the bedroom doorway, his thanks dying on his lips.

He started forward again with Diana, not knowing what else to do, releasing Diana's arm just long enough to pat his right coat pocket.

They started down the stairs. Mick came to the foot of the stairs and stood looking up, unsmiling. Oh, he was big. He was wearing loose pants with an elastic waist, and a black shirt.

David kept coming. He felt anger, indignation, and, oh yes, a strong dose of fear. Mick's neck came out of his black shirt like a bronzed pillar.

Diana was supporting herself completely now, and she was beginning to resist forward motion—to resist more strongly, the closer she got to Mick.

David pulled her on.

"Stop," Mick said, when David and Diana were on the bottom step. Mick put his hand out and placed it against David's chest. David stopped, his left arm about Diana's waist, his right hand plunged deep into his pocket.

"You're going to let her go, Mick," David said.

Mick smiled. "Go upstairs, baby," he said to Diana. "Now."

She turned and started up. David grabbed her hand.

"You don't have to do what he says," he said, trying to make eye contact. "We're going to go straight out the door to my car." She turned back toward him, and he let go of her hand.

She turned away again and ran.

David looked at Mick.

"She's a good girl," Mick said.

"Just back from Dallas?" David asked him, and fear rose in him, causing him instantly to regret his words.

"You think you're pretty smart."

"I think you're a real son-of-a-bitch," David

said, but his tough words made him feel no tougher.

Mick took his arm. "Come on," he said, leading him toward the den. His grip on David's triceps was iron. "Why don't we have a little fun?"

"Diana," David called out. "We're in the den. The front door is clear."

The blow he expected to his midsection didn't fall. They both waited. From upstairs there was no sound.

Mick chuckled softly and released David's arm. "She's a good girl," he repeated. "She'd better be."

"Where's the Monet?"

"I don't know what you're talking about." Mick backed off a couple of yards. "Ever do any boxing, kid? It's been years for me."

David brought his right hand out of his pocket, without the gun. He knew he lacked the will to shoot Mick in cold blood, whatever he had done—and if David did shoot him, here, now, David would likely face a prison sentence. Perhaps he could back out the front door behind the gun—alone, without Diana—but perhaps Mick would sense his lack of will, reach out, and take the gun away. Besides, he couldn't leave Diana, not with Mick.

When Mick stepped forward, raising his fists to his chin, David brought his own hands up. Mick came forward another step, and David stepped back with his right foot, turning his left shoulder toward Mick on the theory that his body in profile made a smaller target.

They were in the open area between Mick's weights and the brick fireplace. David thought about running, about turning and sprinting for the door, but Mick would be all over him if he tried it. Besides, he couldn't leave Diana. If Mick wanted to fight, David was going to have to fight him.

"You a boxer?" Mick said from behind his left shoulder. With his left hand he was brushing at a nonexistent smudge on his cheekbone. It kept his arm up and a good part of his upper body behind his left forearm.

"A lawyer."

"Yes, I know that, but what else are you? *Enumeratio unius non est exclusio alterius.*" Mick giggled, incongruously. "Surprised? Yes, I speak your law-school Latin." He had started to weave.

"I don't," David said. "I just speak your law-school English."

"You won't speak at all, a minute here." Mick jabbed, and David pulled back his chin to avoid it.

David then lunged forward with a jab of his own, but his jab, too, came up short. He jabbed again and came underneath it with his right hand. Mick slapped down the jab. The right cross—it just missed somehow.

David was breathing hard, but he was a runner. No matter what happened, his wind should hold.

"Tell me the truth, you've done some boxing, haven't you?" Mick said.

David tried a combination that caught a piece of a shoulder and glanced off a twisting midsection: no square hit, no real damage.

"Maybe you're familiar with the counterpunch," Mick said.

Dave jabbed, and, as his hand came back, Mick's left came over it to crush into his face and numb it. Still moving, dancing, David gave his head a couple of tiny shakes in an attempt to bring things back in focus. He swung his right hand at Mick's head, and Mick's left arm brushed it aside on its way back into David's face.

Mick said, "If you don't keep your hands up, you're going to get hurt," but David had already learned that lesson. His fists were hard against his cheekbones as he tried desperately to keep Mick's hands in focus. He couldn't punch, because he didn't dare remove his hands from his face: Another hit in the head, and he was going down. There was no pain. Just numbness. He felt strangely disassociated from his body, as if he were standing back and watching the fight from the sidelines.

Mick delivered three explosive mule-kicks below David's elbows, and David fell forward, blood from his face splattering the carpet in front of him as his knees hit the floor.

"Keep your hands up!" Mick shouted, and kicked him in the face to punctuate the instruction. David sprawled backward over the back of the couch. Still, he felt no pain; in fact, no sensation at all. His one feeling was of disembodiment, of drifting upward from his lifeless clay as Mick pulled it back to collapse on the carpeted floor.

Mick seemed to go away, though what he did was to go to his squat rack and, squatting slightly, put the front of his shoulders against the York barbell. He straightened, arms crossed over his chest to hold the bar in place, the massive plates at either end of the bar bobbing and clacking together. He had to move slowly, walking toward David, to keep the weights from bouncing out of control.

David's eyes went wide when Mick appeared above him, so wide that the whites of his eyes showed all around the irises, but it was wholly an automatic response. His hand was in the side pocket of his jacket, but no intelligence directed it, no intelligence recognized the need to hurry. The revolver's hammer had caught in the fabric of David's suit, and David tugged mechanically as Mick unloaded the barbell.

The revolver tore free of the suit pocket just as the barbell hit, just in time for David, in extremis, to fumble it away. The plates boomed on the floor, one set of them on either side of David, the bar whipping across his chest below the sternum, snapping ribs and, when the bar was still, bearing down on his chest in a line of fire that prevented any movement and all but the shallowest breath. The dead hand groped for the gun in a strained, extended effort, then lay palm up, twitching, as his legs jerked in mindless spasm. The Ruger revolver lay useless, a foot or a foot and a half from his hand.

Mick turned back toward his weights, smiling. With a heave of his shoulders he cleared a second barbell from the arms of his weight bench. He carried the barbell across and dropped it from waist height across David's ankles, effectively pinning his feet. Then Mick went to the bottom of the stairs.

"Hey, Diana! Come here, I want to show you something." There were pliers in his left hand, snicking open and closed. "Diana! Don't make me come after you, baby." He continued to work the pliers. When Diana didn't appear at the head of the stairs and he didn't hear her coming, he started up to get her.

But Diana wasn't upstairs. When she fled upward from Mick, she came first to the bathroom where Mick had nearly drowned her, came next to the bedroom with its open closet door behind which she had lain for so long, listening for Mick in the darkness, hearing only the whistle of her tortured ears. There was nothing for her there.

When David called to her, she went to the top of the stairs and stood looking down, fighting with some impulse to self-destruction, to curl into herself and die, which she did not fully understand. From below there were the sounds of shuffling, of harsh grunts, of meat striking meat. She crept softly down the stairs, cringing at each call of Mick's voice though he wasn't calling to her. At the door she heard the sound of David's knees striking the floor. She heard Mick's shout and the wet, jolting thud of Mick's foot against David's face, and she heard the sounds of David's loose-jointed collapse. She hesitated, her hand on the door-lever that would break open the claustrophobic box of Mick's apartment.

The building shuddered suddenly as if struck by a giant. Diana staggered back from the door. The building shook again, and she spun wildly. Then Mick was coming. Numbed by terror, she looked at the stairs to her right, at the archway into the living room at her left. She heard the first snick of pliers, and she went left.

Mick was calling to her. She stood in the doorway between den and kitchen, her eyes on David. He lay on his back, pinned to the ground by massive barbells. His breathing was a thin, irregular whine.

Her gun was on the floor, just beyond David's reach.

She went to it and picked it up. Pulled the hammer back. Stood looking thoughtfully down at it. Mick came in from the kitchen, unexpectedly, and she almost failed to turn in time to cover him.

He stood very still, his arms half-raised. Her arms, held stiffly in front of her, were trembling.

His voice was gentle, almost a sigh. "Diana," he said.

"I'm going to enjoy this." Her voice was harsh.

"Put the gun down, Diana."

Her back touched the wall, putting a stop to her unconscious retreat. He was moving toward her with hypnotic slowness. Her breath rasped in her throat.

"Stop." But he was still coming. She squeezed off a shot, and the gun jumped in her hands.

Mick smiled. He was still easing forward, though she could see the hole in his black shirt. She thumbed back the hammer and shot him again.

"Bitch," he breathed. There was a hole in his shirt over the abdomen. Her next shot went wild. Mick lunged for her, and, though she staggered back and he fell prone on the floor, he caught her ankle. She fell, and her head snapped back against the floor.

From outside came the rise and fall of a siren,

getting louder. "One shot left," a voice said. David's.

She still held the gun in both hands, she realized, though her arms were extended above her head and the gun was pointing the wrong way, away from Mick. He was crawling up her body, grabbing ankle, then knee, then hip.

"His face," David said, wheezing, and there it was above her, Mick's breath warm on her cheek. She had the hammer back. As Mick's hand came down to pin her wrist, she moved, jamming the gun at his face, splitting his lips and splintering teeth as the barrel drove into his mouth.

The sound of the gun, this time, was not loud, little more than a cough. Mick's body became a dead weight, forcing the air from her lungs in a single hard gust, making her next breath an effort. Blood drained from Mick's mouth, and she struggled to free herself.

It required too great an effort.

"Jack Rupert, he's dead, isn't he?" she said, breathlessly, but David didn't answer. "David?"

The front door slammed open. Then men in uniform stood above them, their pistols pointed downward.

20

Two ambulances came, as well as the medical examiner's meat wagon, and somehow David and Diana wound up in different hospitals. In the emergency room at St. Luke's a pale intern took some skull X rays of David's head, a chest X ray, a KUB, and some facial films. David was most worried about the blood he was coughing up, but it was the intern's opinion that the blood was draining back into David's oral cavity from his broken nose, sliding down his throat and triggering the cough. "And there's not a thing we can do about broken noses," she said cheerfully.

David was coughing as she told him this. "It hurts so bad when I . . . cough," he said, gesturing vaguely at his chest.

"Yes, well you did break four ribs. None of them in more than one place, so you shouldn't have any trouble breathing. Except for pain."

David, gasping shallowly, understood about the pain. The intern strapped a rib belt on him and taped his nose. "That's it, you'll just have to wait for it to heal. Now, we send you home."

"You're not going to keep me . . ."

"For observation? Well, your skull's intact. Four ribs puts you right on the line—five and we'd keep you—but I think you can manage okay at home." She gave him a bottle of Tylenol with codeine. Al and Frank were waiting for him outside the E.R. Al drove him home, glancing curiously at him from time to time.

"Don't ask," David said. He sat stiffly and didn't turn his head. "I'll tell you all about it tomorrow."

Al nodded. "They took your girlfriend to the Baptist hospital."

"Is she all right?"

"You admit, then, that she's your girlfriend."

"Is she all right?"

"Okay, sorry. Yeah, I think she's all right. The latest I heard they were keeping her overnight for observation."

The news left him with a desolate feeling. "Oh," he said.

The next morning he couldn't get out of bed. He swallowed one of the Tylenol every three hours, swallowing it dry because of the difficulties of getting up for water. For toilet facilities he used the Gatorade jar that had sat neglected beneath his bedside table for a month or longer.

At some time around noon Frank set up a conference call with Danny Trevillian, the district attorney. David told his story again, and Frank and Danny talked. Danny wasn't planning to prosecute either David or Diana for anything: He agreed that Diana was justified in shooting Mick; under the circumstances, he was willing to overlook David's forcible entry into Mick's townhouse. The bad news was that the police had failed to recover the Monet.

David said, "I was thinking they'd find it in the trunk of Mick's car." He was sitting up in bed, alone, propped on his pillows.

"The frame was in the trunk. The frame and some tools. Let's see . . . handsaw, couple screwdrivers, vise-grips, staple gun, a roll of strapping tape. A socket set. Oh, the important thing, a stretch frame, minus its canvas."

"Uh-oh."

"Yes. What we're looking for may be just the canvas, maybe rolled up, who knows? You know that the two bullets fired into the trunk of Rothgut's body failed to penetrate the muscle wall?"

It just gave them one more thing to talk about. When David hung up, he put his head back and stared dully at the wall at the far end of his bedroom. He had a Delacroix print on that wall; he could only assume that the original was somewhere. His conference call had left him hurting, and he had to breathe shallowly. The doorbell rang, and he called out, but his voice was weak, maybe too weak to be heard. He waited, but the doorbell didn't ring again.

He picked up his phone and dialed Diana's number, but he got no answer. He was thinking about Diana when he heard the sound of a key in the lock of his front door.

It wasn't Rhonda, but Diana, tanned and slender in faded Wranglers and a white cotton blouse. She stopped in the doorway to look at him.

"I'm not sure they got your nose quite right," she said.

"Does every woman in town have a key to my apartment?"

"I don't know, how many keys have you given out? When you didn't answer your doorbell, I got this one from the apartment manager, who's a friend of mine."

He smiled at her, though weakly.

"They kept me overnight for observation, which is why I haven't been by sooner. You want me to empty that for you?" She started toward the Gatorade jar, which gleamed darkly on his bedside table.

"No." He got it first and, checking the lid, pushed it underneath his covers.

"That hurt you, didn't it? Just that much movement. Yes, it did, too. It bleached the color right out of your face." She sat on the side of his bed, though he winced when she did it, and she smoothed back his hair from his forehead. He relaxed and closed his eyes and, without meaning to, fell asleep.

When he woke up, his Gatorade jar, emptied and washed, was back on his bedside table. There was a glass of water there, too, with one of the Tylenol tablets beside it.

"Diana?" There was no answer. He put the pill in his mouth and washed it down, then threw back the sheets and swung his legs over the side of the bed. He had to sit still for several minutes until his breathing steadied. When the pain was manageable, he eased onto his feet. He found he could walk only by keeping his knees bent and moving slowly, like an invalid. Which maybe he was. In the living room, he stopped by the window, squinting into the reflected sunlight of midafternoon.

It was then he noticed the man in the apartment across from him, standing just inside his sliding glass doors with a pair of binoculars. David moved closer to his window and looked down, but he couldn't see what the man was looking at.

He eased his way down the stairs outside his apartment to Diana's door. Her eyebrows went up when she saw him.

"What are you doing up?" She was wearing the same cotton blouse, now with shorts. "Am I going to have to tie you down, or maybe you would like that? Well, come on in. Easy, easy. I swear, I come down for five minutes to change my clothes and you're up catting around."

"There's a man watching your apartment with binoculars."

She left him sitting on the sofa and stepped to the glass doors that opened onto her patio. "Where?" she said. "I don't see him."

"He was there. The apartment directly across from mine." Uh! He had to remember to breathe shallowly. "You know, you're a dangerous woman to become involved with, what with all the psychopaths you attract."

"Good grief. I see him. I'm going up there."

"No." He struggled to his feet.

"I am, too. He's not watching you, he's watching me, and I'm fed up with it." Her jaw clamped shut, and her lips pressed together in a fine line.

"I'll go with you," he said, which precipitated another argument. This time he won.

*   *   *

Otto opened his door, and, as he focused on Diana, his eyes widened and his head went back.

"Ah-hah. You know me, don't you?" she said.

"I don't believe I've had the pleasure."

He looked at David, whose nose was taped and knees carefully bent, then back at Diana.

"I'm Diana Puller, and this is David Loring. May we come in?"

"Uh. Sure. Otto Lempert."

"Who?"

"Otto. Lempert." He was big, nearly as big as Mick had been, but without the iron-hard muscularity. His size did not seem to lend him confidence.

"Are those your binoculars on the coffee table, Mr. Lempert?"

He seemed confused.

"Do you limit your voyeurism to when I'm out sunbathing, or do you customarily peer inside my windows when I'm dressing as well?"

Otto's face had flushed a dull red. "I'm sorry," he stammered. "I read about you in this morning's paper, and I was curious, is all."

"Curious? You wanted to see if he left visible marks on me? You were maybe thinking if I looked good enough I might be worth kidnapping yourself?"

"Well, see, I knew the guy that did it to you, kidnapped you, I mean. In fact, these are his binoculars."

David felt the shock of that disclosure ripple through him. Whatever was said next he missed as his gaze swept the apartment. There was a *Video Review*, a *Playboy* and a ten-pound dumbbell on the coffee table with the binoculars, a neglected beer can sitting on the floor at the end of the sofa. A dirty plate and glass sat on the pass-through into the kitchen. And a large sheet of cardboard stood against the wall, folded into the shape of a flat, shallow box, but now standing partially open, bits of strapping tape still adhering to the edges.

He looked back at Otto, whose mouth was moving, smiling, whose head bobbed agreeably now that Diana's anger had begun to dissipate. Otto's head stopped bobbing, though, and he looked at David.

"What?" Otto said. "Why are you looking at me like that?"

David went past him and picked up the dumbbell, gasping at the pain that shot through him as he stooped.

"What the hell do you think you're doing?" Otto said. "What is he doing?" he said to Diana.

Armed with the dumbbell, David walked to the cardboard box. He picked it up, holding it shut with one hand. "Where's the painting that went in this box?" he said.

Otto stared at him. "Right there on the damn wall."

It was a medium-sized, square picture of dogs playing poker, and it hung above the sofa. David held the cardboard up to it and saw that the picture was the right size for the box.

He put the box down. "I'm sorry," he said. "I . . . don't know what I was thinking."

"I don't either. Sheesh," Otto said. "Not that I like it all that much. Looks kind of dorky there over the sofa."

"I like it," David said. "I guess someone gave it to you?"

"Sort of."

Diana said, "Sort of?"

"I found it in the closet. I figured my girlfriend got it for me, planning to surprise me."

"I guess you're stuck with it, then," David said.

"Nah. I called her, and she didn't know nothing about it." He shrugged. "Go figure," he said.

"Huh," David said. "I'd give you ten bucks for it."

"Oh, I don't know. Ten bucks."

David started to reach for his wallet, then stopped. "Uh. Diana, it's in my hip pocket. Will you? How much have I got?"

"Sixteen dollars."

David looked at Otto and raised his eyebrows. "Oh hell, why not?"

They walked slowly down the sidewalk toward their own building, David's careful shuffle setting the pace. Diana, who carried his just-purchased painting, seemed almost to vibrate with nervous energy.

"I can't believe it. I can't believe it," she kept saying. As David eased down onto the sofa in her apartment, she said, "You are smooth. I can't believe it, you're so smooth."

"I figured Mick kept his binoculars there, why not a six-and-a-half-million-dollar painting? Obviously, it's a long shot."

"No, you were right. There's another canvas under here, I can see it. What shall I do? Shall I pry the staples out of this dog canvas and get it off? Maybe I should take the whole thing out of the frame first."

"Maybe you should put it down, you might damage something. Remember, I paid sixteen dollars for it."

"Oh, I love you." She bounded toward him, then stopped. "I guess you're not up to a big bear hug."

He smiled. "Maybe I could handle just a little hug."

She sat on the sofa beside him to put her arms around him.

"Uh, Diana?" He sounded like he was strangling. "I'm afraid I was wrong."

She let go of him. "Well, what can you do?"

"Maybe if I could . . ." He was trying to lie down. She had to help him.

"You know, for a big tough guy, you're kind of a wimp," she said. She was kneeling by the sofa, looking down at him. "Can you handle a kiss?" She gave him a soft peck at the corner of his mouth.

"A kiss is . . . nice."

She kissed him again. That much he could handle.

SIGNET **ONYX**

AND JUSTICE FOR ALL . . .
(0451)

☐ **AGAINST THE WIND by J.F. Freeman.** A courtroom explodes in a case of sex and murder . . . "A high-octane blast that makes *Presumed Innocent* seem tame."—Stephen King. (173082—$5.99)

☐ **PLAYING THE DOZENS by William D. Pease.** A game of criminal law and cunning disorder . . . "One of the best novels of the year!"—*Washington Post.* "A vivid, strong, brisk thriller . . . stylishly gritty and thought-provoking."—*Publishers Weekly* (169867—$5.99)

☐ **THE SUNSET BOMBER by D. Kincaid.** The hottest courtroom drama since *Reasonable Doubt,* this explosive novel spotlights a hard-driving attorney in search of justice—no matter what the cost. (151267—$4.99)

Prices slightly higher in Canada